Forest Grove Library - you keep the masses... keep it up! J.D. Garrett

Sinister Services

J.D. Garrett

This is a work of fiction. All of the characters, places, and events portrayed within this novel are products of the author's imagination or used fictitiously. Any resemblance to actual people is purely coincidental.

SINISTER SERVICES

Copyright © 2014 J.D. Garrett

Cover and Authors Photos

Copyright © 2014 Mariah D. Alderete & Seth M. Alderete

Printed in the United States of America

ISBN-13: 978-1497534841
ISBN-10: 1497534844

First Edition

DEDICATION

For my beautiful husband, John. "There's nothing better than a hard-ass in a sexy package with intelligence shining in his eyes."

CONTENTS

ACKNOWLEDGMENTS

Special thanks to my family for putting up with my temperamental hours of writing, acting as my sounding board, offering suggestions and corrections, and being generally supportive during the writing of this book. Special thanks to my daughter, Mariah D. Alderete, and her husband, Seth M. Alderete for the wonderful photography used on the cover and author photos. Also, thanks to Kevin Doohan at Washington County Corrections for answering my calls and emails when I had endless questions that needed to be answered. Finally, thanks in great part to my High school English teacher, Mr. Rick Osborne, for believing in me and teaching me that I can do anything I put my mind to; this would not have been possible without you.

TO THE FOREST GROVE POLICE DEPARTMENT:

The contents of this novel in no way reflects my true opinion of the honorable men and women that bravely serve the Forest Grove and surrounding communities. All of you are truly an asset to the community and your sterling service is greatly appreciated!

~ J.D. Garrett

CONTENT ADVISORY

This book is intended for mature audiences. This book contains adult situations and circumstances, foul language, sexual situations, and violence.

1 EARLY APRIL -SATURDAY 6:00PM
KRYSTA MALLORY

I'm not sure what I expected to find as I rounded the corner, but this – man – was certainly not it.

"Sumofabitchinmotherfuckincocksuckin *Whore!*"

The whole time he was saying this he shook his hand as if trying to rid it of some invisible object clamped to his fingers or thumb. I suspected the hammer currently embedded in the wall behind him, as I doubted it was his usual manner of storage. Plus, there was blood on the handle… and dripping from his thumb. Altogether, he looked decidedly pissed-off. I debated creeping back the way I had come. Except my car was stalled in the parking lot outside, and the shop owner told me the guy working on the renovation was also a mechanic. I was already late. My daughter was on her way home from college for the weekend. I promised I would make spaghetti, her favorite. Great. Sighing, I took a step forward – and tripped over a box of nails. He swiveled, stopping my plunge with the hand he had just injured, and resumed his litany as if I had never interrupted him.

"Sumofa *Bitch!*"

I didn't know if I should be amused or terrified. Clearly, he knew I was there he'd stopped my fall. Aside from that, he showed no indication of acknowledging my presence. If home weren't ten miles away, I'd hoof it. But I had groceries, and it was starting to rain. With embarrassment, I realized that he had stopped and was watching me. I met his eyes and froze. There's nothing better than a hard-ass in a sexy package with intelligence shining in his eyes. I felt the heat as blood rushed to my face. The answering smirk on his confirmed he was used to this response in women. My face grew hotter.

"What do you need?"

His eyes held mine. They had gained an intensity that made it impossible to look away. I swallowed and hoped I didn't sound as scared as I felt.

"The owner – he said you're a mechanic?"

"I know a thing or two."

"Oh. Well, my car, there's something wrong with it. It won't start, and I need to get home."

"Okay."

He didn't move. We stood in frozen tableau for an eternity. I swallowed.

"Can you help me; please?"

"Hold on."

I watched entranced as he rummaged through a beat up tool chest and pulled out a half-used roll of duct-tape. Wiping the bloody thumb on his none-too-clean pants, he proceeded to wrap the wounded appendage with tape. He used his teeth to tear his makeshift bandage from the roll before tossing it back into the toolbox. After lighting a cigarette and taking a long drag, all the while watching me, he stuck a screwdriver and a wrench in his back pocket, produced a flashlight from somewhere, and headed for the door.

"Let's go."

I hurried to catch up as he strode out the door and down the sidewalk into the parking lot. He stopped suddenly – I walked right into him. He automatically caught and steadied me as I back peddled and nearly fell – again. I'm certain he was trying not to laugh.

"Where's your car?"

"Over here."

I brushed past him and quickly closed the distance between us and my rusted out 1976 Pea green Plymouth Volare. This time he nearly ran into me. He managed to stop centimeters behind me, his chest brushing my back, breath hot on my neck. I attempted to suppress the small thrill that ran through my body…

"Get behind the wheel."

And tried not to jump out of my skin at his voice in my ear. Fumbling with my keys, I unlocked the door and got in. The car is a piece of shit. I don't know why I lock it; habit I guess. He gave me a look that begged the question. I shrugged. He propped the hood open and leaned in over the engine. Stepping from behind the hood, he caught me trying to catch a glimpse of him through the tiny slit it allowed me while open. The smirk again; and a glint in his eyes that promised I don't know what.

"Give it a try."

I turned the key. The choking that ensued, while not the sound of a purring engine was better than the nothing I had gotten before.

"Fuck."

Or so I thought. He closed the hood.

"I'll be right back. Just wait here a sec."

"Okay."

The rain picked that moment to turn torrential. I decided to wait in the car. A few minutes later, an old Ford 350 pulled up beside me. The carpenter/mechanic at the wheel; he was on the phone. He held up his finger in a 'just a minute' gesture while he finished his phone call, then came over and tapped on my window. I rolled it down.

"Car isn't going anywhere tonight. I can fix it for you tomorrow, but I'm going to have to get parts. Where do you live?"

"About ten miles west of here."

"Hop in; you can give me directions while I drive."

"What about my car?"

"I told you, I'll fix it tomorrow. Now, get in."

By this time, he was thoroughly soaked. He opened my car door, and waited while I clumsily rolled up the window and got out, then closed it. I didn't bother locking it this time. Then he opened the passenger door on his truck and waited for me to climb inside before stalking around and getting into the driver's seat.

"Wait, my groceries, they're in the trunk!"

Briefly, he rested his forehead on the steering wheel. I swear he was praying for patience. He got back out and transferred the groceries from the trunk of the Plymouth to the back of his truck. I wanted to say something about the bags getting soaked, but decided not to push my luck. He got back in the truck and used the front of his shirt to wipe the rain from his face, then started the engine. We drove in silence for five minutes; I think we both forgot he didn't know where I live.

"Where do I turn?"

"Um, do you know where Cornelius is?"

"Yes."

"I live a little ways past that."

"Forest Grove?"

"Ya, my apartments are on B Street."

We lapsed into silence again. In typical schizophrenic Oregon, fashion the weather shifted from torrential rain to sun, then hail, and back to rain again. He smelled good, like an intoxicating mix of musk, dirt, rain and oil: all man. The drive home never felt so long. I realized I didn't even know his name, and I hadn't bothered to tell him mine. I was letting a total stranger that I truly knew nothing about, drive me home. He caught me watching him again. He winked but kept his eyes on the road. My face grew hot. This was becoming a habit. We got to Forest Grove and slowed to a crawl down Pacific Avenue. He turned Left onto B Street without asking. There was only one apartment complex on B Street. I guess he knew Forest Grove. He turned into the apartments; there was nowhere to park. He pulled up behind three parked cars, blocking them in, and turned off the engine.

"I usually park on the street."

He smirked and got out of the truck. It was sunny again. I was about to open the door when he opened it for me and helped me down out of the truck. I couldn't figure this guy out, so many contradictions. He grabbed both bags of groceries from the bed of the truck with one hand, and motioned for me to precede him with the other. With nothing else to do, I led him between the cars and down the walk to my apartment. The number on the door was supposed to say "22" but the bottom of the second two was broken off so it looked like a misshapen "27" instead. I put the key in the lock, jiggling the knob while I turned it. If you didn't jiggle the knob just right, the door wouldn't open.

"You should have that fixed."

I glanced over my shoulder at him as I opened the door and tripped over the doorjamb. My hand on the doorknob kept me from falling. God, he must think I'm a total klutz. I'd lived in the same apartment since I was 19 years old. It was a small two bedroom, and rent controlled. I kept to myself as much as possible. I pointed to the small, beat up dining table just off the living room where we were standing.

"You can set the bags on the table over there."

I watched as he sauntered over to the table and set the bags down. The way the Levi's hugged him as he walked suggested some excellent legs underneath, to say the least. As he turned around, I quickly redirected my gaze to his face. I smiled. He smiled back. Dimples – Oh My God, he has dimples.

"So, about my car, should I call you or just take the bus back to the shopping center where you were working and find you there?"

"You can call me any time you like, but I'll bring the car by when it's done."

"Oh. Okay."

He smiled again; dimples. We stared at each other in silence.

"My name is Krysta, by the way, thanks for helping me out."

"Caden and not a problem."

"Can I get you anything? Something to drink?"

"Do you have beer?"

"No, sorry, I have tea, Pepsi, milk, and this funky kiwi-strawberry stuff my daughter likes."

"Uh, no, I'll take a rain check. I'd better get going anyway, keys?"

"Huh?"

"For your car, I'll need the keys while I'm working on it."

"Oh, I have a spare set, I'll get them."

I could feel his eyes on me as I went to get the spare keys from my bedroom. I wondered if he could feel me watching him that way. It was nice to know I wasn't the only one doing some noticing, though.

The spare set of keys weren't in the jewelry box where I swear I had put them. I quickly dug through various hiding places in my room, swearing under my breath, until I finally discovered them in the bottom of my underwear drawer below a pile of bras. I have no idea how they got there. When I turned around to leave the room, he was leaning against the doorjamb watching me. I jumped.

"Sorry, it took so long; I forgot where I put them."

He stayed where he was as I went through the doorway so that my body brushed up against his as I passed. I *know* it was intentional. Trying to ignore my own reaction, I walked back into the living room. He followed lazily. I handed him the set of spare keys.

"Thanks again for all your help. My daughter should be here any time now, so I should get dinner started. She's coming home for the weekend. Would you like to stay for dinner?"

He seemed to think about it for a minute while studying my face. Pulling a card from his front shirt pocket, he shook his head.

"No, I should get going. Here's my number if you need anything. I should be able to get your car fixed tomorrow morning. I'll bring it by when I'm done."

He left, closing the door softly behind him. I could hear his steps echo down the concrete stairs outside the apartment door. After the sounds of his departure faded, I looked down at the card I held in my hand. '**Caden Neely, Call for Services**' the number was hand scrawled across the bottom; strange. The apartment door closed with a bang. I nearly fainted.

"Hi, Ma, who was that guy?"

"Evin; hi baby."

My daughter rolled her eyes as she dropped her gargantuan bag and about three layers of sweatshirts and jackets on the couch.

"Nooo, *I'm* Evin, who was the guy just leaving our house?"

My daughter's spirit, intelligence, and beauty is surpassed only by her sense of sarcasm and singular wit. In short, she's a total smart ass. I love her to death.

"Funny. His name is Caden Neely, and he's fixing the car. He gave me a ride home after it decided to quit in the Winco parking lot."

"Oh, cool. When's dinner, I'm *starving!*"

"Haven't even started it yet, but I'm making spaghetti, so it shouldn't take too long."

"Yay, spaghetti!"

At this news, Evin rushed me like a linebacker about to tackle and gave me a giant bear hug. Her hugs tend to be a bit on the violent side, if always enthusiastic. I disentangled myself and kissed her forehead. She grimaced. I grinned. Thus, was our usual routine.

"I love you, baby girl."

"Love you too, Mama."

With that, she was off to her bedroom, probably to chat on the computer with some friend she'd just left, while I made dinner. I made the sauce, and started the water to boil. While the noodles cooked, I put away what groceries remained not used for dinner, and wiped up the pool of rainwater left in their wake. As if on cue, Evin emerged from her bedroom, right as I was taking the garlic bread from the oven.

"Smells great, Ma."

"Thanks, Baby. Wanna taste the sauce and tell me if it needs anything?"

"Sure." She picked up the wooden spoon from the counter beside the stove and took a small sample of sauce from the pan, blowing softly on it before tasting. "Mmmmm, perfect doesn't need a thing."

Most family dinners, I assume, consist of parents asking their children about school, and other idle chitchat. Our little twosome were far from normal. Instead of parent questioning child about how college was going, my daughter proceeded to question me about the stranger she saw leaving our apartment as she approached. Total role-reversal, but normal in our household, so I didn't even blink.

"So, *who* was that guy *again*, and *how* did you meet him?"

"He's just some guy that's working on the renovation at that new auto-parts store in the Winco shopping center in Hillsboro. I went in to see if someone could help me when the car wouldn't start after I went grocery shopping, and the storeowner said the carpenter was a mechanic too, so I should ask him. I didn't even know his name until after he drove me home."

"MA!"

Okay, it was a *little bit* irritating when my daughter grilled me like a child.

"*What?* It's not as if I had a choice! The engine wouldn't even turn over! I had to get home."

"You could have taken a bus or called a tow truck."

"You know I only carry my debit card and tow trucks are expensive as hell."

"What if he'd been some sort of serial killer or rapist or something?"

"He wasn't."

"But what if he *was?*"

"He was very polite."

"Oh my God, Ma!"

She glared. I glared back.

"You totally like him."

"I do not!"

"Do too!"

"Do not!"

We stuck our tongues out at each other, and then laughed. I got up to clear the dishes.

"Want help, Ma?"

"No, I got it, baby."

"Okay, I'mma go to bed then, I'm beat. Love you!"

"Love you too, baby."

"Goodnight, mama."

"Goodnight, baby."

2 SATURDAY JUST AFTER 7:00PM
CADEN NEELY

The woman doesn't know her own power. I shifted uncomfortably and pulled my phone out of its holster. Looking up from dialing the phone as I headed to my truck, I narrowly avoided colliding with a teenage girl – the daughter. She looked like a little spitfire. I nodded to her as she glared suspiciously, her tall platform boots pounding up the steps beside me. Some poor soul is going to have his hands full with that one.

"Tony? Hey, bro, I need you to meet me at the Winco parking lot with the flatbed trailer. I have to move a car. Look for the green Volare. Yes, you have to empty it first. Fuck you, pay for it yourself! No, it's not mine. Some chick that came into the auto shop today I'll tell you about it later. Yes. No, I didn't fuck her. I don't know. She has a daughter, college, I think. No, fuck you, dude. Love you too, bro. Bye."

Tony has been my best bro for years. He's a pain in the ass, but he always has my back. We've worked more jobs together than I care to count. Some of them legit, even more not so much. He has a habit of borrowing my shit and bringing it back broken, dirty, or not at all. I wouldn't know what to do without him, but I want to kill him some times, crazy son of a bitch.

My mind wondered back to the woman with the Volare as I drove towards Hillsboro. I suspected half the 'damsel' act was total bullshit. Something told me that woman was a lot more dangerous than she seemed. Either way, I knew I wanted to get to know her better. A fifteen-minute starter swap in the parking lot of Winco wasn't going to accomplish that. I fibbed a little, no harm done. She gets her car fixed, and a free ride home; I get to see her again.

Tony was going to be awhile before he could meet me with the trailer, and I was starving. I decided to stop at Burger King while I was waiting for him to finish at the dump. He always brought the trailer back full of shit and expected me to pay the dump fees. At least this time I knew it would be empty, even if it did mean I had to wait.

By the time I rolled into the Winco parking lot, Tony was waiting for *me*. He'd pulled into the six parking spaces parallel to the Volare and was leaning casually against the side of the trailer. I parked beside him and got out of the truck.

"Fucker, where have you been, I've been waiting for 15 minutes."

I gave him the bird. He sent it back.

"Burger King, I was starving. Help me switch the trailer."

"Did you get me anything?"

"No, buy your own fucking food."

He laughed and unhooked the trailer from his truck. In no time, I was backing it up to the Volare. Getting the boat-sized piece of shit onto the trailer would take a little longer.

"What's wrong with this POS, anyway?"

"Bad starter."

"What?"

He let go of the crank on the pulley. The car rolled backwards a couple of feet before I could slam on the break.

"What the fuck, dude?"

"It's the fucking starter, and we're hauling this massive POS onto a flatbed to tow it back to the shop? You could swap that out in 15 minutes right here. Couldn't you get the part or something?"

"Part's in the truck."

"What the fuck, dude?"

I grinned.

"I wanted to see her again. You know, get her back to the shop."

"You're one pussy-whipped bitch."

"Fuck you."

"Fuck you, too."

We finished loading the Volare in companionable silence. The shop, and not so coincidentally my apartment, was only a three-minute drive from Winco, five hauling the car-encumbered trailer. It took us half as long to unload the car, as it had to load it. We were kicking back drinking beer inside 20 minutes.

"You gonna swap out the starter tonight?"

"Nah, I'll fix it in the morning."

"You need me to follow you to her place when you drop it off?"

"Not gonna drop it off."

"So what's your excuse to call her?"

"Tune-up."

"Clever. Get her phone number?"

I grinned. Tony was going to love this.

"Didn't need to."

"Why not? Where does she live?"

"B Street Apartments."

"You're shittin' me, really?"

"Yep, apartment number 22."

"*She's* the recluse in 22?"

"Yep."

"Alright, fucker, tell it from the top. I want the whole story."

I told him everything. The B Street Apartments were just one of many of the properties that I did maintenance on for various property owners in the area. 'The recluse in 22' had been an ongoing source of irritation over the years. No one knew what she looked like. She'd lived there since before any of the current property management came on staff. None of the other tenants spoke of her. She rarely answered the phone when anyone called to do routine maintenance and always had a reason why she didn't need it. No one ever got inside. She was a ghost. People knew she had a kid. What they didn't know was if the kid was actually hers, a grandkid, or a foster. Theories varied. Many people thought she was an old hag or a widow. Now I knew different. I wanted to know more.

"Seriously, dude, she's hot?"

"Yep."

"Wow, you lucky fuck."

I grinned.

"You gonna do *maintenance* on her?"

"Fuck off."

"Pussy-whipped!"

"Get out!"

Tony laughed and drained the last of his beer before tossing it in the can with the other empties. He stretched and burped loudly then ambled towards the shop door.

"Later, dude."

"Later."

I finished my own beer then locked up the shop and headed to bed. My apartment was upstairs from the shop. It wasn't large, but it suited me. On the other hand, the shop downstairs had plenty of room. It was perfect.

The generic ring of a disposable Nokia woke me from a dead sleep. I rolled out of bed, dug in my bottom dresser drawer for the current throw away, and hit the send button.

"Neely."

"I have a job for you."

"Type?"

"Collections."

"Address?"

The voice on the other end of the line rattled off an address in SE Portland where few reputable people would want to go during the dark hours of the night. I jotted it down on a piece of paper, even though I was sure I could drive straight there. The conversation continued its brisk pace for a few more seconds, covering other details like amount to collect, and I ended the call. There's a reason there is no number on my business card. I have a personal cell but only a select few get to have that number, and it's not in my name. It's under a shell corporation. I don't have a regular business number. For legitimate business, it's in person unless you are one of those select few. The other stuff, well, that's a little more complicated. If you want me for a job and you check out, I will get you the information needed to activate a Nokia disposable phone in my possession via discreet and untraceable means. This will give you a phone number with which to contact me. This number will be available for 72 hours and 72 hours only. After that, I will turn off the phone and dump it. If a job is going to take more than 72 hours, I repeat the process via the same channels. It's a sound system. I don't hand out very many business cards, most of the people I do work for already have all the info they need.

I threw on my clothes and headed for SE. Any tools I might need were in the toolbox of my truck. I was right about the address, I drove straight there.

As expected, my loud knock on the door of the dilapidated house got

14

no direct answer. A slight movement of the ragged bed sheet acting as a curtain to the front-facing bedroom window told me that the occupants were indeed home. I kicked in the door.

"Holy fuck! Who the hell are you?"

"Shut the fuck up and sit down."

This was the usual greeting in such situations. Most people aren't expecting to have their door broken in at three am, not even tweakers. The scrawny little man obeyed my order as if a pig had issued it. Hell, he probably gave them *more* lip. My guess was he suspected I was working for the dealer, whom he hadn't paid, that made me more dangerous than the cops.

"Anyone else here, Lawrence?"

The fact that I knew his name and he didn't know mine didn't seem to faze him. He shook his head in immediate answer, his bottom lip quivering as if he were about to cry, fucking punk.

"Where's the money, Lawrence?"

"I was gonna pay, I swear. It's just that rent was due, and I had to pay the heat bill, and…"

"Sure you were Lawrence."

There wasn't a light on in the place. The only illumination came from the street lamps outside. It was obvious the heat hadn't run in days, at least. I was willing to bet the electricity was off. Hell, he was probably just a squatter here.

"You were seen with another dealer. You put the money in your arm didn't you, Lawrence?"

I tapped my kneecapper against my thigh. More lip quivering.

"Word is you came into some cash, Lawrence. Where's the money?"

His eyes moved involuntarily towards the kitchen, then up; freezer. So predictable.

"I – I need it."

In a flash, I had his scrawny throat in my grip and the kneecapper ready to strike.

"More than your knees? Let's get the money, ok?"

He swallowed and nodded. I shifted my grip to the back of his neck as he rose to his feet. We made our way through the dark the short distance to the kitchen. He opened the freezer, no electricity. I smirked. The money was in an empty ice-cream container, cute. He owed my employer $1500.00, there was $2000.00 in the box; I took it all. As well as the baggie of pot rolled up next to it: bonus. I left Lawrence trembling in the crappy old house with promises to come back if he didn't meet his future obligations.

By the time I made it back to the shop, the sun was rising. I took a shower to wash the stink of SE off me, put on fresh clothes, and went to work on the Volare. It was going to be a good day.

3 SATURDAY NIGHT – LATE
KRYSTA MALLORY

It's always so nice to have her back home. The weekend visits were becoming more infrequent as she made new friends at college and got comfortable with campus life. I gently pulled the glasses off her face and set them on her bedside table, she'd fallen asleep wearing them again. She looked so young and fragile when she was asleep. Even with the piercings glinting in the light at eyebrow and lip. It was easy to forget how strong she is. Poor baby has had such a hard life. I haven't really helped that any, but we've made it through, and we are closer for it. She's a tough little thing, my little lifesaver. Sometimes I think she spends as much or more time worrying about me as I do her. Indulgently, I watched her sleeping for a moment more before tucking the blanket tighter about her shoulders. I closed her door softly behind me.

The living room clock read 11:30pm, but I didn't feel like going to bed. Instead, I made a cup of tea and curled up on the couch to watch the late news. Somewhere between the droning of the newscaster and thoughts of the past, I dozed off…

~*~

Spring, 1992

Halfway through reapplying my lipstick there was a knock on the door. I somehow managed not to smear it, calling out "just a minute" as I finished, before going to answer. The man waiting outside my apartment door held out an extravagant bouquet and flashed a charming smile.

"I wanted something to match your beauty; this was the best they could do."

I laughed and invited him in while I found a vase. We'd met at the little market where I worked as a part time clerk. He was a rookie police officer. He was funny and charming, and always knew the right thing to say. He asked me out five times before I said yes. I was barely 20 and had just moved into my own apartment. I hadn't dated much, but who could be safer than a cop is? After setting the vase of flowers on the table, I leaned in to smell them. They were lovely, but lacked fragrance.

"They're beautiful, thank you. So, what are we going to see?"

"There's a new comedy called 'Encino Man', I thought we'd go see that."

He walked in front of me to his car and got into the driver's side. Leaning across the front seat, he unlocked the passenger door so that I could get in. The first few minutes of the drive were especially quiet; I guess we were both nervous. I made an attempt at small talk to break up the tension.

"What made you decide to become a Police Officer?"

His laugh was a little unnerving. I tried to shake it off.

"You know; guns, bad guys, and fast cars – what's not to love."

"Don't you worry it will be dangerous?"

"Dangerous," he flashed a smile, "to me?"

I shivered. Perhaps I'd had enough small talk. We rode the rest of the way in silence. At the theatre, he bought our tickets and a giant container of popcorn, which he offered to share, but mostly ate himself. I've never been a big fan of the stuff, so I only picked at it a bit. I allowed the smooth movement of his arm around my shoulder, as we laughed and commented with the rest of the viewers. Brandon Frasier was great, and Polly Shore was his usual hippy self. The movie was hilarious. As we joked our way back to the car, I guiltily reassessed my earlier misgivings as nerves. He was just a regular guy, and I was having fun.

It was late when we got back to my apartments, but I wasn't tired yet.

He walked me to the door. Hesitantly, he kissed me goodnight. Suddenly, he seemed a little unsure of himself. It was sweet.

"Would you like to come in for a little while? I can make coffee."

He smiled shyly. "I would like that."

The new brass doorknob gleamed brightly under the fluorescent porch light as I inserted the key and smoothly turned the knob. Stepping inside, he closed the door behind us and leaned back against it. Setting the coffee to brew, I glanced over as I heard the click of the door locking.

"You can never be too safe. You would be surprised how many home invasions occur while people are watching TV in their living rooms with the door unlocked."

"That never would have occurred to me."

"It happens all the time."

Casually, he stepped forward and held out his hand.

"You're beautiful, come over here a minute."

"You're just saying that."

I took his hand. He pulled me close and wrapped his arms around me.

"You really don't know it, do you?"

Sliding one massive hand up to cup the back of my head, he leaned down and kissed me. Starting out softly, he let me warm to the kiss as it gradually heated up and became more passionate. Soon the kisses were frantic, and we were fighting for air. Practiced and smooth, in moments he had me pressed up against the wall, hands roaming my body through my clothes. His kisses grew rougher and moved down my neck as his hands moved to the buttons on the front of my shirt. Instinctually, my hands went to draw his away.

"Not yet."

Fingers lacing with mine, he drew my hands above my head and kissed me again, even more fierce than before. His body ground against mine, pressing me hard against the wall. Once more, his hand went to the buttons of my shirt, the other still clasped mine above my head. I tried to pull them free. His grip tightened.

"Not yet, I'm not ready."

When his eyes met mine, they'd gone cold.

"*I* say when you're ready."

Roughly, he pulled the front of my shirt open, sending two of the buttons skittering across the floor. I whimpered and struggled.

"No! Please stop!"

My words were lost on his ears. His hands moved roughly over my body. I fought to push him away. I begged him to stop. His breath was hot as he kissed my mouth and neck roughly, then moved down and tore the material of my bra away from my breast. He used one hand to keep my wrists bound while he pulled my jeans open and down with the other.

"Please stop, please stop, plea—"

My cries were a mantra that he interrupted by covering my mouth with his. I tasted the salt from my own tears on his lips after he had kissed my cheeks and neck. It was over quickly. His full weight sagged against mine when he finished as he rested his head against the wall above my shoulder. Tears streamed silently down my face, and I choked back a sob. Finally, he shifted his weight back and stood, pulling up and fastening his jeans as he did so. He brushed a casual hand through his sandy colored hair and smiled at me. He smiled at me. Like nothing was wrong.

"I have to use the bathroom."

I all but ran for the bathroom door, locking it behind me. He didn't attempt to stop me. I collapsed onto the toilet seat and sobbed uncontrollably for a few minutes. Gradually, I got my crying under control. I used a hot washrag to clean myself up some, adjusted my torn clothing, and returned to the living room. He was sitting on the couch, completely relaxed. What do I do now call the police? He *is* the police. I just wanted him out of my apartment so I could wash his filth off me. As if he could sense my thoughts, he looked at me and smiled coldly.

"I have an early shift, I should get going."

"Okay."

"Don't forget to lock your door."

With that astoundingly expert advice, he was gone. I doubt many criminals were more dangerous than the *officer* that just left. I locked the door and went to take a very hot shower.

~*~

Present Day

Drenched in sweat, I fought free of the blanket and sat up on the couch. It was 3:00am; an infomercial blared loudly from the TV, advertising some new miracle product for "the one time only introductory price of $19.95." I picked up the remote and shut it off. I wondered what prompted me to relive that nightmare. It had been a very long time since I'd had that dream. After the rape happened, I relived it in my sleep every night for months. He sent me flowers the next day. The card read, "Had a blast," bastard. It was the same arrangement as the one he handed me at the door the night before. Come to think about it, I don't think I've let a single man inside the apartment since that night, until yesterday. Well, that explained the dream. Caden Neely was about as different from that cop as you could get. I awoke feeling dirty. I went to take a hot bath.

4 SUNDAY EARLY AFTERNOON
CADEN NEELY

I hate when a plan bites me in the ass. I finished the starter in *less* than 15 minutes. I had to drive all the way to Beaverton to get the alternator. By the time I got back and put the damn thing in, the morning was gone. The car finally started but it ran like shit, and oil leaked from every orifice. It really *did* need a tune-up; at least. Fuck. I couldn't give it back to her like this. I massaged my forehead for a minute, and then went to dig out the tenant numbers for the B Street Apartments. Her number was on the bottom of the page. I dialed it from my personal cell, anticipating a quick answer; after all, I'd given her my number so she should know who it was. It went to her voicemail: perfect.

"Krysta, it's Caden Neely, your car is going to take longer than I thought. Got it to start but its leaking oil everywh—"

Fucking voicemail cut me off. I called back. This time I rattled off the address of the shop, my number, and told her to call me if she needed a ride anywhere. I hung up and went back to work on the car. Why do I get myself into this shit?

The deeper I got into the engine of the Volare, the more problems I found. It was as if the woman *never* had any work done on the thing. You can't just drive a car into the ground and never change the oil. That does damage. I was spending more time tracking down parts than under the hood. The car was a fucking relic. It was starting to get expensive. I was going to eat every fucking dime. She had better appreciate it.

I was covered in oil and hot as hell when I got to the timing. Like the rest of the car, it wasn't cooperating. I pulled freshly installed spark plugs and removed the brand new distributor cap. Watching the rotor closely, I turned the fan. The distributor didn't move – bad timing chain.

"Is it as bad as it sounds?"

I quickly straightened and slammed my head into the hood of the car.

"FUCK!"

The teenage girl standing beside her tried to smother a giggle. She brought her daughter, great. The giggle contradicted the tough-girl image the girl's gothic clothing and scathing 'fuck you' glare gave off. More than meets the eye, just like her mother – who was watching me curiously.

"What?"

"My car – is it as bad as it sounds?"

"Worse. I fix one thing and find something new."

"Oh. Is it going to be expensive?"

"Don't worry about it."

"I really don't have much money."

"I said don't – Look, it's on the house, ok?"

She looked both relieved *and* worried. Don't look a gift horse in the mouth, lady.

"I like working on cars. It's ok, really."

"Are you sure?"

"Ya."

"Hey grease monkey," the kid interrupted, "your head is bleeding."

The smile on the girls face was positively evil; as if she was happy I was bleeding.

"Thanks, kid. I'll be right back."

I went to get a paper towel from the rear of the shop. As I walked back, I heard Krista whisper to her daughter.

"Evin, *be nice!*"

"Why," Evin said loudly, "I don't even know him."

I laughed.

"She's right. I could be dangerous."

"*See* mom!"

"Evin, Stop."

They glared at each other. Then the girl – Evin, moved her glare to me, but somehow it didn't seem quite as sincere.

"So, do you need something, or did you come by to check on your car?"

"Actually, it's kind of both. I have a bunch of errands to run, so I need my car."

"Not ready."

"Well, do you know how long it's going to take?"

"No."

She looked a little flustered. I tossed the blood soaked paper towel in the garbage barrel and lit a cigarette. I was enjoying myself immensely.

"It's an old car. Have you *ever* taken it in for a tune up or oil change? You should check the oil every time you put gas in it."

She glared at me. I could see where the daughter gets it. Maybe I shouldn't push it. I took one last long drag off my cigarette and tossed it on the ground.

"I'll give you a ride. Just let me get the grease off my hands."

"Thank you."

"Mom, we should just take the bus."

"The bus takes too long."

"Fine – whatever."

I watched the mother-daughter exchange in silence, wondering if I should back out now. Unfortunately, I was already in waist deep.

"We'll take you up on the ride, thanks."

"Ok, just give me a sec. I'll be right back."

'Running errands' consisted of driving all over hell and back from store to store and then waiting an eternity while the kid tried on clothes. I gathered from the semi-heated argument between mother and daughter as we drove, that the kid needed new clothes – but didn't want them. She thought her taped-up boots and holey jeans were just fine. Her mother clearly didn't agree.

"If the kid wants to wear ripped jeans, why don't you let her?"

Two razor-sharp glares swiveled in my direction.

"I'm not a kid."

"Because –"

I held up my hands in defeat.

"Okay, okay, I'll stay out of it."

Having given them a new target for their animosity, they stopped arguing and shifted to teasing each other instead: women. After three stops, they apparently had the jeans conquered and we were off after shoes. Another argument started.

"Mom, I got these online. They aren't going to have anything like them around here."

"They're falling apart, Evin, the sole is almost completely torn off. You have to get new shoes."

"No it's not, look, I fixed it."

In an amazing display of flexibility, the girl twisted her leg around to show her mother the bottom of her boot. Duct-tape held it firmly together, which looked like it had been colored black with a sharpie. I laughed. I was beginning to like this kid. Krysta sighed loudly.

"You're getting new shoes."

"I won't like anything they have around here."

"Well, I don't know what to tell you. You are going to have to find something."

I decided it was a good time to score some points. It would probably cost me, but it would be worth it.

"I have an idea."

"What?" they demanded simultaneously.

"Why don't I take you girls to Washington Square? I'm sure she can find some boots she'll like there."

"That will be expensive."

"I'll cover it."

"Mom, can we, please?"

The kid gave her mom a look that would melt ice. I had the feeling I'd be seeing more of that in the future. I felt my wallet lighten.

"I'll pay you back."

"Don't worry about it."

An hour and a half later, we sat in the food court at Washington Square eating fast food and chatting like old pals while Evin happily examined her new steel-toed, knee high gothic boots. I paid almost $200.00 for them. They were worth every penny.

"Mama, aren't they pretty?"

"Yes, Evin."

Evin stuck out her booted feet and turned them from side to side. The buckles that ran up the length of the boots gleamed. She grinned evilly. The same grin she'd flashed when my head was bleeding.

"I bet these could do some damage!"

Krysta and I both laughed. The girl was positively violent. I got the feeling it covered a soft interior. It usually does. I really liked this kid. The mother – well, I'd still like to get to know her better. This wasn't a bad start though, not bad at all.

The ride back to Forest Grove was much quieter than the earlier part of the day. Evin fell asleep almost immediately. The fierce, tough-girl image fell away when she was sleeping. It made her look a lot younger. Krysta's face was tender and unguarded as she watched her daughter sleep. I felt like I was witnessing something sacred and private. I suppressed the urge to reach for her, startled at how strong it was. Way too soon for that. I focused my eyes on the road and tried to clear my head.

"Thanks for driving us around today. And thanks for getting Evin the boots, she really likes them."

She still had that look on her face when she turned toward me. It wasn't helping my thought process.

"No trouble, I was ready for a break anyway."

"I'm sorry if she was harsh earlier, she's pretty protective of me. We're all each other have."

"She's a good kid, I like her."

Krysta looked surprised.

"Yes, she is."

I turned into the B Street Apartments and turned off the engine. Krysta watched Evin for a moment more before gently shaking her awake.

"Evin, we're home, wake up."

I got out and gathered the bags from the back then opened the passenger door to let them out of the truck. Evin climbed groggily from the cab and stumbled towards their apartment. She was still half-asleep. Krysta got out after her.

"She goes back to school tomorrow; I'm going to miss her."

"Where's she going to school?"

"Portland State University, this is only her third term, I'm still adjusting."

"It must be hard."

"It is. I would like to keep her at home forever. Evin would never allow that."

"Couldn't convince her to live at home and commute?"

"She's far too independent for that. I think I stifle her."

She looked sad. Once again, I ignored an impulse to touch her.

"I'd better get going, I'll walk you up."

"Okay, thanks."

The truck felt empty and too quiet as I drove back home. I turned on the radio and flipped through the stations. Only one station wasn't playing commercials, so I left it there. The sounds of Van Morrison's 'Brown Eyed Girl' filled the cab of the truck. Krysta has brown eyes. I turned the radio back off and drove the rest of the way in silence.

5 MONDAY 9:45AM
EVIN MALLORY

"I'm leaving, Ma!"

"Evin, wait, I want hugs and kisses."

Mom rushed from the bathroom still tying her robe. She looked like she hadn't slept – again. I pretended to grimace while she kissed my forehead and gave me a giant hug. She expected the little rebellions. The truth was I loved her hugs and kisses. I missed them like hell when they took me away.

"Are you sick again, Ma?"

"No, baby, I'm just not awake yet. Do you have everything you need? Do you have your bus pass and money?"

"I'm fine, Ma. I can take care of myself. Get some sleep while I'm gone."

"I will baby. Have fun at school. I'll see you next weekend?"

"Ya, I'll be home Friday night. Be careful around that *guy*."

"Evin, I'm an adult, I can take care of myself."

I laughed.

"Right, Ma, love you. See you in a few days."

I could feel Mom watch me as I walked down the steps from the apartment and across the parking lot. Sometimes I swear she thinks I'm still a child. Of the two of us, I think she's the one that needs the most looking after. I learned how to fend for myself a while ago. Being in foster care will do that to you, not to mention growing up with a suicidal mom. If that doesn't make you mature quickly, I don't know what will. She tries though. Honestly, I think losing me for a while might have been the best thing to happen to *her*. She's been a lot healthier since she got me back home. She seems *almost* happy sometimes. I wish she would make some friends though. She needs more than just me. I hate leaving her alone during the week. I never know what I'll find when I get back from school. But, *damn it* I need a life too! I can't live at home forever. She has to let me go eventually. *She* needs to get out into the world. Mama has locked herself in that apartment for way too long. You can't just shut the world out. Eventually, it's going to break in on you whether you want it to or not. God knows I had to learn *that* the hard way.

Bus 57 idled at the end of the line stop on the corner of B Street and 19th Ave. That early on a Monday there were usually only a few people waiting for the bus but today, there were at least 12. I stopped a little outside of the group and waited for the driver to come out of the break room and open the door so we could get on. If there were this many people already, by the time we got to the stop by Hatfield Government Center in Hillsboro where I could transfer to the Max, it was going to be packed. Great fucking start to my day.

When the 57 reached Cornelius, the bus was standing room only. Screeching to a stop at 10th street, the driver opened the doors. A *very* pregnant Latino woman struggled up the steps with a toddler on her hip and a stroller packed to the brim pulled behind her. I had long since abandoned my seat to an elderly woman, but no one budged when the about to burst woman and her child came aboard. She braced the stroller with her leg and held onto the overhead bar with one hand while she kept her squirming toddler in the other. There was an obviously healthy kid, a year or two younger than I am, sitting in one of the front seats. He ignored her and fiddled with his phone. I lightly kicked his foot to get his attention. He looked up with attitude all over his face.

"Give the pregnant lady your seat."

"Fuck off."

"Don't fuck with me, you little punk, I said give the pregnant lady your seat."

He looked about to argue some more, then flipped me off and got up, pushing his way to the back of the bus. I smiled at the woman with the little kid and signaled for her to take the seat. She smiled back, if a little warily, before slowly easing into the seat and positioning the toddler on her lap.

"Thank you, that really wasn't necessary."

"Yes it was; that pisses me off. He should have offered it to you."

Every time I ride the bus or the max, it's the same thing, and every time it pisses me off. I guess that today I'd just had enough. I was surprised it actually worked though. There is always some asshole taking up a handicapped seat that refuses to move when someone gets on board and needs it. Kids today just don't give a damn. Most people look at me and think that I'm one of those kids. They are usually surprised to find out I'm not *normal*. I have nothing in common with most of the adolescent jerks my age. I hate it when anyone assumes that I do.

The rest of the trip back into Portland was uneventful. Once I settled on the Max, I plugged the headphones into my cell and blasted my music to block out the noise. The crowds and confined space of the Max train always made me claustrophobic. The music helped. I let the tunes and the gentle motions of the train lull me into a light sleep.

~*~

Kicking the door closed behind me, I dumped my backpack on the couch and pulled off my headphones. School didn't actually let out for another two hours. I was suspended. Mom was not going to be happy, but she'd probably threaten to sue the school board, not be mad at *me*. It's not *my* fault I'm hyperactive. It's not as if I was disrupting class on purpose, although that's exactly what the teacher called it. According to *her*, I am *always* 'generally disrespectful to authority and disruptive in class on a daily basis'. All because I tap my pen or pencil or generally fidget with something when I have excess energy. As if I can control how much energy I have. I hate stupid people. Just three and a half more years and I'll be *done* with fucking high school.

"Mama, I'm home."

No answer, she must be in the bath reading her book. I finished unloading my jackets and headed for the bathroom, note from Principal in hand. There was a fancy bouquet of flowers on the dining room table. I stopped to smell them and read the card. They didn't really smell at all. The card said, "Happy Anniversary – See you again soon, we'll have a blast." Happy Anniversary? What the hell? I decided to question Mom later. After tapping briefly on the door to warn her I was coming in, I opened the door and stepped inside. The first thing that hit me was the smell. It smelled like wet pennies. Seconds later the blood registered. Mama was in the bath, knife lying on the side of the tub, her head resting on the back as if she was sleeping. The water was a sickening diluted reddish pink color. There were drops and smears of varying shades of brown and crimson smeared over her face and the sides of the tub and shower tiles. Her arms floated listlessly, little red ribbons gently flowing off the jagged tears in her wrists into the hot water in which she lay. I screamed and ran back into the living room for my phone and dialed 911.

"Please state your emergency."

"I think my mom tried to kill herself. There's blood everywhere, she looks like she's sleeping, and there's a knife. It looks like she cut her wrists."

"Okay, Miss, calm down. Is she breathing?"

"I don't know I didn't touch her. Please just come."

"Okay, I'm sending help. I'm going to stay on the phone with you until they arrive. Where are you located?"

"The B Street Apartments, Number 22, Forest Grove."

"Okay, Miss, help is on the way. They should be there in just a few minutes. There is a station just a few blocks from you."

"Thank you, I don't know how long she's been like this, the water was still steaming though."

"Okay, help will be there soon, you are doing fine."

I could already hear the sirens. Still holding the phone to my ear, I flung the door open. An ambulance was pulling into the parking lot. I ran down the steps and waved them over. Two EMT's jumped out of the ambulance and started gathering their supplies, then motioned for me to show them where the patient was. I ran back up the steps and into our apartment, the EMT's following closely. I pointed at the bathroom. I couldn't bring myself to go back in there. I couldn't see her like that again. The EMT's rushed toward the bathroom. I could hear them pull her from the water and start to work on her. Their voices blurred together as they issued commands to one another. After what felt like an eternity, they were loading her onto a gurney that someone had brought into the living room. I realized the apartment was *full* of people, cops, firefighters, and at least two more EMT's. I realized I still hadn't hung up the phone that I held limply in my hand. I ended the call and put it in my pocket.

"Excuse me, Miss, are you the young lady that called 911?"

There was a cop standing over me where I sat on the couch in the living room. He was tall with sandy blond hair and faded blue eyes. He smiled at me; I shivered. Who smiles at a moment like this?

"Ya, I'm her daughter, why?"

"I just need to ask you a few questions."

"Can it wait? I really want to go with her to the hospital."

"Sure. If you like, I can give you a lift to the hospital and we can talk while we're waiting for word from the doctors."

"I guess that would be ok, thanks."

The cop was somewhat creepy, but then, I think *all* cops are creepy. I guess he was just trying to do his job. I put my sweatshirt and jacket back on and followed him out to his police car. We followed the ambulance to St. Vincent Hospital on Barnes road in silence. After we got into the emergency room one of the EMT's approached us and told me that mama was stable and the doctors would tell me more when they could. The cop asked the nurse at the desk if there was somewhere private we could talk. She led us through a door to the left of the ER entrance, down a couple of maze-like hallways, and motioned us into a small conference room. After holding the door open, she closed it softly behind us. I answered his questions in a daze, recounting the events from the time I opened the door to when he showed up asking his questions. He kept going back to the flowers. He asked me to repeat what they looked and smelled like twice and recite the card to him so he could write it down word for word. It almost seemed like he was getting off on it. I was just about to tell him I didn't want to talk to him any more when the social worker came in. She was a squat, olive-skinned, Hispanic woman with a pudgy face and bad skin. She had poorly died auburn hair twisted into a clip at the back of her head, and shifty small dark eyes. I disliked her instantly. She walked toward me, pudgy hand outstretched, and plastered on a fake smile that didn't touch her eyes. I ignored her hand until she dropped it.

"Hello, sweetheart, you must be Evin Mallory. My name is Violet, but my friends just call me Vi. Do you mind if the nice officer and I step out into the hall and chat for a moment?"

"No, *Violet*, I don't mind. Go right on ahead and have your *chat*."

Violet and the cop went out into the hallway, closing the door firmly behind them. I could hear her cheap Payless pumps clicking on the linoleum floor tiles as they moved a little bit down the hallway away from the door. I jumped up from the chair I was sitting in and looked out the small square window in the door of the conference room. They seemed to be arguing about something, but I couldn't tell what. After a few minutes, the cop stormed off and the fat little social worker headed back in my direction. I hurried back to my chair and sat down. I was exactly how she left me when she came back in.

"Sorry about that, sweetheart, adult business you know. The nice officer had to respond to a call, so it's just you and me now. How are you holding up?"

I stared at her blankly. Was she a fucking idiot? My mom just tried to kill herself, how the hell did she *think* I was doing? I resisted the urge to jump up and slug the bitch. She took my silence as encouragement to continue.

"It will be alright, sweetheart, we're going to take good care of you while your mom is getting better. The doctors told me she just needs some time to rest and TLC and she'll be good as new. In the meantime I'm going to take you to visit a nice family where you won't have to be all alone, okay?"

"What? I don't want to go with you I want to go home. I need to be with my mom."

"Your mom is in good hands, sweethea—"

"I'm not your fucking sweetheart, stop calling me that! My name is Evin!"

I was reconsidering decking the bitch. Suddenly her voice lost the saccharine edge to it and became a whole lot nastier.

"Listen, *Evin*, you don't have a choice. You are 15 years old, a minor. Your mother is a danger to herself and therefore unfit. You are going to a foster home. End. Of. Discussion."

~*~

"The doors are closing. The doors are closing. Please keep all belongings out of the yellow marked areas when the train is in motion."

The electronic voice of the transit recording cut into my music and jarred me awake. The last vestiges of the dream melting from my consciousness and quickly forgotten. My stop was up next. I ride the Max so often that I usually wake up just in time to get off. Occasionally I have to double back, but not very often.

I love the city. I love how you can get lost in the crowds of people but still not *feel* crowded. I love the sounds, the smells, and the noises. Most of all, I love the old buildings. Portland has such personality. I love Forest Grove too; Portland is just so much *more*. Someday, I am going to travel and see the world. So many other great cities out there that I want to visit. First, I have to finish college. I have priorities. Another thing I *don't* have in common with most of the teenage population. I just hope that Mom will be ok when I'm gone. She needs me.

I don't actually have class on Mondays. I usually meet with my counselor around two but she had to reschedule this week. Monday is the day to have *me* time; Doctors orders. It takes about two hours to get to my dorm at The Broadway downtown from our apartment in Forest Grove. I dumped out the contents of my backpack and quickly repacked it for a trip to Forest Park. It takes a while to get there from the dorms, but I had all day and it's my favorite place to go to walk and write. You can get lost out there if you want to and people leave you alone. It's crazy, a giant forest in the middle of the city. I found it by accident a couple of weeks after I started school. Now I go there all the time. I thought my counselor would flip when I told her, but she actually encouraged me to continue doing it. "It's important to reward yourself..." *blah blah blah*. I didn't really pay attention to the rest of the psychobabble. I actually used to go to a completely different area of the park than I do now. My therapist recommended the Lower MacLeay Park and Wildwood trails. I guess she does a lot of hiking and stuff and she told me about the ruins of an old building out in that section of Forest Park she thought I might like. I guess it used to be bathrooms in the 1930's or something, but everyone calls it the Stone House now. Either way, it's my favorite place to go sit by myself and write.

After repacking my bag, I locked my room and headed to the Starbucks downstairs on the corner of Jackson and 6th to get a Carmel Mocha Frappuccino. As usual, there was a variety of college students and business professionals crowding the place. By the time it was my turn at the register, Joe, the Barista, was already making my Frappuccino. I get the same thing every time I go in. They all know my order by heart.

"Hey, Evin, off to therapy?"

"Not today, therapist cancelled, spending the day at the park."

"Going to the ruins again?"

Joe handed me the Frappuccino. I paid with a five and put the change in his tip jar.

"I'd tell you but then I'd have to kill ya."

I grinned and waved. He waved back as I left Starbucks and headed down 6th to Harrison to catch bus 17. The bus ride to NW Vaughn and 27th was supposed to take 24 minutes according to the Tri-met trip planner. In reality it was more like 45, with all the stops and people getting on and off in between.

Talking to Joe at Starbucks made me think about my therapist. I actually rather liked her. Most of them are idiots. She seemed to get me though. Like how she totally knew I would love this area of Forest Park. By the time the bus got to my stop, the Frappuccino was gone. I dumped the empty cup in the trashcan at the front of the bus and got off. The Stone House ruins are about a mile from the bus stop, but I don't really mind, I like walking. The only vehicle in the Lower MacLeay Park parking lot was a white delivery van with its emergency lights flashing and no one in sight. Probably went to get gas.

April in this part of Oregon is soggy at best, with a few sun breaks to make sure you're paying attention. Today it was trying to be sunny with the occasional burst of thunderous drizzle and hail: typical Oregon weather.

Therefore, the trail, once you got past the paved part, was muddy, but I'm used to that. Tracks littered it from hikers and various animals but I didn't pass anyone as I made my way toward the ruins. Many people avoid the trails until the weather dries up in July; others wait for the few dry stretches in between. A handful of die-hards like me hit the trails regardless of the weather, but the park is so big that unless you are in a group you may still never run into anyone. There are some guided tours and such I think, but that's just not my thing. Those are for tourists.

The Stone House was deserted when I got there, which is exactly the way I like it. I dumped my backpack at the bottom of the moss-covered steps and shrugged off my sweatshirt. The hike in had me roasting. My sweatshirt took up residence next to the backpack as I dug out one of the Kiwi-Strawberry Arizona's I stashed from the mini fridge in my dorm. Despite the fact that sweat was practically pouring from my back, the can was still cold. I held it to my forehead for a minute before I opened it and gulped about half.

"Well you are a pretty little thing aren't you?"

I dropped my Arizona and tried not to choke. The guy came out of nowhere. He had to have been hiding around the other side of the ruins just waiting. He was fucking *huge*, like over six foot and 200 pounds. Of course, I'm only five foot five, so that's not saying much. He was greasy looking, as you would expect to find running drugs or pimping whores. I involuntarily shivered. I made these assessments in about the time it took my Arizona to travel from my hand to the ground and splatter my new, and relatively muddy, boots.

"Fuck off, dude, I'm not interested."

"A mouthy little bitch too, isn't she?"

This last bit came from another guy, who stepped out of the trees to stand a little back down the path from the direction I had come. He was smaller than the other one was, but looked just as mean, not good.

"I bet we could teach her a better use for that mouth. Whaddya say, C?" The short one inched closer.

I eased the lipstick mace out of my pocket.

"You know the rules, A, can't touch the merchandise. Let's pack her up and get out of this shit hole."

The tall dude strode forward, ready to grab me. Waiting until he was actually reaching for me, I grabbed his wrist and yanked him forward, simultaneously kneeing him in the groin and emptying the mace into his eyes. He fell to the ground screaming like a baby. I turned to the other one.

"Lucky shot, little girl, but whatcha gonna do now? You ain't got no more mace."

I straightened my left leg and brought my right leg forward, bending it slightly, while also squaring my shoulders and bringing my fists into a forward guard position. I grinned at him.

"You're quite the little fighter, aren't you?" He said, stepping forward.

"That's my name, don't wear it out..."

I sprang into motion, going into a full roundhouse kick, my right leg snapping up and out quick as a flash. I'm fast as hell. He was faster. He caught my foot inches from his nose. I felt a needle slide into the back of my neck; the partner was back up.

"Fu—"

All of my muscles melted. I collapsed to the ground in a boneless heap. *That's* going to bruise. My brain was working in slow motion. I could hear but I couldn't move or speak. What the fuck did he *give* me?

"I can't believe the bitch fucking maced me!"

"Did you see that roundhouse she threw at me, C? You're lucky *you* got the mace! I'd like to see *you* try and catch a kick like that!"

"Fuck off, Alan. Get the bag and help me haul this bitch out of here."

"*Hey,* no full names!"

I don't think they realized that I could still hear them. Maybe whatever they gave me usually knocked people out completely, but I could hear them just fine. There was some scraping and shuffling then one of them threw me over his shoulder like a bag of potatoes. I think it was the tall one. I tried looking around but everything was so blurry it just made me nauseous.

After a few minutes, rough hands pulled me from the shoulder and positioned me into some sort of wheelchair, strapping me in. They must have had one of those all-terrain wheelchairs stashed. One of them pulled a baseball cap from somewhere and put it on me, pulling the bill down to hide my eyes. I'm sure it went really well with my black ripped jeans, gothic boots and crimson lace-up top. Idiots. Any moron could have seen something was wrong with the girl in the wheelchair *besides* the fact that she was in a wheelchair. Fortunately, for the idiots, or *unfortunately* for me, we didn't pass anyone on the trail back to the parking lot. At least not that I could hear anyway.

"Throw her in the back of the van, C; I'll get rid of the chair."

Of course, the fucking delivery van in the parking lot. God, I'm stupid. There's no way this was random. They were totally waiting. They knew I was coming. They were prepared. The realization filled me with fear, and I whimpered involuntarily.

"She's still awake, A."

"Not for long."

Searing pain blossomed across my head, and then everything went black.

~*~

My therapist was on the phone when I got to her office. She motioned me in, and pointed to the leather couch against the wall parallel to her desk. I dumped my bag and shrugged out of my jacket, then sat down and waited for her to finish her call.

"Uh huh. No, two pm should be perfect. Yes, that's fine. Ok, she'll be there. Bye." She hung up the phone.

"Sorry, about that, Evin. I'm afraid I'm going to have to reschedule next Monday's session. That was about my daughter. I have to take her to an appointment. Normally my ex-husband would take her but he's going to be out of town on business. Perhaps you can spend a little extra time at the park next week, instead. Give you a bit of a break from the routine."

"That'd be nice."

"So why don't you tell me how things are going. Did you go see your mom this last weekend? How is school?"

"School is school. I didn't go home last weekend, had too much homework to do. I'm going home this weekend; I can't stay away too long, or mom starts bugging me."

"You worry about her too, though, don't you?"

"I guess."

"Are you still journaling?"

"Ya."

"Spending a lot of time at the park?"

"I like it there."

"It's a nice place."

"Have you explored any new areas? Forest Park has a lot to offer, you know."

"I pretty much stick to the Stone House area. I like to go there to write. It's quiet."

"Yes, I can see how it would be a relaxing place to write."

~*~

Confused images of my therapist's office faded into the background as I tried to get my bearings. I was lying on some sort of padding in the back of a vehicle – the van. That fucker cold-clocked me. Sweat ran from my forehead into my eyes, and pooled at the small of my back. The pungent smell of Juniper trees filled my nostrils. The back of the van was dark. I tried to wipe the sweat from my eyes and realized my hands were bound to something above my head. My ankles were also constrained by something attached to the floor of the van. They weren't taking any chances. There was some sort of soft gag in my mouth. I turned my head and blinked my eyes rapidly, trying to stop the stinging from the sweat. I could hear voices coming from the front of the van.

"Why the fuck we gotta drive all the way to Sisters, anyway, Charlie?

Why ain't we taking the bitch to the auction house in Salem like usual?"

"Because, *Alan,* like I told you before, this one is special order. The boss has had an eye on this one for a *long time.*"

"Special order – what the hell does that *mean* anyway? One pussy is the same as the next, far as I'm concerned."

"Means she was *bred* for someone specific and now that she's of age it's time to deliver."

For the second time since encountering these men, raw fear overwhelmed me and I cried out. Bright light temporarily blinded me as the curtain separating the front of the van from the back parted and a head poked through.

"Passenger's awake, C."

"Well, go dose her. Better give her a double this time, too, don't want her waking up before she's settled in."

"OK."

The one I now knew was Alan came into the back of the van holding a syringe. Alan sat patiently while I kicked and fought against my restraints until worn out, then held my head down with one hand and inserted the needle into my neck with the other. I felt myself slip back into oblivion.

6 MONDAY EARLY AFTERNOON
KRYSTA MALLORY

Evin always left a trail of debris in her wake when she visited home as evidence of her passing. I grumble to her about it from time to time, but as long as it means she keeps coming home, I really don't mind. Her weekend visits tend to group together sporadically, depending on her current level of stress or worry for me. Sometimes I'll go for weeks without getting any more than a text saying, "I love you, Mom". Then, she'll come home every weekend for a month straight. That's just how Evin works. Her moods often seem inexplicable to the outside world, but I understand them completely. She is so much more like me than she will often admit. The extreme swings between childlike playfulness and seriousness beyond her years. Hours lost in thought, and then that very same evening giggling like a little girl over the silliest of things. She is full of so much innocence *and* wisdom. It takes a hard life to result in such a contradicting personality. Creating an exceptionally unique and special person: like my Evin. Oh yes, we are alike, my baby girl and I. It's why our fights, when we have them, are so heated, and our play is so childlike and wholehearted. I missed her already, and she hadn't even been gone a full day yet. As I followed her trail of discarded clothing, food wrappers, and dirty dishes through the apartment, gathering as I went, my mind drifted backward.

~*~

It had been five months since the rape. My reflection in the mirror grew more haggard by the day. I didn't even recognize myself anymore. Dark brown hair laid listlessly about my shoulders, and deep, bruise-like circles underscored the green-flecked brown of my eyes. Avoiding my own gaze, I picked up the razor off the edge of the sink. My arms were already a network of scars. Hesitation marks. I relived that horrible scene every night in my dreams. I couldn't take it anymore. I saw him everywhere. Pressing the blade to my left wrist, I watched entranced as the first drops of blood rose to the surface. Then I felt it – not a flutter, but that first full kick from within my abdomen. As if the unborn child were protesting my intention. The razor blade fell into the sink, forgotten, as my hands flew to embrace the life growing within me. I collapsed to the toilet seat, consumed with tears of remorse.

The following weeks were a flurry of activity. Hours spent at the closest DHS office applying for social services. Then, even more time filling out forms for services like WICS and medical history forms for the doctors. There were countless trips to the Goodwill, K-Mart and other low-end stores and thrift shops hunting for bargain baby supplies. I learned how to properly strip down, sand, and re-finish an old baby crib so that it was just like new. I became so absorbed in the preparations and excitement surrounding, (now I knew), the baby girl growing inside me, that I had even stopped having the nightmares. It was a new start, the day I first felt my baby girl kick, my little lifesaver. Before I knew it, my due date had arrived…and passed.

I was putting the baby's name and meaning, "Evin – My Little Fighter," with pastel rub-on transfer, on the end of the crib when my water broke. I rubbed on the last three letters and carefully used the end of the crib to pull myself to my feet. I was doing this alone. I *knew* I was doing this alone. Therefore, I'd taken every class and workshop the state sponsored health care covered. Which meant I knew I had a little bit of time, yet, before my baby girl was truly ready to make her appearance. I waddled to the bathroom to get a towel and back into the nursery to clean up the mess. Then, I went to change into clean clothes. Once I was certain that both the nursery and I were satisfactorily dry again, I called the cab to take me to the hospital. By the time the driver knocked on the door, my contractions were still a good 45 minutes apart. It took about that long to get to the hospital.

Slightly less than three days later, another cab brought me, and eight pound, 16 ounces, little Evin back home again. My baby girl had been a fighter from the start. That first swift kick she'd given me was my wakeup call. I named her for that fighting spirit, and she'd kept it growing up. There's a lot more in a name than people realize, I think.

~*~

The ringing telephone snapped me out of my reverie. I set the dirty dishes I was holding on the table and picked up the phone. The caller ID said 'Property Management'. As I read the display, there was a knock on the door; I went to answer it with the ringing phone still in my hand. Caden Neely stood outside the door.

"Answer the phone."

"What?"

He had a cell phone pressed to his ear; I looked down at the phone in my hand in confusion, then back at him.

"Answer the phone." He grinned.

I hit send on the phone in my hand, held it to my ear and listened.

"Hi," Caden's voice came from in front of me and echoed through the phone, "This is Caden with the Property Management for your apartments. I hear there's a problem with your door lock?"

Caden held up a new exterior doorknob kit in his other hand and winked at me.

"I was wondering if today would be a good day to come by and fix it."

Shaking my head and smiling, I hung up the phone and then motioned him inside.

"You're a bit strange, you know that, Caden?"

"I figured it was the only way I'd get you to answer your phone."
I laughed. "Probably true, I'm a little leery of the outside world these days."

"Didn't you recognize my number? I wrote it on my card for you."

"Comes up as 'Property Management' not your name, I didn't even notice the number."

"Didn't think of that."

"Would you like a beer?"

"You bought beer?"

"Yes, would you like one?"

"I can't believe you bought beer."

"So is that a yes or a no?"

"Sure, I'll take a beer."

The man is exasperating. A simple yes or no answer would have sufficed. You'd think no one had ever bought him a beer before. I figured keeping some on hand was the least I could do after all the work on my car and running us around he'd done. Getting a Bud Ice out of the fridge, I used my sleeve to twist the top off and handed it to him. He took the bottle, and then looked at me pensively.

"How'd you know what kind I drink?"

"I saw the empties at your shop."

"Oh. You're wonderful."

I laughed.

"So, how about I fix that door lock for you?"

"Are you *really* the maintenance guy for the Property Management?"

"Yep, for several years now."

"Why haven't I seen you before?"

"Probably for the same reason I haven't seen *you* before. You're a bit of a legend around here, you know."

"What? Why?"

His deep bass chuckle at my response was very pleasant. His dimples flashed and I automatically smiled back at him.

"They call you 'the recluse in 22.'"

"Oh my God, I have a moniker?"

"What's a moniker?"

"A nickname."

"Oh – then yes, you have a moniker."

"Great. I guess I should get out more."

"I could help with that."

"You could, huh?"

"Sure, would you like to come by the shop later? Some of the guys and I are having a barbeque. You could check on your car."

"Is it ready?"

"Not yet, waiting on a part."

"Then why would I need to check on it?"

"I thought you might like to use it as an excuse to come by."

"Oh, Okay…"

"Well, I better get that lock fixed."

"I'm used to it like that."

"It's not safe. I don't like the idea of you girls here alone with a broken lock."

I didn't know how to respond to that. His gaze was serious and possessive as it met mine. Then, he picked up the doorknob kit he'd set on the kitchen table, strode back to the front door and went to work installing it without another word. He was worried – about Evin and me? That's interesting. I gathered the dishes I had set down when he called, and began washing them as he worked, then finished tidying the living room. The simple chores kept me from fidgeting too much in his presence and gave me an unobstructed view of him while he worked. Not that it took him

46

long. I was folding the couch blankets when I felt his eyes on me and realized he'd finished. I looked up to find him leaning against the doorframe of the open front door. He dangled a set of keys from his finger. I spread the folded blanket across the back of the couch and accepted the keys from him. The casual graze of his fingertips across my palm sent a spark of electricity up my arm.

"All done, I put in a deadbolt too. Make sure you lock it at night."

"Thank you, I will. I'll have to let Evin know there are new locks in case she comes home early. She does that some times. Is there a second set I can give her?"

"Usually the second set goes to the Property Management, but I can get a copy made for you."

"That would be nice, thank you. She should have her own set."

"Ok, I'll get another set made tomorrow. I have to go finish up for the day at apartment 18, and then I'll be heading back out to the shop for the night. Let me know if you would like to come out."

"Apartment 18?"

"Ya, tenant moved out, I'm cleaning the place up and getting it ready for carpet and paint. I'll be over there for about another hour and a half if you want to come by."

"Okay."

He left, softly closing the door behind him. I stood where I was until I could no longer hear his footsteps echoing down the concrete stairs outside the apartment door. Apartment number 18 was actually directly below ours. I didn't even know they had moved. The second the echoes died away, I went to the door and opened it a crack to peek out, when I didn't see him, I opened it all the way. Slipping the key Caden had given me into the shiny new doorknob; I locked it from the outside and then extracted the key. I tested the knob with my hand; it wouldn't turn. I unlocked it with the key and tested it again then locked and unlocked the deadbolt, watching the bolt slide in and out of the door into the air with the delight of a child with a new toy. I *hated* that old doorknob. I returned the deadbolt to the unlocked position and closed the door, locking both the knob and the bolt from the inside, then went back to cleaning with a satisfied smile.

Thirty minutes later, I turned off the vacuum cleaner and called Evin's cell phone to let her know we had new locks and I would have a set of keys ready for her some time tomorrow. I got her voice mail. I left her a brief message then hung up and checked the time; three pm, she was probably at her counseling session. She may call back or she may not. I sent her the same message via text, knowing she would see it when she wasn't busy and I probably wouldn't get a reply for hours. If she were in class, therapy, or even just on the Max listening to music she would ignore her phone entirely. It did annoy me sometimes, but I was used to it.

I decided to go downstairs and check in on Caden. I found myself thinking about him a lot since that afternoon at Winco. At first glance, Caden Neely seemed like the kind of man one might want to cross the street to avoid. He had trouble written all over him. He has a foul mouth and a quick temper. Especially when he thinks no one is looking. He also, I was beginning to realize, has a golden heart. It made me wonder if the tough exterior is real or cultivated. In a way, he reminded me a lot of my daughter. Maybe that's why I knew I could trust him. He is most definitely an Alpha male. He's not the conventional male 'pretty' that society advertises through the media. Caden is somehow – *more*. I felt myself smile as I contemplated his appearance. He's rough looking, but in a *good* way. Taller than me, but only just, about 5'9" to my 5'7". Broad, well-muscled shoulders, back and chest; he's what you would call 'barrel-chested'. I surmised those muscles came from 30 plus years of hard labor and not working out at some gym. He just didn't strike me as the type of man that had the time to work out that way. I'm guessing he has a decade on me, and that would put him close to, if not, 50. The eyes that are so intensely expressive are a deep cerulean blue with bits of olive green around the pupil. His mustache and goatee are a light copper speckled with white and add to a slightly devilish appearance. The throaty chuckle and knowing gleam he periodically gets in his eyes amplify the effect.

The door to apartment 18 stood wide open. Rolls of frayed and dirty old carpet and carpet pad leaned up against the living room wall, leaving the sub-floor exposed. Tack strips ran along the floor by the walls, threatening the improperly clad or placed foot. Unopened cans of paint were stacked haphazardly to one side of the room next to a Home Depot paint bucket with rollers and various other items sticking out of it. Next to the paint bucket sat a couple of very used paint trays and a paint-splashed DeWalt radio/CD player from which Van Morrison's 'Brown Eyed Girl' was loudly playing. Caden was singing along while taping up plastic sheeting over the cabinets in the kitchen. He had a very nice singing voice. As he hadn't noticed my presence, I decided not to say anything. I leaned up against the frame of the door, watching, while he continued to sing and work. 'Brown Eyed Girl' ended and Marvin Gaye came on. Caden picked up the lyrics to 'Sexual Healing' in his strong, sexy bass without missing a beat. Marvin was just getting to *"it ain't right to masturbate"* when Caden turned around and saw me standing there watching him. He stopped singing and blushed bright scarlet.

"Don't stop on my account, I like your voice."

"How long have you been there?"

"Long enough to know you can sing."

"Humph."

He crossed the room and switched the DeWalt from CD to radio, cutting off the beginning of another Marvin Gaye song. I suppressed a laugh. Walking the rest of the way into apartment 18, I surveyed his work. It looked like he was doing more than paint and carpet. Store tags still adhered to the cabinetry and appliances he had just been covering. There were several interior doors, still wrapped in plastic, leaning against the wall in the hall leading off the living room, and the residue of the manufacturers' stickers was plainly visible on the new storm windows.

"Did you do all of this yourself?"

"I sub-contracted the windows. They're a pain in the ass."

I laughed.

"The totally new kitchen isn't?"

He just shrugged. The work was beautiful. The rent-controlled apartments didn't get many upgrades. I knew the property had changed ownership a few years ago, but I didn't think it would make much difference. Of course, I rarely let anyone in my apartment, so it wouldn't really matter if it did. Being directly below mine, apartment 18's layout was identical to my own, so the new cabinets, countertops, linoleum, and appliances instantly had me picturing myself in the new kitchen. The cabinets in my unit were decades old and none of the doors or drawers closed right. The laminate coating was peeling off most of them, completely gone on some. The green speckled Formica countertops were atrocious, and the matching green GE range and refrigerator screamed 1970's; and neither worked correctly. I'm not certain, but I think I may have visibly drooled. Caden noticed my reaction and chuckled.

"I know the contractor – I could put in a good word."

"Wouldn't it affect my rent?"

"Nah, I know the owner too. Besides, the plan is to upgrade all the units as they come open. If a tenant is willing to allow the work while it's occupied, the owner will be good with that."

"Really?"

"I'd need to make a couple of phone calls, but ya, pretty sure."

"I *hate* my kitchen and *none* of the windows in my apartment open or close right. It really sucks during the summer."

"You know, if you answered the phone when the contractor called once in a while, some of that might actually get fixed."

His eyes positively twinkled when he said it. I laughed.

"I just might do that now."

"Are you *sure*?"

"Pretty sure."

I'd programmed him into my phone right after calling Evin. Now when he called me, it would show up as 'Caden Neely' instead of 'Property Management'. I even gave him his own ring. I didn't tell him any of that, of course. I just smiled.

"So are they getting rid of the linoleum tile in the bedrooms and hall too, or just putting new carpet in the living rooms?"

"New linoleum."

"Bummer."

"In the kitchens and bathrooms and carpet throughout the rest."

I smacked his shoulder.

"Ouch! What was that for?"

"You did that on purpose!"

"Maybe," He laughed. "Wanna hit me again?"

"Not when you're expecting it." I grinned.

"Well, I better lock up for the night. Do you want to come out to the shop for barbeque?"

"When?"

"You can come with me now, or I can come back and pick you up."

"I'd really like to take a shower."

"How about I pick you up around six?"

"Sound's perfect."

"I'll see you later then."

He began hauling tools out to his truck as I headed back upstairs to get ready. Closing the front door behind me, I momentarily contemplated whether to lock it. Briefly, I entertained the fantasy that Caden might come up the stairs and climb into my shower. The idea brought a smile to my lips, but I quickly discarded it, sensing Caden would never do such a thing without first knowing it would be welcome. I locked both knob and deadbolt and headed for the shower, still smiling. I'm not sure how one man can come across as both dangerous *and* safe, but he managed to pull it off seamlessly. Maybe I would extend that invitation.

Most of the time I didn't bother with make-up, I just didn't see the point. However, that doesn't mean I don't know how to use it effectively. Kohl-lined, Smokey eyes in earthen tones were balanced perfectly by deep plum lips and just enough blush to emphasize high cheekbones and a strong jaw. Without cosmetics, I am, perhaps, average or slightly above in appearance. On the rare occasion I choose to use them, I *can* be downright striking. It is a weapon or tool, depending on the situation, that I use sparingly. Tonight, I decided to go all out and took the time to do it right. I decided to leave my hair loose, hanging in gentle waves around my shoulders, with a little teasing of the roots with the hair dryer for body. Surveying the results in the mirror, I decided I was pleased with my efforts and went to conquer the wardrobe. It was still cool this time of year, and would cool more toward nightfall. Since I wasn't one of those women that owned many dresses, or *any* for that matter, it simplified my choices some. I paired slim fitting, stonewashed Levi's, and leather, thigh-high boots with a shelf bra that emphasized my already ample bust, under a deep-scooped neck forest sweater that brought out the little bit of green in my eyes. A necklace that dripped Swarovski crystals in a matching shade nearly to my cleavage emphasized the effect. That ought to knock him back on his heels. I was dabbing a bit of musk scent on my neck and bust line when I heard his knock on the door. I smiled and went to answer it.

The first thing I noticed when I opened the door was his scent. It wasn't overpowering, but unlike the other times I had seen him, there was no lingering *work* mixed in with it. He was truly intoxicating. Then, I actually *looked* at him. He was wearing all black. Black Levi's hugged his thighs; a crisp black button down shirt with the top three buttons undone exposed just enough of his neckline and upper chest. There was a trace of chest hair showing. I'd never really liked chest hair on a man; somehow, I still had the overwhelming urge to run my fingers through his. Over the crisp black shirt was a leather biker jacket, also black. All the black made his blue eyes even more striking and the *dangerous* part of his persona that much more evident. I wanted to tell him to forget the Barbeque and drag him into the apartment.

We assessed each other for several minutes before *either* of us could act. I could tell by the expression on his face that he was just as floored by my appearance as I was by his. The glint in his eyes shifted and I caught my breath. His hand came up smoothly, sliding around the back of my neck and into my hair, pulling me to him. The kiss was hot, desperate, and abrupt. My body reacted to his touch instantly, and with my mind completely muddled, he released me and stepped back.

"You'll want a coat; it's going to be cold on the bike."

Then he was gone, back down the stairs into the parking lot, leaving me standing there, and reeling, to follow him or not. A few more seconds passed before I could move. He was pure electricity. Then I had to laugh. I guess my preparations had worked; obviously, so had his. I got my coat and went after him.

Even though he had said 'bike', it didn't really register until I got to the parking lot and saw it. He was leaning casually against a monster of a Harley Davidson motorcycle, all chrome and leather, with a blue tank, fenders and ghost flames. It was beautiful, and it suited him perfectly. Without a word, he handed me a helmet and got on, waiting patiently while I got the helmet fastened and climbed on behind him. The intimacy of riding behind him on a motorcycle didn't escape me, and I'm certain it didn't him either. Our positioning on the bike pressed us together closer than we had been when he kissed me minutes earlier. The fact that he *had* just kissed me made it that much more so. I could feel the heat of his body through the length of my thighs, and even through our jackets. I jumped when he revved the engine to life. This motorcycle wasn't one of those quiet ones you found at the dealerships; it *screamed* its power. I found myself comparing the Harley to its owner. Riding the bike to his shop in the diminishing sunlight was brisk, and intoxicating in its own way. I found myself wondering what it would be like to have that kind of power at my command.

When we got to Caden's shop, there were already several other motorcycles and additional cars parked haphazardly around the gravel drive and parking lot. An assortment of lawn and folding chairs arranged in a semi-circle near a burn-barrel that was fully ablaze. Rowdy, biker-looking men, who had obviously gotten a head start on the evenings drinking, occupied most of these. Two mammoth grills, one propane and one briquette, gave off the pleasant aroma of roasting meats. The two giant drive-in doors of the shop were wide open, and loud music issued from several speakers strategically hung from various corners inside. Where my car had previously sat in the main bay was a large table covered with an assortment of dishes, drink makings, and condiments. A cacophony of catcalls and leering comments greeted me as I dismounted Caden's Harley and removed the helmet. I was the only female present.

"Woo-hoo, Sexy Mama!"

"Hey, baby, bring some of that over *here*!"

"Wanna come sit on my lap, honey?"

"Hey, *I'll* take you for a ride!"

Caden graced his rowdy friends with an evil looking smile, and then pulled me into another kiss. This time I'm sure he was staking his claim. The kiss was long and deep, his hands caressed my body for the duration, filling me with a heat that the cool evening didn't allow. The catcalls became whistles, and then gradually faded as I lost my ability to focus on anything but him. When he finally, reluctantly released me, I was lightheaded and dizzy. His eyes had darkened considerably, and burned with passion as they met mine.

"They'll still tease you, but they won't cross the line."

I just nodded. I didn't trust myself to speak coherently at that moment. He tightly grasped my hand and led me into the fray. Most people respect the biker crowd, if not fear them. They definitely live by their own set of rules. They work hard and play harder. To describe them as a rowdy bunch is really an understatement. Free spirited; yes, fearsome; some of them, conformist: never. The camaraderie among them was difficult to define and strongly apparent. Unspoken, yet also apparent, was the knowledge that they would be there for one another, unquestioningly, should the need arise. They were a family of brothers.

I seemed to have passed some sort of test; the banter continued, but looks of respect replaced the leers. As though being so obviously tied to Caden gave me status.

"Hey, 22, you got a real name? Caden's a little tight-lipped with the details."

"Can you blame him?"

"I'd wanna keep that one to myself too!"

"Hey – What's the '22'? I can see it ain't her *bra size*!"

The last bit met another round of laughter as I ignored it and tried to figure out which of the crowd had asked the first question. Caden caught my eyes briefly, seeming to search my reaction to the men's banter. When he saw I was amused not offended, he nodded toward a tall, thin man with shoulder length blond hair minding one of the grills.

"That's Tony, my best bro." Caden said.

"Tony," I hollered, "my name is Krysta."

"I kind of like '22'!" Tony replied.

"Wait," a younger looking kid piped up, "22, as in, *The Recluse in 22*?"

"That's the one!" Tony said.

"That's Frank," Caden pointed to the kid, "he helps with painting and stuff sometimes."

"I thought '22' was a hag." Frank sounded confused.

"She's definitely *not* a hag!" an older, Santa-like man hollered.

"Hey 22," Tony hollered, "maybe you could hook Frank up with your daughter. I hear she's in college."

I felt Caden stiffen beside me: curious.

"My daughter would eat him alive!" I called back.

My response met raucous laughter and I felt Caden relax. As the laughter died down, Tony declared the meat cooked, and the men descended upon him in a rush to get their share. Conversation, food, beer, and various other inebriations filled the next few hours. I was drinking something light and fruity one of the boys made me when they found out I only drank 'chick drinks' that still packed quite a punch. I was a little tipsy, but definitely not close to the level of drunk many of them were displaying. Gradually, Caden's friends left. Soon he was waving goodbye to the last of them. He saw me suppress a shiver.

"I'll give you a ride home in the truck so you don't freeze."

"Thanks."

In stark contrast to the rough and ramble feel of the evening, Caden still formally held open the truck door, and then closed it behind me. I watched him walk around the front of the truck and climb into the driver seat, not averting my gaze when he looked up. I didn't see the point in avoidance. It was clear the attraction was mutual. Once he settled behind the wheel, he patted the center of the bench seat.

"Scoot over here. There's another seatbelt tucked into the seat."

I slid over next to him, and we both struggled a few minutes trying to pull the middle belt free before it came loose. Finally, I had it snapped into place and we were off. We pulled out on to T.V. Highway and headed for Forest Grove. Casually, Caden took his hand off the shifter and slid it down my leg.

"Did you have fun tonight?"

"Yes, but I think I may be stuck with the nickname '22'."

"Does that bother you?"

"Not really."

"Good."

It was small talk. His right hand was smoothly running up and down the inner length of my left leg from knee to thigh and back again. Periodically he would lightly knead his fingers in a circular motion. It was driving me crazy. Neither of our eyes left the road. Like some unspoken pact, we didn't acknowledge that he was seducing me on the ride home. I decided that two could play that game. I slid my left hand over his well-muscled thigh and down, feeling every flex and ripple as he drove; and allowed myself a satisfied smile at the evidence that I was affecting *him* just as he was affecting *me*.

There was no question whether he was coming inside. He parked on the street, in a place the truck would be safe overnight. As he walked me to the apartment, his hand left a trail of heat from my neck to thighs and up again. I couldn't unlock the door fast enough, and was thankful for the new locks that opened smoothly instead of fighting me. The second the door closed my back was against it, his mouth hot on mine, hands roaming my body.

"Not here. It can't be here."

"Then tell me where."

He'd stepped back, was waiting for me to act. I felt a flood of relief from a fear I didn't know I still possessed. No, Caden Neely was *nothing* like *him*. He saw the change in me and I watched a mix of emotions cross his rugged features, curiosity, sympathy, and finally anger, but still he said nothing more. My chest constricted in response. Taking both his hands in mine, I pulled him closer, and then kissed his lips softly.

"Thank you."

He only nodded, we both understood. I led him to the bedroom. This time he let me take the lead. It was clear he was more than capable of being the aggressor. It was also clear he was simply *capable*. Our silent exchange just inside the door, somehow told him I was fragile right now, and he was determined to handle me with care. I was both grateful and frustrated. Now that I was certain Caden would never hurt me, I wanted him to *act*. I slid his jacket off, tossing it on a chair in the corner. Then, I placed his hands back on me myself and unbuttoned his shirt, pulling it off. Once fully exposed, I indulged my earlier impulse to run my hands across his chest and through his chest hair. It was firm, and the hair soft, unlike other men I've encountered. I followed my hands with my mouth, kissing his chest, and then worked my way up his throat back to his lips. I felt the heat rising in us both as I kissed him and my hands explored. He was still holding back, I could feel him fighting it. I moved my mouth to his ear, and gently sucked and nibbled his earlobe before whispering.

"Don't hold back, I want you."

That was all the permission Caden needed. With a groan, he was pulling off my clothing, straining to touch every inch of me with hands and mouth. The frenzied passion he'd fought back just inside the door, resurfaced, stronger than before and more demanding. He knew exactly how to kiss me, exactly how to caress, where to touch. I'd never experienced anything like it. I knew I would never find another man that would evoke the same reactions in me. I took his hand again and led him toward the bed – and my phone rang. It was a very distinctive ring and assigned to only one person: Evin. I glanced at the clock on the bedside table: 1:29am. She wouldn't be calling at this hour unless something was wrong.

"Evin – something's wrong, I have to answer."

I barely registered the look of resignation that passed over Caden's face as I hit send on my cell phone.

"Hi, baby, what's wrong?"

"Misses Mallory?"

The voice on the other end of the line was most definitely not Evin, and male to boot.

"Who is this? Why do you have Evin's phone?"

"My name is Sean, I'm Evin's boy – I'm a friend of Evin's. She was supposed to meet me back at her dorm room by six at the latest. When she didn't show up, I let myself in; she gave me a key a while ago. Her backpack was inside on the floor. Her phone, keys, journal, and make-up bag all still there. The only thing gone is her wallet. Evin *never* only takes her wallet. She's – something has happened to her. I know it."

"Stay put, I'll be there as soon as I can, and *lock the door!*"

I hung up the phone and began getting dressed as quickly as possible. My hands were shaking so bad I couldn't get my stupid bra fastened. I felt Caden's rough, sexy hands on my shoulders. Automatically, I turned into his arms and cried. He held me in silence while I sobbed the panic out of my system, and then helped me finish dressing. He was already dressed.

"Are you going to tell me what's going on?"

"My daughter – Evin's missing. That was the boyfriend she's been avoiding telling me about. Calling on *her* phone, from *her* dorm, where *she* isn't. I have to go. I have to find her."

7 TUESDAY NEARLY 3:00AM
CADEN NEELY

"If you're so sure she's not out with friends, why don't you call the police, have them check into it?"

"The police can't be trusted; besides, they won't even *consider* doing anything for at least 48 hours. Evin is 19 years old, they'll say she's an adult and she took her wallet, therefore she is *not missing*."

It was nearly three am in the morning, and I was driving east on Highway 26 towards downtown Portland. Krysta was positive Evin was in some sort of major trouble and wouldn't listen to reason. I didn't like most cops either but they had a point when it came to this kind of stuff. When I was 19, I didn't come home at night all the time. It didn't mean I was missing. It meant I'd been out partying too hard somewhere and had to crash where I was. I always stumbled back home at some point over the next day or so. I'm sure Evin would too. Kids forget things, like their phones. Sometimes they even forget them on purpose; say, so boyfriends and moms can't track them down and ruin their fun. Evin was probably trying to *avoid* her boyfriend. Hell, she was probably just out with another guy. Most likely, she left her phone behind so this Sean kid wouldn't bug her. I tried to reason with Krysta, I wasn't getting very far.

"Has it occurred to you that maybe she left her phone behind on purpose so this other kid would leave her alone while she was out with someone else? She'll probably be home tomorrow."

"Evin's not like that. She would *never* leave her phone behind. She would just ignore his calls if she were trying to avoid him. She'd take it with her in case of an emergency if for no other reason."

"Okay, fine. We'll check it out, but I'm sure she's just out partying with friends. She's 19; kids don't come home a lot when they're 19. It's not a big deal."

"You're wrong. If she took her stuff I'd agree with you, but she didn't. Evin doesn't know how to pack light. She *always* carries a backpack. Leaving her phone and backpack behind means there is something wrong. You don't know Evin, she's *always* prepared."

Finding parking in downtown Portland is usually a bitch. At three in the morning, it's a bit easier. I parked on the street around the corner from the entrance to Evin's dorms, and we walked to the front door, finding it locked. Krysta called Evin's phone and told Sean to come let us in. Evin's dorm room was on the fourth floor on the Broadway side, room 444. It was a single so she didn't have a roommate.

The first thing I noticed was the place was a wreck. Clothes covered the bed and strewn about the floor. Assorted books, papers and other debris scattered and piled haphazardly about on every available surface. In other words, it was a typical teen's room, no matter what the setting. I saw nothing wrong. Krysta bee-lined for the backpack sitting against the wall by the bathroom door.

"This is the pack she was carrying this weekend. She just got it. Did you take anything from it, Sean?"

"Only the phone, I looked through it, but I didn't take anything else out."

"Did you notice if any of her other bags are gone?"

"They're all in the closet, I checked."

"Show me."

The kid looked like he was about the same age as Evin, and reminded me of a gothic hippy. His black wavy hair hung to his shoulders, he wore bright red, skin-tight girl pants, purple doc martin boots, a black t-shirt with a band on it I didn't recognize, and thick black eye-liner. He also really seemed scared. I wasn't sure if I should laugh at his costume or ask if he was ok. I settled for keeping my mouth shut and letting Krysta handle things for the moment. He opened the closet and pulled out a giant tote bag full of other types of bags. Krysta dug through them, examining each one, and then put them back.

"They're all there, she didn't take a different bag, and even her keys and lipstick are in the backpack. You've spent an afternoon with Evin, Caden, how many times did you see her re-apply her lipstick?"

"A few, but that doesn't really mean anything. It's odd she left her keys, but kids forget things. I still think you should give her till tomorrow and *then* if she doesn't show up, call the police."

Krysta sat down on the clothing covered bed. She looked deflated. Fuck, I didn't think anything had actually happened to the kid, but I couldn't stand seeing Krysta this upset. I crossed the room and squeezed her shoulder. She looked up with tears in her eyes.

"Let's call the police, file a report, at least get it in the system. If she shows up, great, if not, they have a head start looking for her. It's their job, Krysta."

"Alright, I just don't think they'll help, but I'll call and file the report anyway. I suppose it can't *hurt* the situation any."

I sat beside her and gently rubbed her back as she dialed 911. After a couple of minutes of frustrated conversation and scrambling for pen and paper, she was writing down another number. They told her to call the non-emergency line. The next conversation was brief also, and after giving some basic information, she hung up the phone.

"They're sending someone here to take the report. They said to stay here and wait."

"See, they took you seriously, they're going to take a missing person report."

"Ya, they're taking a report. We'll see how much good that does. They didn't even ask anything about her on the phone. As soon as they find out she's 19 and has been gone less than a day they'll change their tune."

"Let's just file the report and go from there."

It only took about 15 minutes for the cop to get here. He didn't call Krysta to let him in, but knocked directly on the dorm room door. I have no idea how he got through the front entrance. I stayed next to Krysta on the bed and the kid let him in. As soon as Sean moved out of the way, and the cop stepped forward, I felt Krysta's sharp intake of breath. I looked at her questioningly, but she just shook her head so I left it alone for the time being. He was a little over six feet, with light hair and eyes. I recognized him, he used to be a Forest Grove cop; he must have transferred. His nametag read 'Officer Richard'; we used to call him 'Officer Dick'. The title was fitting; the guy was a real asshole.

Officer Dick asked Krysta an assortment of questions and wrote it all down in his little black notebook. He kept the condescending look and tone in his voice that had earned him the nickname the whole time. Krysta's voice was toneless as she answered his generic questions about why she thought her daughter was missing. She took him through the phone call from Sean, to when he had arrived at the dorm in that same monotone voice. Not once did she look up at him, but Officer *Dick* studied *her* with an interest that made me want to wipe the look off his face with my fist. At Officer *Dicks'* request, Sean found him a photograph of Evin out of one of her albums, which he stuck in his breast pocket after studying it briefly. I didn't like how he looked at the photo either. He made a cursory inspection of the room and the backpack, still taking notes, and then closed his notebook.

"I'll get back to the station and get this entered. At her age, I'm sure she'll show up on her own, but we'll get the report filed anyway. Here's my card, call me directly if you have any questions."

Krysta didn't budge. I stood up and took the card myself. He shrugged and left. I could see some of the tension leave Krysta when he left the room. There was definitely something going on there. Maybe they'd been involved at some point. It was obvious they'd known each other. Either way, I didn't like him.

"You two wait here, I'll be right back."

Sean nodded; Krysta seemed to be lost in her own world. I left the dorm and followed Officer Dick down the hall. He took the stairs; I waited a minute, and then followed. On the ground floor, he exited into the lobby and stopped by the trashcans. I paused with the stairwell door cracked and watched as he took something from his pocket and threw it away. Then he went out the front doors, locking them behind him with a key before sauntering away. Why would he have keys to the exterior door of a college dorm building? Something was definitely wrong here. I went to the trashcan and looked inside. It was nearly empty; the only thing in it was a handful of crumpled together papers. I reached in and took out the papers Officer Dick had thrown away. They were his notes for the missing persons report, and mostly just scribbles. Obviously, he didn't intend to enter anything into the system. Whether this lack was out of laziness, contempt, or something else entirely, was unclear. I headed back to the dorm room to find out what the history was between him and Krysta.

As I waited for the elevator, I noticed it was already starting to get light outside and checked my watch. It was nearly six am. Officer Dick had been there for over an hour asking questions and pretending to take notes. Why even put up the front? How would he account for the time spent on the call? What kind of a report *would* he file to cover his time, if not the missing person's? The bigger question, why was Krysta afraid of him? Because that was definitely, *fear* I was reading there. The elevator chimed, I got on and rode it to the fourth floor. I was certain Krysta wasn't going to tell me anything with her daughter's boyfriend in the room, so I made up my mind to send him downstairs to the corner Starbucks for coffee so we could talk. They should be open by now. Krysta was still sitting on the edge of the bed where I had left her. Sean sat in a desk chair next to the overcrowded desk. He looked positively glum. I felt for the kid. They both looked up when I came into the room.

"Hey, Sean, here's a 20, why don't you go down to Starbuck's and get some coffee. Give Krysta and me a chance to talk for a few minutes. Take Evin's phone, we'll call and let you know what to get us when we're done. Just hang out down there for a bit."

"You want me to ask them some questions? She knows most of the employees down there."

"Sure, why don't you do that, see if they remember anything from yesterday?"

I watched the kid leave, and then sat down in the chair he had been occupying. I watched Krysta and waited. I knew an explanation was coming, and she would tell me when she was ready. Finally, she looked up briefly, before reaching for my hand.

"Do you remember last night in the living room, just inside the door, I stopped you – I was afraid?"

I nodded. How could I forget? She was hot then cold, the fear washing over her plain as day. It was clear in that moment that someone had hurt her, right there, in her own apartment. I wanted to track the fucker down and kill him.

"I was raped – that was him. It happened 20 years ago; I was barely 20 myself. He was a rooky cop. I figured, what could be safer? Boy was I wrong. We'd gone out on a date, I asked him in for coffee. He wouldn't take no for an answer. Then he acted as if everything was normal. He wasn't even worried about me reporting him. Why should he be? He was a cop. He sent me flowers the next day. The card said, 'Had a blast'. Periodically, on the anniversary of the rape, he would show up somewhere I was, or send me flowers again – always the same ones. He kept tabs on me. Then he transferred to Portland where Evin just happened to be going to college. That can't be a coincidence."

"He's the father isn't he?"

"Yes, and no, Evin doesn't know, and I'd like to keep it that way. She's *my* daughter, *not his*."

"I'm guessing, even if Evin doesn't know that, *he* does."

"I know he does, one of the times he *accidently* ran into me at the grocery store while I was pregnant with her, he commented on me 'having his bun in the oven', but I didn't put him on the birth certificate."

"I doubt he'd be interested in playing daddy anyway. I've encountered him around Forest Grove in the past. He's not the type."

"*Now,* do you believe Evin is in trouble?"

"There is definitely more going on here than meets the eye. I have some contacts in law enforcement *and* other – areas; I'll do some digging. We'll find her, I promise. Why don't you call her boyfriend back up? Tell him to bring us some coffee, make mine black and whatever you want. We'll send him home and head out. I have a couple of people I want to go talk to; I'll take you back home first."

"I'm going with you. There's no way I'm sitting at home while you're out looking for my daughter."

"Some of the people I'm going to be dealing with are pretty shady."

"I don't care, I'm going with you."

"Fine, whatever, but first I want to change her door locks. Something tells me *Officer Dick* knows how to get inside; I want to make sure we have the only keys."

"Officer Dick? And what if she *does* come back and is locked out?"

"That's what we called Officer Richard in Forest Grove, he's a dick. She knows your number right? She can call you and we'll come get her. It's obvious she's not safe here anyway, not with *him* hanging around. He has a key to the lobby door, there's no telling what else he has keys to."

"Oh my God."

"Ya, you were right. Now, call the boyfriend, I'm going down to the truck to get a new lock and some tools."

Officer Dick was nowhere in sight when I got down to the street. He probably went back to harassing whatever local kids he usually was this time of morning if he hadn't just gone home. I didn't know what shift he had, but I intended to find out. I had my sources. I had one matching set of individually keyed locks, deadbolt and knob, in the truck for a job next week. They weren't the kind you get at Home Depot where you can just match the number and get matching keys; a locksmith individually cut them to be unique. There *were* no duplicate keys. They were special ordered by the customer. I'd have to get another set made, but I didn't care. It guaranteed Officer Dick wouldn't be getting into Evin's room to move or change anything while I checked things out with my own contacts. I suspected he had something to do with all this; too many coincidences. I don't believe in those, there's always an explanation.

When I got back to the lobby with the locks and my tools, Sean was there waiting for the elevator with three coffees in a holder. The door chimed before I got there, he got on and held it open for me.

"Thanks. Did you find out anything at the coffee shop?"

"One of the Baristas talked to her yesterday but he won't be on until this afternoon."

"What time?"

"They said he starts at 1:30 today, his name is Joe, and another worker saw him talking to her yesterday around noon when she stopped in for coffee. What's with the tools?"

"I'm putting new locks on her room, I don't trust that cop. Have you seen him around the dorms much when you're here?"

"At the dorms, all over Portland, he's a Portland cop. I think the campus is his beat. I never thought anything of it, he's a cop."

"Try and stay away from him."

"Okaaaay…"

"We're pretty sure he's involved in this somehow."

"Oh, you know, Evin and me run into him all over the place. Evin told me once that she knew him from Forest Grove that he used to be a cop out there."

"Did she tell you anything else about him?"

"Only that she thinks he's kind of creepy, but she thinks all cops are creepy. So why do you think he's involved?"

"A few reasons, too many for comfort. You should get out of here. Leave us your contact information so we can get a hold of you if we need to. I'd rather he not have anyone close to Evin nearby, do you have somewhere you can go that's not in his district?"

"I have family outside of Portland, I can go there, but I'd rather wait here for Evin."

"I don't think it's safe. Go to your family, we'll let you know when we find her."

"I'd like to help."

"You already have, I'll call you if you can help any more, just get out of here for now."

He wanted to argue, I could tell. I think if I'd been anyone else, he would have. As I was the one he was facing down, he thought better of it. By this point, we were back in the dorm room. He set our coffees on the desk with the change and Evin's phone, got his stuff and left without another word. I think I pissed him off, too fucking bad; he'll get over it. I didn't want to have to deal with a pissed off Evin if something happened to her boyfriend while I was trying to find *her*. He forgot to give us his phone number but I'm sure it's in Evin's phone so no big deal. I handed Krysta my clipboard with notebook attached, and a pen.

"Write down everything you can think of that's important. Any contact with Officer Dick – I mean Richard, anything else strange you can remember. Write down 'Joe at dorm Starbucks starts 1:30pm, talked to Evin the day she went missing'. Anything about her room you think may be important. I'm going to change the locks so only we can get in here. I'll take everything to someone I know can be trusted. Oh, and find another current picture of Evin, Officer Dick dumped his notes, which were mostly useless scribbles, but kept the photo so we'll need another one."

"Who are you going to talk to?"

"A biker buddy of mine, someone I've known a long time."

"How is a biker buddy going to help find Evin?"

"He's also a County Sheriff."

"Another cop, are you sure he's safe?"

"Like I said, I've known him a long time, he can be trusted, and he can go where we can't."

"I'm not sure I like this, cops tend to stick together."

"Don't worry; I know what I'm doing. Now get to writing, I've got work to do."

I put in the new locks while she did what I told her. While I worked, I wondered if she was going to argue with *everything* I asked her to do. Of all the women to get involved with, I had to tangle myself with a bullheaded one mixed up with an asshole-crooked cop. Straight-laced cops were trouble enough; crooked ones were dangerous as hell. There were plenty of shades in between where the rest of them fell in line. Most of them just did their jobs and went home, but some were power hungry assholes. When you got a power hungry asshole that was *also* dirty, you could be in real trouble. Then there were the ones that were determined to take the latter down. That's where Al came in. Though you'd never guess it if you met him off duty. You'd think he was just a regular guy, hell; he didn't even look like a biker. Like all of us, he had a past, and his past set him on a mission to bust dirty cops. I never could get him to tell me what happened. Only that being a cop was the best way to do what he needed to do. He was one of those that fell in the middle. As long as you weren't hurting the innocent, he could turn the other cheek, but if you were, he'd be the first to set you straight. He had a strong sense of Justice that he stuck to, though it wasn't always the law. I learned a long time ago never to argue morals with him.

When I finished changing the locks, I put the old ones in a bag to take with me. I figured I'd give them to Al too, so he could check and see if there was anything off about them. They didn't look like they'd been jimmied, but he could check for other stuff. I figured it was worth a try.

"Are you about ready to go? I'm done here. We still have a while before we can talk to the Starbuck's employee. I want to go find Al and maybe get something to eat."

"Who's Al?"

"The friend I was telling you about. I'll call him; see if he can meet us for breakfast somewhere."

"Ya, but check this out. I was looking through Evin's calendar on her phone. Usually she has therapy every Monday, but this week the appointment says 'therapist canceled'. She didn't even mention it to me. She usually tells me that kind of stuff, I guess she forgot."

"Maybe she didn't think it was a big deal. It might be nothing, but I'll have Al check into it anyway. Add it to the list and make sure to put down the therapists name and number."

By eight am, we were back on Highway 26 on our way to meet Al at a little hole in the wall called 'Mary's' out in Cornelius. The owner had a thing for Elvis. Elvis posters, clocks, life-sized cardboard cutouts, and every other kind of Elvis memorabilia imaginable crammed into every available space. There were about a dozen tables, as well as a semi-circle counter in the middle with bar seating. The tables had checkered plastic tablecloths under glass tops to hold them in place, and an arrangement of plastic flowers graced each one. The dining area was crowded and tiny but the food was great, cheap, and the employees were always cheerful and friendly. It was one of our favorite places to meet.

I spotted Al sitting at a table in the corner as soon as we walked in. He waved us over. I pulled out a chair for Krysta opposite Al, and then took the one in between. I figured with as nervous as she was about *any* cop, I should probably give her the buffer. About the only thing that makes Al intimidating is the fact that he's a County Sheriff, at least in appearance anyway. He has an iron will and his mind is sharp as a tack. He's got a thick shock of short, dark brown hair and dark brown eyes in a cherubic face that has earned him the nickname 'pretty boy' from all the girls. He catches a fair amount of shit from the guys about it, but takes it well. He's not big either, about my height, maybe an inch taller, but with a lean frame. He looks more like the kind of guy you'd see on one of those billboards selling men's underwear than a cop or a biker. He's frequently underestimated, no one expects him to be dangerous – he's too pretty. He exploits it shamelessly. The second we sat down, he flashed Krysta his biggest smile, extending his hand across the table to her.

"Al Truman at your service, you must be Krysta."

Krysta gave him half a smile and shook his hand briefly. "Yes, though, I have to admit, you aren't what I expected."

"Caden didn't warn you that I'm not a big, scary-looking biker?"

"He just told me you were one of his biker friends and a County Sheriff."

"So you didn't expect a pretty boy?"

Krysta laughed nervously and shook her head. Al gets a kick out of teasing the girls. He knew I didn't tell her what he looked like, he asked me. He also knew she was off limits and would never cross that line. Teasing her was his way of setting her at ease. It worked pretty well.

"So, Caden tells me you may need my help with something?"

Krysta looked at me before saying anything; I nodded for her to answer.

"My daughter is missing, and I think a cop is involved – one from my past."

"I'm going to need more information than that."

"He – Caden, would you please tell him?"

"It's ok, Krysta. Al, do you remember the Forest Grove cop we used to call 'Officer Dick'?"

Al's reaction was immediate and distinct, his shoulders and back became rigid as he stiffened in his chair. His easygoing manner vanished, his eyes sharpened and jaw clenching. The non-threatening 'pretty boy' had just transformed into a viper ready to strike. *I wouldn't want to cross him.*

"Officer Richard is the cop you think is involved in her daughter's disappearance? Tell me everything."

8 TUESDAY 8:30AM
AL TRUMAN

I've known Caden since a little after I joined the Washington County Sheriff's department at age 25. That was ten years ago. The first time we met was when I pulled him over for speeding on his Harley in a construction zone. I liked him immediately. I still gave him a hefty ticket; it was near a school, he should know better. We bull-shitted for ten minutes after I gave him the ticket and made plans to go for a ride together the next weekend. He's a good guy, but he chafes at the rules a little. I've had to kick him in line every now and then, never mind that he has 15 years on me. Of course, he's always flicked me a fair amount of shit too; he's one of the few I'll allow.

I've never asked Caden what he does in his 'off' hours, but I really don't need to. I have resources. I know enough to know not to ask specifics unless I want to have to arrest him. I also know that most of what he does only makes my job easier. As long as he's the one out there doing the collections and evictions for the shady underbelly of our society I know no one is going to die in the process. There are much worse men out there. I also know many of the users he 'collects' from suddenly decide to clean up their acts and go straight. I don't think that's a coincidence. Some of the missing girls on the streets turning tricks to pay off their debt suddenly show up back home clean and sober too, debts paid. There's a soft center in that beast. He would have made a good cop. I don't tell him that – he'd laugh in my face. He'd also tell me there are too many rules. Like Caden, I believe some rules should be broken others can be bent. I'm here to enforce the good ones, whether they are law or not. Being a law enforcement officer is just the best means by which to accomplish my goals.

I have a big problem with cops that think they can break any rule they want, especially when the rules they choose to break hurt other people. The bad cops that really piss me off though, are the ones that hurt women and children. Cops like that are the reason I went into law enforcement in the first place. I figured out that the best way to take them down was to join their ranks, get inside, and get them to trust me. So far, it has worked like a charm.

I first met Officer Richard 20 and half years ago. I was 14 years old at the time. I never knew my real father. My mother married my stepfather when I was eight. He was a police officer with the Forest Grove Police Department. He'd transferred there from one of the larger precincts in Washington County. My stepfather was a real piece of work. He was one of those men that became a cop because he liked to push people around, and used the badge to hide behind. Mother and I were no exceptions to this rule. I tried to protect her; usually this just got me beaten too. There were never any police reports, and the hospital records magically disappeared. Cops protected each other and everyone else was afraid of them.

One day my stepfather brought home his new partner, Officer Bill G. Richard. He was a rookie cop that he'd taken under his wing. I could tell they were the same type. They both had that cold aloofness in their eyes that said they could turn vicious at any moment. The comradely fashion in which they talked and bantered made it clear that they had hit it off. One of my stepfather in the house was bad enough; two of him was downright terrifying. My mother was still at work. I casually got up off the couch and headed toward my bedroom, planning to climb out the window. I didn't get far.

"Where are you going, son?"

My blood chilled at the sound of my stepfather's voice.

"I'm going to my room to do my homework."

"Hey, Richard, he says he's going to do his homework. You ever hear of a teenager volunteering to do their homework?"

"Nope, I sure haven't, I say he's lying."

"I think so too. It's not a good idea to lie to an Officer, son."

"I wasn't lying, I'm go—"

My stepfather's fist cut me off mid-sentence. He beat me for a half an hour straight that time, all the while his new pal cheering him on. When he finished, I was in too much pain to drag myself to my room, so I got to witness the after show with my mother when she got home a bit later. I was in too bad of shape to stop it. Officer Richard stayed and watched everything, chatting and joking with him the whole time like beating a kid and his mother to a pulp was some great sport.

My stepfather and Officer Richard became the best of friends. They were always at my house together. Though Officer Richard never touched me directly, he was present for more beatings than I care to remember. He always cheered my stepfather on. Then, one afternoon when I got home from school, I could hear my mother crying in her bedroom along with both of their voices. I pounded on the locked door. After a few minutes, my stepfather opened it. I could see Officer Richard inside. He was only wearing boxers. My stepfather came out similarly clad and beat me unconscious. When I woke up it was dark. I was certain I had broken ribs and a concussion. My face was bloody; I had a broken nose. I could only see out of my right eye, the left was swollen shut. I painfully pulled myself to my feet and made my way to my mother's room. It was empty. The bed was soaked with blood. No one else was home.

They never found my mother's body. My stepfather and Officer Richard covered up everything. They had to have help higher up in the system. There was never any mention of my Mother's murder. They sent me to a home for wayward boys, saying I was 'troubled'. When I was 17, my stepfather simply disappeared. I guess *he* pissed off the wrong person. That left Officer Bill G. Richard for me to deal with. So began my plan to join law enforcement. I knew someone was protecting him, probably *lots* of some ones. The best way I could figure to find out who, and take them down, was to join their ranks and gain their trust.

Over my years as a Washington County Sheriff, I've had my eye on Officer Richard, but I've never been able to put together anything concrete. There are some high-powered people protecting him, as far as I can tell. I know he's corrupt. I know he has helped to murder at least one person. I just can't prove it. I've exhausted every trail and angle involving my mother's murder to its end and come up with nothing. I don't think he's ever connected me with that teenager from his rookie days; I took my mother's maiden name when I turned 18. Truthfully, I was a bit of a chunk when I was a teenager, many people wouldn't recognize me. Still, I've failed to get close enough to him to gather enough dirt to take him down. A new angle to pursue on *'Officer Dick'* as Caden likes to call him is just what I've been looking for. At the mention of his nickname, I involuntarily tensed, bad memories cascading through my mind as if they happened yesterday.

"Officer Richard is the cop you think is involved in her daughter's disappearance? Tell me everything."

Caden answered this demand by handing me a clipboard with a variety of papers attached to it. The first several pages were too legible to be Caden's, and were on the kind of yellow legal pad I was used to seeing him carry for job notes. The pages contained what appeared to be a timeline starting from approximately twenty years ago. They outlined an ugly course of events starting with the rape of Krysta by a then rookie Officer Richard, when she was only 20 years old. Things did not get much prettier from there. Officer Richard essentially stalked Krysta throughout the pregnancy that resulted from him raping her, and continued to do so intermittently over the course of the following 20 years. Things really took an ugly turn when Officer Richard sent Krysta flowers on the 16th anniversary of the rape with a threatening card attached. It was one thing too many and Krysta attempted to take her own life. The Department of Human Services caseworker had Krysta placed on a psychiatric hold and put her then, 15 year old daughter, Evin, into foster care. It took her two years to get Evin back home, Officer Richard plaguing her the entire time. Then he shows up at Evin's dorm to take the missing person's report having transferred to the same Police Precinct in which Evin happened to be attending college. I paused, trying to decipher Caden's illegibly scrawled note next to Krysta's much more readable cursive.

"What the hell does this say, Caden?"

"Come on, bro, my handwriting isn't *that* bad!"

"Caden, my five year old niece can write better than this."

"Fuck you; you don't even *have* a niece. It says 'he has a key to the front door'."

"The front door to what?"

"The front door to the dorm building."

"Oh – ohhhh, that's not good."

"Exactly, that reminds me. I put a unique lockset on Evin's dorm room door; I didn't know what else he has keys to and didn't want him getting in there. I have the old ones in the truck, thought you might want to get them checked for prints or whatever. Mine will be on them, obviously, as well as Krysta's, Evin's and Evin's boyfriend, Sean."

"Good thinking, I'll get them from you when we leave. I'll need elimination prints."

"That shouldn't be a problem."

Krysta watched the way Caden and I talked to each other in a sort of shocked daze. I'm not sure what surprised her more; the way Caden spoke to me or that it didn't bother me. Caden just is; you accept him as you find him or leave him be. Anyone that knows me would probably say the same thing. I'm just more charming – and less scary. It usually works to my advantage, and I'm not afraid to use it.

After Caden's illegible scrawl Krysta had written what she deemed important things to note about the dorm room and Evin in particular. Her backpack with her cell phone, keys, journal, makeup bag and other toiletries were in the dorm room but her wallet was missing. Nothing else seemed to be missing from the dorm as far as Krysta or the boyfriend could tell. Evin talked to a Starbucks worker named Joe around noon before she went missing.

"Caden, did you talk to this Joe character?"

Caden shook his head; his mouth was full of food. The waitress had delivered our breakfast without making a sound.

"Hey, why didn't you tell me the food was here?"

"Couldn't you smell it?" Krysta asked.

Caden swallowed and then laughed. "He gets focused and blocks everything out."

"All I can say is my pancakes had better not be cold."

Caden laughed. The pancakes were still hot. We finished breakfast and talked a little more. Krysta turned Evin's phone over to me and I took separate prints from her and Caden to eliminate them from the lockset. Krysta told me Sean's phone number was in Evin's phone if I needed to call him, she'd already sent herself the name card. I could go through the rest of the notes on my own and get back in touch with Caden later. I already had enough to give me a couple of starting points to investigate. I got the locks from Caden and we parted ways, him to go track down Joe at Starbucks, and me to do some digging on my own.

The first order of business was to get back to the Sheriff's Department and pull any digital files I could find associated with Krysta or Evin Mallory. There should be a record of the 911 call in the central database from when Krysta attempted suicide. It was a good starting point.

The Washington County Sheriff's Department is located on the second floor of the Washington County Jail in Hillsboro. It is only about a seven-minute drive from Mary's; I made it in four. Caden would have told me to write myself a ticket. I would have responded it's a perk of the job. One of the rules it's ok to bend on occasion, as long as no one gets hurt.

There were only a few people in the office when I got there. The usual admin staff was there, secretaries and such, and a couple of other Deputies doing paperwork. I went to an empty computer terminal and entered my search criteria. As of yet, nothing had been entered into the central database about Evin being missing. The listing for the 911 call was the only thing to come up. There was a digital log in the database and the physical tape and file was in central records. I scanned the digital file; it should contain everything the physical file did, except the actual voice recording.

If you've seen the transcript of one attempted suicide call, you've seen them all. Sure, the methods vary and the faces change but other than that, they look a lot alike. There was the transcript of the 911 call itself, between the daughter and the operator, which was relatively typical. The address and name information of Krysta and Evin Mallory, then the list of responding emergency workers. As well as that, there was a list of attachments with photos of the scene and the attempt victim. Individual reports from the various emergency workers attached to the very bottom of the file. I scanned the list of responders and stopped when my eyes fell upon one name: Officer Bill G. Richard. He was the second on scene. I hit "Ctrl + P" on the terminal keyboard and printed the entire file. Suddenly the handful of other people in the office felt like too many. Casually, I waited by the laser printer for it to finish its job, and then took the entire inch thick file and left the office.

I'm not sure why I felt eyes on me as I got back into my cruiser and left the county jail parking lot. I think I'm starting to get paranoid, but I breathed a sigh of relief as I pulled out onto Baseline and headed towards Forest Grove. Putting a little distance between the Government Center and me while I perused that file just seemed like a good idea. Taking a right onto 20th in Cornelius, I continued north until I hit Zion Church Rd. I didn't think I was likely to be disturbed on the back roads of Cornelius. I drove west down Zion Church a bit and pulled into an empty industrial parking lot where I knew I wouldn't be bothered.

Officer Richard's report *may* have appeared normal to someone else, but had a coldness to it that bordered on callous. Not to mention he'd left out *a lot* of important details. Of course, those details would have cast more than a few suspicious shadows on him. Like his extensive history with the attempted suicide victim, or that the flower arrangement and menacing card *that he sent* were what pushed Krysta Mallory over the edge. Then, of course, there was that little piece of information about him having raped her nearly 16 years before the incident. Obviously, he'd chosen to leave that out as well. Really, the report didn't tell me anything other than the fact that Officer Richard was second on the scene, is a lying sack of shit, and... Ahhh – he gave young Evin a ride to the Hospital in his cruiser and questioned her alone in a conference room until the Social Worker arrived. That's interesting, and unusual. Perhaps I'll have a talk with that social worker.

One of the good things about spring in the Northwest is that we get periodic stretches of sun between all the gloom and drizzle. One of the *bad* things about spring in the Northwest is that we get periodic stretches of sun between all the gloom and drizzle. Everyone is so damn used to the rain; they forget how to drive when that bright yellow ball is in the sky. Let's not forget all the road construction crews that come out to play. They're a real blast to get around too. I hate spring in Oregon. All the idiots come out of the woodwork. It easily took three times longer than it should have to get back into Hillsboro. As if the regular stop and go traffic isn't bad enough, everyone slows down even more when they see a police cruiser. It makes me want to shoot someone, but that would be breaking one of my own rules – and the law. So instead, I flashed my lights and sirens a couple of times to get the last few sun-zoned drivers out of my way: another perk of the job.

According to the 911-call file, Violet Skazony was the responding social worker. I didn't recognize the name. After a brief conversation with Alice at the front desk, I knew why.

Violet Skazony wasn't just *any* social worker; she headed up the entire Washington County Children's Protective Services Division. It made absolutely no sense for her to be the one responding to a typical call like this, or *any* for that matter, she wasn't a field worker. Why didn't she send someone else out on the call? Why was Evin Mallory so important? It definitely piqued my curiosity.

After getting directions from Alice at the reception desk, I punched in the six-digit security code to the door and entered the maze. The main work area of Child Protective Services was crammed into what seemed to be an endless circuit of hallway, conference rooms, and offices with an oversized bullpen of cubicles in the center. If you didn't know exactly how to get where you were going it was extremely easy to get lost. The building really wasn't very big. How they fit that many desks and cubicles into so little space always amazed me. Leave it to the Government to get the most out of the least available. The result was that the place seemed bigger on the inside than it looked on the out; and made you lose all sense of direction.

Violet wasn't in her office. A six-foot high dividing wall ran parallel to this section of offices for about 50 feet, or five offices. Violet's was second to the last. About every ten feet, there was a break in the dividing wall into the central maze of cubicles created from the dividers. While there were easily dozens of cubicles, many of them were unoccupied, probably due to caseworkers being out in the field. The cubicle closest to Violet's office was, however, by an attractive, dark-haired woman hacking away at her keyboard with enough speed to make her fingers blur. Her nameplate said 'Angel Fairbairn' and she wasn't wearing a wedding ring. I leaned against the edge of the cubicle wall, and put on my most charming smile.

"It's a wonder there's *any* evil left in the world with such an Angel on our side."

I saw her shoulders stiffen, and then she swiveled in her chair to face me. She cautiously took in the smile, badge and Sheriff's Deputy Attire before coolly smiling back.

"Can I help you with something Sheriff—?"

"Truman, Sheriff Al Truman, and yes, I was wondering if you could tell me where I could find Violet Skazony, she's not in her office."

"She had to go to Salem for conferences; she won't be back in until tomorrow at the earliest. Is there anything else?"

"Does she often work cases herself? Her name came up as the caseworker on something I'm following up on and I didn't recognize it. I'm familiar with most of the caseworkers."

"*I've* never met you before."

"*My* world has definitely brightened now that you *have*."

"Do those cheesy lines and false charm actually ever work?"

Ouch, okay, new tactic.

"Frequently, but apparently not on intelligent women like you." I bowed. "Okay, I have a missing girl. She was in foster care for a while several years ago when her mother attempted suicide. Violet is listed as the caseworker, I just wanted to ask her a few questions, see if I could get any leads on where to look for the girl."

Her countenance softened; mental note – Angel Fairbairn is a straight-laced, no bullshit type.

"Violet hand picks a few special cases, usually situations where there is a suicide or attempt involved. She has a soft spot for kids dealing with that kind of situation. I think there may have been something in her own past that makes her feel a connection with those kids."

"Thank you, Angel, you've been —"

"Don't say it."

I laughed. "— a lot of help."

"I'm sorry; the 'Angel' jokes just never stop. I get really tired of them."

"I'll remember that. Have a wonderful afternoon, Angel."

She flashed a genuine, if brief, smile before turning back to her work. I attempted to make my way back out of the maze. Instead of the exit, I ended up in a conference room. Backtracking, I tried again and found bathrooms and the copy and print area. I decided to take it as a sign and used the restroom instead of pounding my head against a cubicle wall. The men's bathroom didn't have urinals, just three regular stalls and a handicapped on the end. Someone talking on the phone occupied the handicapped stall. I took the first one. The man on the phone sounded agitated. I couldn't help listening.

"No, Charlie, she can't handle it tonight she'll be at *the Conference*. No, she can't pick the girl up in Salem. The bidding starts at ten so she won't be available until midnight, at least. Fine, I'll tell her to call you after the Conference, but she won't be happy. If Alan is giving you that much trouble, get rid of him, you know he's expendable. Just take care of it."

I heard the phone click shut. It was obvious the man didn't know I was in there. I sat on the toilet and pulled up my feet before he left his stall, and waited. As soon as I heard the bathroom door close, I cautiously followed; keeping enough distance that he wouldn't notice me behind him. When we got close to the exit into the waiting area he stopped, I ducked into an empty conference room just before he turned around. A few seconds later, I heard the heavy security door close and I continued into the lobby just in time to see him getting into his car through the large windows. I recognized him instantly as an Assistant to the District Attorney. I stopped by Alice's desk.

"Hey Alice, why was he here?"

"DA sent him to pick up some files for the Conference in Salem."

"Okay, thanks Alice, have a nice day."

"You too, sweetie."

Alice was old enough to be my grandmother and doted on any single male of legal age. She hated most females unless they were children and them she spoiled rotten. She's worked as the receptionist at the Hillsboro CPS office for as long as it's been there and several others before that. She was also close friends with my mother before she died. I always knew she'd tell me the truth, at least what she knew of it. However, she was one of those people that thought there was a reason for everything and saw the best in every*one*, which meant that she closed her ears on gossip. An investigation thrives on gossip, at least to some extent. Alice's job included recording the purpose of every individuals visit to CPS, so she could always tell me why someone was there, which in this case, was helpful.

The phone conversation ADA Mitchell was having in the men's

restroom was strange to say the least. It was most definitely suspicious. Whether it has anything to do with my missing teenager is anyone's guess. What kind of *Conference* had bidding at it? I wonder if this is the same *Conference* that Violet Skazony is attending. Who are Charlie and Alan? Not to mention the girl Mitchell had spoken of, if not Evin Mallory. There were so many questions to answer, definitely some food for thought.

9 TUESDAY 10:45AM
KRYSTA MALLORY

The hodgepodge of people that Caden claimed as friends, or 'buddies' as he referred to them grew stranger the longer I was associated with him. I didn't know if I should question his odd assortment of connections or just be happy that he has them. For now, the fact that he was willing to utilize the vast and varied resources at his disposal to help find Evin was enough, more than enough, really.

He'd taken us back to his shop so that he could pick up a few things and make some phone calls while we were waiting for Joe to start his shift at Starbucks. We still had some time to kill, Caden said, and he had 'networking' to do. I contemplated what that might mean for a man like Caden as I watched him pace back and forth, cell held to his ear. It was now clear that he was even more complex than I ever could have guessed. The little bits of conversation I overheard as he paced by me hinted at connections to people I'm not sure I'd ever want to meet under normal circumstances. Still, I was undeniably certain I was completely safe in his company. The two pieces of knowledge are totally contrary to one another. At least most sane people would think so. Perhaps sanity is slightly overrated. As I made these assessments, Caden snapped his phone closed and briskly sauntered towards me.

"Al called. Officer Dick was the second on site at your suicide attempt. He drove Evin to the hospital and talked to her alone until the social worker, a lady named Violet Skazony, arrived. Al went by DHS to talk to Violet but she's in Salem for some Conference. Only Al doesn't think it's any normal conference because on his way out he overheard the ADA on a

82

phone call in the men's bathroom mentioning 'the conference' in a way that made it sound suspicious. I have some of my contacts checking into it. We should know for sure pretty soon."

"Violet Skazony is the Social Worker that was in charge of our case. Evin hated her. I didn't especially like her either; she felt – wrong."

"She's not just any Social Worker; she's in charge of the entire Washington County Children's Protective Services Division. Apparently, she only handles 'special cases' where there is a suicide or something similar involved."

"Maybe she just isn't used to working directly with people, she was always awkward."

"Could be, but Al has her going to a conference in Salem, and suspects that the suspicious conference the ADA was speaking of on the phone is the same one."

"What could be suspicious about a conference?"

"There was mention of a girl and bidding during the conversation Al overheard the ADA having, among other things less savory."

"Oh." With the images that snippet immediately brought to mind, I didn't want to know what was 'less savory'.

"Anyway, Joe should be on shift at Starbucks in about 45 minutes, so we should get going. Noon traffic on Highway 26 is a bitch."

Caden was right about the traffic. I drove into Portland as little as possible, myself. On the rare occasion that I went to visit Evin at college I usually went to a Tri-met Park and Ride and took the train. I *hate* driving down town. As for work, well, I telecommute. It's not difficult to hide from the world when your job is telephone customer service and you can do it from home. I have a dedicated landline that's solely for work and nothing else. When I'm done for the day I just log out of the system, it's perfect.

Everything was going just fine – until it wasn't. Now I've lost Evin again, and this time she could be in *real* trouble. There's so much Evin doesn't know. Like whom her father *really* is – and how dangerous he is. What if I somehow caused this by not warning her? Could I have prevented this from happening if I had reported the rape all those years ago? If he'd gone to prison maybe I would have been more stable, a better mother, not been so afraid all the time. If he'd gone to prison, he probably wouldn't have sent those flowers. If I'd never received them – but there really is no going back.

"We'll get her back," Caden gently wiped one of my tears. "I promise."

I hadn't even realized I was crying. Nodding, I leaned into his strong, firm hand and took what comfort he offered. Nothing can fill the void of a lost child; it helped some not bearing it alone.

The snarling frenzy of lunch hour traffic finally spit us out downtown around a quarter after one. Another fifteen minutes of searching landed us a parking space five blocks up from the Starbucks and Evin's dorms. It was nearly a quarter of two when we finally made our way up to the counter to ask for Joe. I kept quiet. I didn't trust myself not to burst into tears at any moment if I tried to ask the questions. Besides, Caden seemed to know exactly what he was doing. When it was our turn at the register, Caden stepped forward, his bearing one of command.

"Are you Joe?" Caden asked the kid at the register.

"No, he's in back stocking. Can I help you with something? I'm the manager."

Caden looked like he wanted to laugh; the kid was probably barely in his twenties and flamboyant as hell.

"We need to talk to Joe, it's important. He may have been the last person to speak to a girl before she went missing."

"*Did he* do something illegal?"

He said it with flair of attitude that only a gay man could manage. I could tell Caden was getting frustrated.

"No – look, are you going to get Joe or do I need to come back there get him myself? We're in a bit of a hurry here."

"Well you'll excuse *me* if I need to know what's going on with *my* workers before I let some *brute* have at them!" The boy pirouetted in place, hands planted firmly on his hips, before marching to the back. "Jose*pher*, there is some brute and a woman out here that *insist* on speaking to you –

quite rudely I might add!"

A speckling of laughter broke out throughout the coffeehouse, as the manager's voice carried clearly to the patrons in the front. I couldn't help joining, despite the circumstances. It *was* comical. Joe came out of the back with the manager hot on his heels. After pausing to make a whispered exchange with one another, Joe blushed, and then continued around the counter toward us. It became obvious why the young manager was giving Caden trouble. The two of them were together and he was being protective of his boyfriend. I nearly laughed again. The thought of Caden being a threat to a gay man in *that* manner was *extremely* laughable.

Joe was one of those gay men that, if he weren't in the company of his significant other, it would be hard to tell he *was* gay. His speech and mannerisms were more those of a straight man. He did not come across as at all flamboyant, so if it weren't for the interaction between him and his boyfriend behind the counter I probably would not have figured it out so quickly. I would be willing to bet money that he hadn't been 'out of the closet' for very long. Another reason why his boyfriend was being so possessive, he probably wasn't certain Joe wouldn't change his mind.

"Aaron said you wanted to talk to me?" Joe asked.

"Yesterday around noon you spoke with Evin Mallory when she came in?" Caden asked.

"Evin, as in the Goth girl with black hair and glasses that lives upstairs?"

"Yes, that Evin, did she tell you where she was going or if she was meeting anyone?"

"Did she seem ok?" I interjected, "Was she upset or anything?"

Caden looked at me sternly. I bristled but held my tongue. He obviously wanted me to let him ask the questions. I don't know why *I* can't ask any questions – she's *my* daughter. I sat back in my chair and stewed silently while the conversation continued. Joe nervously glanced back and forth between us before answering.

"She seemed happy, and she didn't *exactly* tell me where she was going, but I *think* she was headed out to 'The Stone House' in Forest Park. That's where she usually goes when she has the afternoon off."

"What do you mean 'she didn't exactly tell you'?"

"Well, I asked if that was where she was going, and she said 'I'd tell you but I'd have to kill ya', so, I took that to be a yes in Evin-speak."

"He's right," I said, "that means yes."

Caden glared at me; I glared back.

"Was she alone or did she say if she was going to be meeting up with anyone?"

"She wasn't with anyone when she came in. She did say that her therapist cancelled her appointment for yesterday, but she didn't mention going to meet with anyone else. I heard her boyfriend came in this morning asking questions, though, have you talked to him?"

"I sent her boyfriend in this morning."

"Oh, well, that's all I know. So what's going on with her anyway, is she in some kind of trouble?"

"She's missing."

"Oh. My. *GAWD!* I had *no* idea – I'm *so* sorry. If there is anything else Aaron or I can do to help, let us know. We *love* Evin!"

So much for Joe not being obviously gay, it definitely slipped out that time. Caden pulled a business card from his breast pocket and handed it to Joe.

"Call me if you remember anything else that you think might help."

"Interesting business card. So are you a PI or something?"

"Ya, 'or something', thanks for the help. Let's go, Krysta."

I was barely out of my chair before Caden had the door open, which he impatiently held for me as I hurried to catch up to him. He barreled his way through the crowds of PSU students and business professionals on the sidewalk toward where he'd parked five blocks up. I nearly missed colliding with other pedestrians as I hurried to keep up with him. Half out of breath, I grabbed onto his elbow to avoid falling behind again.

"Where are we going, now, anyway?" I asked.

He glanced at me, a look of irritation on his face, before answering.

"Weren't you listening? We're going to the Stone House to look for Evin, or at least any sign that she went there."

I found myself fuming; again. I took a deep breath and told myself that Caden was *helping* me and biting his head off was probably not a good idea.

"Yes, Caden, I *was* listening. I just thought that perhaps you might want to, I don't know; call your friend, *the Sheriff*, before we go traipsing off into the woods after evidence since you insisted that we enlist his *expert assistance.*"

Okay, so maybe I couldn't help biting his head off – a little. He stopped cold in the middle of the intersection. Other people in the crosswalk stumbled into him before regaining their bearings and going around. A driver in a car that was trying to turn laid on his horn. Caden was oblivious to all but me.

"My friend, *the Sheriff*, is currently trying to run down another lead he thinks may be connected at the DA's office. Possibly, at great personal risk, I might add, and is ditching his regular duties as a Sheriff to do so. Now, do I need to take you home so I can work, or can we go check out the Stone House?"

Caden glared sternly at me, waiting for my answer, while cars honked and drivers yelled for us to get out of the way. It was too much. The terror of losing Evin again, facing Officer Richard, Caden's hot and cold manner towards me. My shell crumbled and I burst into uncontrollable tears.

"Oh my fucking God," Caden said, looking skyward for a moment. "I'm sorry, Krysta, I know you're scared and worried about Evin." Caden pulled me into a hug and held me there while he talked. "I just need you to trust me, okay. I know what I'm doing, and my contacts know what *they're* doing. We are going to find her, I promise. It will be ok."

I struggled to contain my tears and nodded agreement. Taking his hand, I continued across the intersection and back toward the truck. Caden allowed my lead, I had controlled the sobs but tears streamed freely down my face. I couldn't help it; I was overwhelmed. I don't think he knew how to deal with that. Tepid sky mirrored mood, as ugly grey clouds moved in to block the sun, and brisk gusts of wind buffeted back and forth between buildings lining the streets. I didn't mind the wind; it felt good on my face after the hot tears. By the time we got back to the truck, they were dried.

I'd heard of the Stone House, but I'd never been there before. I don't remember Evin mentioning it to me either. She must have wanted to keep it private. I'm just glad *someone* knew she liked to go there. Caden didn't ask anyone for directions, but drove directly to a place in Portland called Lower MacLeay Park. It didn't seem like *much* of a park itself, more like a turn-about with restrooms, a spattering of parking, a few picnic tables, and a trail leading off into a splinter of woods squeezed among the western sprawl of Portland. Apparently, the splinter opened up into the *much* larger Forest Park.

The turn-about style parking area was full, so Caden parked on the street. I had already started walking toward the park entrance before I noticed Caden wasn't with me and turned around. When I got back to the truck, his head was buried in the truck bed toolbox; he hadn't even noticed I'd moved.

"What are you doing?"

"'.'m .e.ting ...plies" Came Caden's muffled reply.

"You're eating flies? What? Caden, I can't understand you!"

"No, I'm not eating flies!" He said, standing free of the toolbox. "I *said*, 'I'm getting supplies'!"

"Oh, supplies for what?"

"C...ec...g ev...nce."

His head was back in the toolbox. I gave up trying to figure out what he was doing and waited for him to resurface. After a few minutes of digging around and much clanging of tools, he reemerged with a handful of latex gloves, a roll of tall kitchen bags, and a flashlight. He handed me a pair of the gloves, then got his clipboard out of the truck.

"Sorry, couldn't find the gloves."

"What do we need all this for?"

"Collecting evidence; we don't want to compromise anything we find by getting our own fingerprints all over it."

"You sound like you've been through this before."

"I help Al out on occasion. Last time I touched evidence without gloves he reamed my ass. I knew I still had some – just haven't used 'em in a while so they were buried. I *told* you I know what I'm doing."

I buried a smile. "Alright, I believe you. Are we going now?"

Caden grunted as he strode past, leaving no choice but to follow. It was a long slow hike to the Stone House from Lower MacLeay Park. The terrain was beautiful, and under any other circumstance, I would probably have enjoyed the hike immensely. Today, all I could think was – *my baby girl was out here all alone.* What was she doing here? Did she come here to think? Was she trying to escape something – our troubled past? What possessed her to come to the middle of a forest alone? There was a stream trickling along the side of the trail, weaving in and out of eyesight, but nearly always audible. The trees towered overhead creating a canopy that blocked out most of the patchy sunlight, so that when it did break through it was breathtakingly blinding. The trail we walked on was a thick mixture of mud, pine needles and rocks marred with the countless tracks of human and animal. I don't know how Caden expected to find any trace of Evin among all of this.

While we trudged on, Caden looked tirelessly, as did I, for any obvious sign of Evin. We shrugged off rain, squinted through sunlight, and battled winds as the weather cycled its usual routine. I was beginning to think we would neither find any evidence of Evin *nor* make it to the Stone House when we turned a corner on the trail and I saw it. The ruins drew me in like a friend offering comfort. There wasn't a lot left. The base of the structure remained, as well as a few walls, the floor and steps leading up to it. The crumbling ruins of the old building showed the signs of age with the growth of plush green moss and ivy meandering its way up the stone façade. It was beautiful. I left Caden behind and ran the rest of the way to the base of the stairs, where I stopped cold. I knew, now, that Evin had been here. A moment later, I felt Caden's hand on my shoulder.

"What is it? What did you find?"

"Look," I said, pointing in front of the steps. "I bought Evin that

Lipstick mace. I had her initials etched into the case. Evin's dorm mini-fridge is full of that kind of Arizona. That's her shade of lipstick on the lip of the can. She was here, Caden, so where is she now? Who did she use that mace on?"

Caden snapped photos of both items before putting on a pair of the purple latex gloves and carefully stowing them in one of the plastic kitchen bags he'd brought. He scrawled the location we found them on his notepad. Together, we scoured the rest of the area but failed to find anything else that showed that she was there. The expended lipstick mace cylinder was undoubtedly hers; it even had her etched initials. The lid was missing, but we were unable to find it anywhere. After an hour of searching the ruins and surrounding area, we grudgingly decided to take what we had back to Al and see if he could get anything off them.

We were both tired and dirty when we got back to the entrance to Lower MacLeay Park. When we reached the little turn-about, Caden stopped abruptly. He intently studied a Parking Enforcement Deputy that was currently writing someone a ticket for parking in a no parking zone.

"What's wrong?"

"Nothing," Caden said, "I just had an idea."

Suddenly he was off again, striding toward the Deputy with determined purpose. I hurried to catch up, tired and disheartened. The Parking Enforcement Deputy looked up defensively as we stopped suddenly in front of him.

"If this is your vehicle, you'll have to oppose the ticket in court, there's nothing I can do now." The Deputy said.

"No, Sir, it's not, I was wondering if I could ask you a question?" Caden said.

"I'm unable to fix or alter Parking Tickets of any kind."

"That's not my question."

"I can't grant permits either."

"Wrong again."

"There's no —" The Deputy began.

"I need to know if this lot was patrolled yesterday!"

The Deputy blinked. Honestly, I think he was just reciting responses from some list he memorized and wasn't even fully awake. Caden cutting him off so abruptly seemed to snap him out of it and he actually *focused* on us for the first time.

"I don't think I've been asked *that* before. Yes, the lot is patrolled several times daily, why?"

"A girl, age 19 went missing some time yesterday afternoon. We know she came here. I was wondering if you or whoever was patrolling yesterday saw anything suspicious."

"Well, that would have been me. I don't know if this is what you're looking for," The Deputy began flipping through the pages of the ticket book in his hand. "However I *did* write a ticket yesterday. Ah, here it is. It was a plain white delivery van, parked in a handicapped spot without a permit. I issued a warning *and* a citation, actually. The first time I came through the van pulled into the spot while I was here. I told them they'd have to move. It was a couple of guys, said because they were going to be transporting a disabled passenger they thought they could park in the handicapped zone. I told them not without the DMV permit, and issued a warning. They apologized and said they'd move the van. That was around 11:30am. I came back by about an hour later and the van was still there, with the emergency lights on and the two guys nowhere in sight so I put a citation on the windshield."

"You got the plate number on that?"

"Of course I do. I also have title and registration info. Can you show me identification that says you're authorized to have it?"

"That, I cannot. However, I can put you in touch with someone who does. Hold on a sec."

Caden pulled his cell out and dialed a number. He left me standing there with the Parking Enforcement Deputy while he strolled a short distance away to talk on the phone. After a few minutes, he snapped his phone closed and came back.

"You should be getting a call." Caden said to the Deputy.

The Deputies radio squawked loudly, causing me to jump, he looked at Caden suspiciously, as he answered.

"Go ahead."

"10-21" said the voice on the radio.

"10-4" The Deputy left us standing there, walking to his cruiser a few feet away. I could see he was taking some sort of a call in the car, but couldn't hear what he was saying. He wrote something down on a notepad then came back to where he left us standing.

"Well, Mr. Neely," he paused to look Caden in the eye; Caden hadn't told him his name. "It appears you have friends in high places. Sheriff Truman assures me this information is safe with you and tells me to remind you to keep your fingerprints *off* any other evidence you collect *this* time." The Deputy's eyes begged the question 'what evidence?', but he didn't actually ask.

"Thanks for your help." Caden took the paper the Deputy offered. "Where, exactly, was the van parked yesterday?"

"In the handicapped spot closest to the restrooms, right over there." He said, pointing about 300 feet beyond where we were standing.

"Thanks, again."

Briefly, Caden examined the information on the sheet of paper the Deputy had given him, before folding it and putting it into his wallet. He replaced his wallet in his back pocket then strode toward the indicated parking spot. After examining the sparse bit of trash in and about the actual parking area the Deputy had indicated, Caden expanded his search to the trees and around the building right next to it. It didn't take long before he was carefully unfolding a crumpled piece of paper, with purple latex covered hands.

"I found the citation. Whoever parked that van here did not intend to pay it. I doubt they thought anyone was going to come digging either. I wonder if they left anything else behind."

"Wait a minute, 'whoever parked that van'? Didn't that Parking

Enforcement cop give you the registration info?"

"Ya, but it's registered in a woman's name and he said it was two men."

"He said it was a delivery van, maybe it's a business owner."

"Or someone's wife, or stolen. Regardless, Al will find that out. Hey, there's a dumpster, I'm gonna check it out."

We walked to the dumpster together, and Caden flipped up the lid. The smell was atrocious. He tossed aside a giant black garbage bag, recently placed from one of the cans. Nestled between the bags of garbage in the bottom of the dumpster was a like new, cross-country wheelchair. It was covered in garbage, mud, and debris, but obviously expensive. Caden wrestled it free from its hiding place and hauled it out of the dumpster. When he set it down on the pavement the frayed sleeve of a sweatshirt hung limply from where the arm rests folded together. I gasped and darted forward. Caden stopped me just in time, restraining me from touching it with a purple-gloved hand; he pulled the dark grey zip up hoodie from the folded seat of the wheelchair. Holding it up, he looked me in the eye, questioning, I nodded.

"It's hers."

10 TUESDAY 6:25PM
CADEN NEELY

I pulled the tattered grey sweatshirt from the seat of the wheelchair and held it up for Krysta to see. She met my eyes and nodded.

"It's hers," she said.

My cell picked that moment to ring. I pulled my phone from its holster and draped the sweatshirt over the wheelchair.

"Neely here."

Krysta took a step toward the chair. I shook my head and waved her off. She looked at me defiantly then stalked around the other side of the restrooms. I think she was crying, again, fucking wonderful. I listened to what my contact was saying with half an ear as I contemplated how else I could fuck up with Krysta. The tinny sound of my name said repeatedly drew my attention back to the call.

"Neely – Neely, are you there?"

"I'm sorry, what did you just say?"

"I thought I lost you. It's some sort of bigwig Black Market auction, held monthly, from what my sources say. There's a $10,000.00 buy in to participate, along with a background check to make sure you have the right kind of connections."

"Of the shady variety, I assume?"

"Right, they don't want anyone too clean. Suspicious applicants tend to disappear."

"What makes an applicant suspicious?"

"You know, 'average Joe', perfect record, the squeaky clean variety."

"Gotcha, that shouldn't be a problem. Did you find out what they're auctioning?"

"No one knows; you're going to have to get inside to find that out. I did learn that there are powerful players from all over the world flying in to bid – it's an in person only event."

"Interesting."

"One more thing."

"Ya?"

"There are a lot of cops and other officials present at these auctions."

"You're shittin' me."

"My sources are accurate."

"Fuck – ok. Thanks, I owe you one."

"I know you're good for it."

The line went dead; I closed the phone and put it back in the holster. Al was gonna have a fit over this. I debated whether I should tell him first and give him the option to investigate it himself, or go investigate it and *then* tell him what I found out. I decided to decide later. I put the sweatshirt in a kitchen bag and picked up the folded wheelchair in a gloved hand. I'd have to get a yard bag out of the truck to put it in, I wasn't about to leave it sitting there. Someone might take it. I was surprised at how light the thing was; like it was titanium.

I rounded the corner of the restrooms expecting to find Krysta waiting for me there. She was nowhere in sight. I didn't see her at the picnic tables either, so continued on to the truck. She was leaning against the front bumper, smoking one of my cigarettes. As I approached, she took a long drag and blew the smoke in my face defiantly. With an effort, I kept the off color remark that immediately came to mind to myself. She was obviously still mad. Instead, I put the wheelchair in a yard bag, placed it in the bed of the truck, and then took the pack from above the visor, and lit my own cigarette. For a few minutes, we just stood there and smoked in silence. I decided it was safest to let her cool down. Finally, she seemed to relax a little. She took one last drag, and then dropped the butt, grinding it out beneath her hiking boot.

"I quit when I was pregnant with Evin."

"Makes sense; did you miss it?"

"At times, yes, like now."

"Do you want another one?"

She laughed. "Maybe later, thanks."

"Just checking. That was my contact in Salem on the phone. He says the 'conference' is really a big Black Market auction, couldn't find out what's for sale. We have three hours and 10 minutes to figure out who we're going to get inside and how, so we better get moving."

"Salem's a long drive."

"That depends on your transportation. I have to call Al, give him the info on the van and tell him what we know so far."

I helped Krysta into the passenger side of the truck before calling Al. He picked up half way through the first ring.

"I was about to call you," he answered.

"Well, now you don't have to. I've got information on the conference."

"So do I. What'd you get off the van you called about earlier?"

"Plate and registration, I also found the citation Parking Enforcement left on the windshield wadded up and thrown into the trees behind the restrooms."

"Okay, hit me."

I dug the paper the Deputy had given me out of my wallet and read the information off to Al, then climbed behind the wheel of the truck.

"We also found several items that Krysta is convinced belong to Evin, by the Stone House as well as a sweatshirt Krysta says is hers in the dumpster behind the restrooms thrown in with a brand new custom wheelchair."

"Could be they knocked her out and used the chair to move her, but why leave it behind? Why leave *anything* behind for that matter?"

"Amateurs? Or maybe there wasn't room for her *and* the chair in the van?"

"That could be, if they were trying to keep her locked down out of sight somehow. Wheelchairs are usually traceable by their serial numbers, so it seems risky for them to leave it behind. I'll have it traced."

"So, what do you got on that registration?"

"I'll have to wait until I'm back to the office, the name rings a bell, but there's no record attached to it so it's not coming up. I'll get back to you on that one. What did you get on the conference?"

"My contact in Salem confirms it's a Black Market auction for the who's who of the world's underbelly. It goes on monthly. There's a $10,000.00 buy in and a background check and if an applicant turns up too clean, they tend to disappear. He also says there's a lot of cops and other officials there. I want to go check it out, but I can't bring Krysta, she'll never make it past their radar. What did you find?"

"Just enough to know I need to get back in and dig deeper, I got interrupted. The DA is definitely going to be at *whatever* is going on in Salem. How about you check out things down there, while I use the opportunity to get into the DA's office and dig a little deeper. I got the impression there was something in there they didn't want me to see."

"You aren't even going to ask me if the background check or buy-in is a problem are you?"

"Do you really *want* me to?"

"Nope."

"Then why'd you ask?"

"Just   curious."

"Let me know what you find."

Al disconnected. I laughed quietly. Al had access to my *documented* criminal record. It was just colorful enough to satisfy most people that I wasn't someone to mess around with. Al also knew that wasn't the only 'background check' these guys were likely to run. They would have their own channels to go through that would give them other stuff. Oh, they'd get the traditional criminal background check too, and that would reinforce what their contacts told them, but that wasn't *all* they relied on. The underground had its own information networks that provided that kind of information. I should know – I used them all the time. The reason Al didn't want to ask those questions was that if he knew the answers he would likely have to arrest me. He didn't want to do that. Not only were we friends. I was extremely useful to him. Those same connections made it easier for him to work his magic, and to *appear* corrupt when necessary, in order to gain the trust of those cops that were. It was an important part of his long-term goals to bring down the dirty cops in the system.

Krysta was giving me the silent treatment. Women did this a lot when they were mad at men. I think because they are constantly trying to get us to talk about our thoughts and feelings they think silence will bother us the way it does them. Generally, men as a whole will pretend not to notice and just take reprieve in the silence. I debated taking this route for the duration of the time it took to get us back onto Highway 26 West; about ten minutes. Unfortunately, I wanted more of an association with Krysta than being the mechanic. So, I took a deep breath and plunged in headfirst, knowing full well I was diving into a shark pit.

"You're awfully quiet, something on your mind?"

"What the hell do you mean, 'I can't take Krysta with me'?" She snapped.

"It's too much of a risk. You're too clean, they'd never let us past the first check point."

"Oh, and you're *so* dangerous. I can *act* shady just like you."

I don't think she meant it as the blatant challenge that it came across as. My reaction was visceral. I couldn't help it; I bristled.

"You don't know what the hell you're talking about. You're *not* going, and that's final."

"Oh, the hell I'm *not*! I'd like to see you *try* to leave me behind, she's *my* daughter!"

We both lapsed into angry silence, too mad to speak. I took several deep breaths and tried to get myself under control. I don't know why she was able to get under my skin like that. I usually have a better handle on my temper. When I was certain I could speak again without yelling at her, I glanced over. She had her arms crossed stiffly as she stared pointedly out the side window. Tears streamed down her face. Why do women cry when they're angry? I swear to God it's because they *know* we can't handle it. Men just don't know what to *do* with tears. I sighed loudly. She glared.

"Listen, this thing that's going on in Salem is going to have some really dangerous people present. They use underground methods to make sure that anyone showing up has enough dirt in their background to be one of them. Yours won't, which will be suspicious and could get you killed. Not to mention, we think several local Social Services Officials are going to be present as well as numerous dirty cops – any one of whom could recognize you for various reasons. We just can't risk it. *I* can't risk it."

"So you're saying that you *do* have the kind of background they'll be looking for?"

I knew the question would come, but still I dreaded answering.

"Yes, I do, enough to fit into the crowd without suspicion anyway."

"But you're friends with a cop."

I laughed. "Yes, I am, and he's even one of the good ones. It's complicated."

"I think I understand you less the more I get to know you, Caden Neely."

"Someday, I'll tell you everything I promise. Now, can I take you home? I don't have much time."

"Can I stay at your place while you go? I don't want to go back to my apartment alone right now. Not knowing that Officer Richard is involved in all of this somehow."

Unbidden, a mental image of Krysta going through everything in my apartment looking for information and secrets sprang to mind. I waited for the possibility to bother me, and then realized it didn't. I tried not to contemplate what that meant.

"Sure, you can stay at my place."

"Really?"

"Yes, really."

She seemed genuinely surprised by my answer. Hell, I was surprised by my answer. I didn't let anyone into my apartment. I had people over to the shop all the time, but never the apartment upstairs. If a woman was involved and didn't want to go to her place, I took her to a motel. No one gets inside. I guess there's a first for everything.

I hauled ass back to the shop from Portland, slowing down only for known speed traps. I didn't have time to play by the rules. I waited for the cloud of dust from the tires to disperse in the wind before I opened the door for Krysta. I've choked through it enough times to appreciate it's worth waiting the minute or two. Besides, I'd made good time on the highway.

I unlocked the steel-barred security and inner fire door to the shop and led Krysta inside. There was no outer entrance to my apartment; you had to go through the shop. It was possible to *leave* from the second floor – but you'd have to jump, that is, unless you knew *exactly* where to find the hand and footholds from the barn style door on the right side of the building. We walked into the first bay of the shop and I flipped on the lights. Slowly, the fluorescent bulbs buzzed into life overhead. An assortment of workbenches, professional grade toolboxes, and various other types of equipment, automotive and otherwise were illuminated. In the center of the bay rested Krysta's Plymouth Volare, still waiting for a timing chain. Black visqueen plastic sheeting acted as curtain, covering the doublewide entrance between the first and second bays. I held back the plastic and motioned Krysta through. Clear plastic enclosed most of the second bay, save for the walkway at the front. I used it primarily for paint.

At the end of the hall like area in front of the second bay was another door, through which was a basic office. What had once been a third bay I had converted. Now, the front of the bay held an office and the back of it a storeroom for spare parts – and whatever else I felt like throwing in there. The door was fireproof and only locked or unlocked with a key. Off the back of the office were a bathroom, shower, and a supply closet. The closet locked from the inside or with a key, was oversized, and had a hidden door in the back. Krysta looked at me strangely when I unlocked and held the closet door open for her, and then closed and locked it behind us. I reached in among the office supplies on the third shelf down lining the back wall and triggered the lever. The wall, shelves and all swung quietly outward, letting us into a hallway with a stairwell leading up. At one time, there *was* a second entrance at this end of the building. The security and fire door remained, so from outside it *appeared* there still was. In actual fact, if you managed to get those two doors open, difficult since they're welded shut, you would find only an equally difficult to penetrate cinderblock wall behind them.

"*This* is your apartment?" Krysta asked as I led her up the stairs.

"No, this is just the stairs to the front door."

"But you have to go through a closet and a secret door to get to the stairs."

"Yep."

"I can't believe you have a secret door."

I grinned. "Cool, isn't it?"

"You're a very strange man, you know that?"

"Oh, come on, you never wanted a secret hideaway as a kid?"

She laughed. "Yes, but then I grew up."

"Exactly, no one to say 'no, you can't have that' anymore."

She shook her head, clearly amused. I unlocked the front door to the apartment at the top of the stairs and let her inside, following her in. The apartment opened into the living room with a kitchenette to the left, an eat-in counter separated the two. A doorway off the right side of the living area opened into the single bedroom, with walk-in closet and bathroom attached. There was a second doorway out of the apartment into the remainder of the second story of the building from the bedroom. It was a fire door and extremely secure. It also wasn't accessible from the front entrance. The area the back door opened on housed the laundry machines and water heater, as well as a huge storage area. It was also an emergency escape route. The entire building had motion sensors and cameras that I could monitor from the entertainment center in the living room. Of course, an alarm would trip if the sensors were set off when the system was active. Some of the people I free-lanced for weren't very nice. Occasionally, through no fault of my own, the people they sent me after would suddenly decide to clean up their act and go straight, which cost the client money. This tended to upset the clientele, who sometimes sent other freelance employees to ask me why. It could get ugly, so I liked a little forewarning.

While the shop below was relatively organized, it *was* a shop, which is to say it had a general disorderly feel to it. The apartment was in direct contrast to this. The furnishings were simple and understated, but nice, and everything was clean. I've been in enough other bachelor pads to know this was unusual. I just liked my living space to be orderly. I kept my bed made, my clothes folded and put away, and my surfaces clean. A stack of motorcycle, automotive, and gun magazines sat neatly on the coffee table, and a small assortment of similarly themed, but tasteful, artwork graced the walls about the living and bedroom. There were more magazines in the bathroom – some of them not quite so innocent. I thought briefly of stashing them, and then decided I didn't care. I'm a grown man; she could deal with it.

"Make yourself at home. Remote for the TV is on the table, and there is food in the fridge if you get hungry. I have to get money for the buy-in then I'm out of here."

"You just happen to have $10,000.00 cash in your apartment?"

I flashed a grin, "Usually."

She followed me through the bedroom into the walk-in closet and watched as I opened the Collector 39 two-hour gun safe. It was one of the best, with a two-hour fire rating, able to store between 13 and 39 guns, made of ten gage solid steel and rated for documents and paper currency as well. It was also pry-proof, self–locking, and had its own security system. I never skimped on tools – the gun safe was one of the most important tools I owned, and housed the *next* important tools I owned.

"Holy crap, just how big of a safe do you need?" Krysta gaped.

"It's a gun safe."

"How many guns do you have?"

"Just a few."

In actuality, I had more than a few, but they served different purposes. I liked to double up. If having one of a tool is good, two is always better. This rule most definitely applies to guns. Handguns, shotguns, semi-automatics, I had them all. The .44 caliber revolvers were my favorites. On the top shelf of the safe were cash and important documents. I took enough for the buy-in and some extra in case I actually needed to bid on something to keep my cover, put it into a small duffel, and then closed the safe door. The 14 bolts slid back into place, locking it shut.

"I'm going to arm the security system when I go, so don't leave the apartment or you'll set it off."

"Any idea how long you're going to be gone?"

"I probably won't be back until early morning. You can sleep in the bed. I'll take the couch when I get home."

I put on my riding jacket and headed for the door, Krysta trailing behind me. As I opened the front door, she grabbed my arm.

"Caden"

"I have to—"

She kissed me, long and deep. If she was trying to make it hard for me to leave, she was succeeding.

"Be careful." She said, and then gave me a gentle shove toward the door.

Shaking my head at the whims of women, and fighting the effects of her kiss, I locked the door behind me. I activated the security system from the panel by the secret door at the bottom of the stairs before going through it. There was a second panel just inside the apartment so it could be disarmed from there if need be.

On the Harley, it's not difficult to cut the time it takes to get from Cornelius to Salem nearly in half, especially taking the back roads. It was nine on the dot when I rolled into downtown Salem. I parked in front of the Center Street Starbucks and sent a text to my contact telling him where to meet me, and then went to get a coffee. I had just sat down at an outdoor table and was lighting a cigarette when he joined me.

"Here's what you'll need." He said, handing me an envelope.

I opened it and looked inside. The enveloped contained a map with GPS coordinates, a satellite photo of an airport hangar warehouse, and an invitation card with my name on it. It didn't occur to me that an actual invitation would be necessary.

"Forged?"

"Legitimate Invitation."

"How'd you swing that?"

"You have your secrets, I have mine."

"Background check?"

"Completed and passed."

"Buy-in?"

"Due at start of auction."

I slid the envelope into my jacket pocket and handed him another with payment for services rendered. He accepted the envelope and left without another word. I lit another cigarette and finished my coffee. I still had time. At 9:30pm, I examined the map briefly, and then got back on the Harley. The auction was going to be at a large aviation warehouse at the Salem Airport. It was conveniently located to I-5 for participants arriving via ground transportation and, obviously, easy access to those that were flying in and perhaps wanted to be able to leave quickly as well. It was also in an area that would be discreet from the casual observer.

The parking lots surrounding the warehouse were near to overflowing. However, I doubt they were the types of vehicles that one would see in proximity to an aviation warehouse during normal business hours. Limousines, Luxury busses, diplomatic vehicles, and other high-end cars packed the lots. There were also numerous vehicles from various social services offices present. Specifically, there were cars used by Child Protective Services, police cars from several precincts, and a spattering of other vehicles with government plates I didn't recognize. Judging by the official vehicles locations in relation to the building, I judged they were the first to arrive, not the last. I was really beginning to suspect that Krysta had somehow gotten involved in something *extremely* dangerous; and coming from me that's saying something. There were many powerful people here tonight. Time to bite the bullet, I wished myself luck and headed for the warehouse entrance the crowds were headed to.

Two armed guards operated entry into the event. Instead of police uniforms, they wore solid black; button down shirts, tactical pants, and tactical boots. It was obvious they had vests under the shirts and, uniforms or not, they were definitely cops. When it was my turn in line, the guard to the left of the door asked briskly for my invitation. He took it from me and then scanned it with a portable black light wand he held in his other hand. The invitation came alive with hidden text. My aliases were listed – all of them, not just those on my official record, as well as my current address and phone number. The number no one has unless I give it to them; the number listed under a shell corporation instead of my name. Below this information was a barcode with a checkmark after it. He picked up another scanner from the podium next to him and scanned the barcode, peering at the results on the monitor of a notebook computer on the podium before stamping the invitation and handing it back to me. He waved me through. On the other side of the door I glanced at the invitation card before slipping it into my jacket, still only my name, the stamp was invisible ink too.

I found myself in a reception area of sorts when I looked up and took in my surroundings. Temporary walls had been set up, separating about a two thousand square foot area at the front of the warehouse from the remainder of the massive aviation building. I estimated the building was probably 80,000 square feet or more with ceilings high enough to house an airliner. Hell, that probably, *was* its actual purpose. There was a broad curtained doorway about halfway down the wall leading into the next section of the building. Fully appointed tables were set up and a wait staff moved among them delivering drinks. For guests that preferred something more casual, there were comfortable couches and chairs placed about the room, both singly and in clusters. Flowers, sculptures, and lamps strategically placed made it feel more like a gallery than a warehouse. Whoever ran this thing went all out for their clients. Interspersed with the crowds were a significant number of guards, attired like the two at the main entrance. There were several large trestle tables aligning the walls, covered with hors d'oeuvres to keep the guests happy until the main event.

I wandered toward the tables and picked casually among the offerings while I scanned the crowd. So far, I hadn't spotted Officer Dick. I wasn't actually familiar with the DA but I was hoping that he would be associating with someone I *would* recognize. Some of the black-clad guards looked familiar, but I couldn't place them directly. I moved through the crowd trying to get an idea what this whole thing was all about but no one was actually discussing the event at hand. They must consider it bad form or something. Finally, some sort of a chime sounded and everyone began to move toward the doorway in the back wall.

As I made my way into the cavernous area, the first thing I noticed was the reduction in conversation levels. There was a recording repeating instructions from overhead speakers. If I was expecting a traditional auction, I was to be disappointed. There were more temporary walls creating countless small rooms. Each room had its own separate door and appeared to open by keycard. Before you could even get to the rooms, you had to get though a guard station, where they took your buy-in and handed you a keycard. This keycard allowed you entry to the rooms to view each individual auction item. If you wanted to bid on the item there was a terminal inside the room from which to do so. Your keycard granted you to access this as well.

After trading the $10,000.00 for my card, I made my way down the hall of rooms. There were indicator lights above each door to show if a room was vacant or occupied. This allowed the participants to place their bids in private. Various patrons came and went from the rooms as I made my way down the corridor past the first several before choosing a vacant one. The door buzzed open as the lock disengaged and I stepped inside. The room was dark except for the quickly receding crescent from the doorway as it closed. When the door clicked shut, I heard the locking mechanism slide into place. Fighting a momentary panic, I was searching for the knob when the lights kicked on. There was another card slot on the interior of the door; it auto locked. I turned around, feeling somewhat silly, to inspect whatever it was up for auction, and froze. Behind what I'm sure was bulletproof one-way glass, was a young girl probably in her late teens. She looked terrified.

"Please slide your card at the terminal to place your bid. Item number WF18R1329."

I jumped at the smooth female voice and looked around. It came from the computerized bidding terminal against the wall. I looked back at the girl. They were auctioning kids.

11 TUESDAY APPROXIMATELY 1:15PM
AL TRUMAN

My assumption that the District Attorney's office would be cleared out for whatever this conference was in Salem and easy to get in to, proved wrong. Since I was a regular visitor to the Washington County Courthouse, blending in wasn't an issue, so I decided to hang out for a bit and listen in to the general chatter. Water cooler gossip is one of the best ways to gather information about a case within the system. This case was a little stranger than most I'd encountered so far, but many of the same rules still applied. People talk, you just have to know how, and where, to listen. I kept my ears wide open as I doctored a cup of coffee in the cafeteria.

"Dodging paperwork again, Truman?"

I smiled broadly. "You know it, Sally."

The question came from one of the many legal secretaries in the building. Honestly, I'm not sure which floor she worked on or even if she was with the DA's office or one of the many other legal offices, but it really didn't matter, they all talked. It was a very small community packed with break-time gossip. On any given day, the courthouse was abuzz with a huge variety of people. Civilians hurried about taking care of personal legal matters or attending hearings, and law and business professionals doing their jobs. The atmosphere was usually one of quiet urgency. Today was no different and one more law enforcement officer in the building didn't even turn a head. I decided to play along with Sally's assumption and see what it got me.

"You know how it is this time of year, construction crews everywhere, traffic slow as hell. I thought I'd get out of the grind for a little while, maybe check up on some of my cases."

"Ya, it took me 45 minutes to get to work this morning and I live ten minutes away! I hate all the spring construction." Sally said.

"So, do you know what's going on up in the DA's Office? I went up there to ask about a case file and it was so crazy in there I decided I'd better wait for it to quiet down a bit first and go back later."

Sally leaned in, smiling conspiratorially as though she were about to share some great secret.

"Word is some higher up has got the DA jumping through hoops for a big conference in Salem tonight and he's got his whole staff in an uproar getting his schedule cleared so he can get out of here on time."

"Higher up than the DA? Interesting, I wonder who that could be."

"I don't know, only that when the calls come in about the conference he closes himself in his office to take them and gets really nervous. Oh, and it's a woman."

"Scandalous – think it's someone he's dating?"

"Well, he's a widower, so I guess it could be, but which female official do you think it would be?"

"You're asking me? What's the opinion around the courthouse?"

"No one has seen him with anyone since his wife died two years ago."

"So maybe there is no romantic connection."

"It would be more interesting if there was."

I laughed. "I suppose it would be. So, do you know how is wife died?"

"It was some sort of progressive crippling disease, really sad story."

"Wow that is sad. It would be good for him to get out into the dating field again after such a tragedy. You think he's working so hard on the conference to impress this woman?"

"Could be, I wonder who she is? All I know is he has the whole office in an uproar so he can be out of here early enough to get down there and help set up. His secretary, Anna, is positively frazzled!"

I chuckled appreciatively. "Poor girl, he's probably going to have his whole staff working overtime covering for him while he's gone, too."

"Oh no, from what she just told me at lunch that's why they're working so hard now. They all have strict instructions to have everything done early so they can close down the office by the time *he* has to leave! He doesn't want to chance anyone doing anything that could pull him away mid-conference. Only the night clerk is staying."

"Well, at least they get the evening off; except for the night clerk of course."

"Tell me about it, they *say* legal secretary is a typical nine to five job when you're in college, but that is so totally *not* true! I'm here every night until after seven."

"That's tough, I'm glad I don't have your job."

"Lucky you, well, I'd better get back to work my time is up. If you want, you can tell Anna that Sally in the Justice department sent you for those files you need, she'll put a rush on it."

"Thanks a bunch, Sally that will save me some time. I'll owe you one."

"You can buy me a coffee next time! Talk to you later Truman."

"Bye Sally."

So *that's* where Sally works, in the Justice Department. That could turn into an extremely useful connection. I may just have to get to know Sally a little better. I finished off my coffee and checked my watch, 1:30pm. Caden should be talking to Joe at Starbucks any time now. Hopefully that lead will prove a little more lucrative than this had so far. I debated going to check out the therapist and coming back later after things had quieted down a bit. It would probably be easier to speak with her in the middle of the afternoon; I doubt she kept evening hours. Deciding this was the best plan; I dumped my empty cup and left the cafeteria, walking past the information desk toward the stairs. I had just passed the bank of elevators when the doors chimed and a voice I instantly recognized nearly stopped me in my tracks. I slowed my pace slightly and glanced casually over my shoulder as I trotted down the steps toward the exit doors; the DA and ADA Mitchell had just left the elevator and walked toward the cafeteria. I stopped as they turned the corner and smiled at the security guard, and then turned and headed back toward the elevators, calling casually to the guard as I passed.

"I just realized I forgot something."

The elevator let me out on the appropriate floor and I went in search of Anna, the DA's legal secretary. I was still trying to formulate exactly what I was going to say when a frazzled young woman precariously balancing an enormous stack of files interrupted my thought process.

"May I help you with something?"

"I was looking for Anna?"

"I'm Anna." The woman tried to blow a stray hair out of her face and the upper-most files in the stack began to slide sideways and tumble to the floor, spilling their contents as they fell. "Damn."

She carefully set the rest of the files on a nearby desk, already overloaded, and began picking up the mess. I sank to the floor beside her.

"Here, let me help you with that, seeming how it's my fault you dropped them."

She smiled. "Oh, I don't know about that, I probably would have anyway."

"Do you always try to carry so much at once?" I asked as I sorted papers into their folders, quickly scanning the contents and handing them back to her with a disarming smile. They didn't look like anything useful to me.

"Not always, but often. You said you were looking for me. Is there something I can help you with?"

"I was, Sally said to ask you for some files I needed from the DA for a couple of my cases, but it looks like you're a little overwhelmed."

"Sally sent you?"

"She said you were the woman to see." I gave her my best smile; she looked about ready to cry. I was seriously beginning to think my innate charm had begun to lose its appeal. This was the second time today it seemed to be failing. Perhaps I was spending too much time around Caden.

"I guess I am," Anna said eyeing her now thoroughly disarranged stack of files irritably, "just let me get these back in order first."

"Certainly."

We sorted her files in silence for a moment, and then I sat back and tapped her lightly on the hand.

"Would it help you out if I went and located the files I need myself? You could just point me in the right direction. Then you wouldn't have to step away from your obviously already over-loaded agenda to help me."

Her relief was immediately evident. "You wouldn't mind?"

"I don't mind at all, keeps me out of the traffic, actually. I'll locate the files, make the copies I need, and be out of your hair in no time."

"That would be a help. Current case files are in the cabinet in DA Berghauer's office right through that door." Anna indicated the door behind her. "I'll be working out here if you need anything."

"Thank you, Anna."

I made my way into District Attorney Berghauer's office praising my good luck and reminding myself to buy Sally that cup of coffee the next time I saw her. Inside the threshold, I paused to take in my surroundings. A large cherry desk with all the usual accoutrements dominated the room; a laptop computer, multiline telephone, leather desk pad, and matching pen, paperclip, and notepad holders all with the same cherry finish adorned the top. File organizers sitting on the rear left corner, also in matching cherry, balanced framed photos on the right. A bronze nameplate rested back center, facing out, with the DA's name on it. Everything was orderly. The wall to my left held floor to ceiling bookshelves stocked with what appeared to be legal books. The shelves matched the desk. On the right wall were more shelves, and two file cabinets, also matching. Two square leather chairs faced the front of the enormous desk and a leather office chair sat behind it. A stack of files neatly placed on the leather desk pad drew my gaze. Stamped across the top in red was the word "Confidential". I walked around the desk and flipped open the front cover. Scanning quickly, I realized I was reading a print out of an email, the first page listing the names of everyone on the forward to list. I recognized Violet Skazony, District Attorney Howard Berghauer, Officer Richard, and several other officer's names immediately. I was about to turn the page and see what else was included in the email when I heard ADA Mitchell's voice outside the office. Closing the file, I quickly moved to the file cabinet and opened it to the "P's"; thumbing through for a case of mine I knew the DA was currently working. I tried not to jump when the door slammed behind me.

"What the hell are you doing in here?" asked Mitchell.

I pulled the folder from the drawer and turned. "I'm getting a file for one of my cases Sally in Justice needs a copy of. Anna was a little overwhelmed out there so I offered to get it myself."

"You shouldn't be in here."

"Just trying to lighten the work load a little, I'll copy this and get out of your way."

"Fine, but next time have Anna or another assistant do it. No one is allowed in this office except the District Attorney's staff."

"No problem."

I could feel Mitchell's eyes on me as I left Berghauer's office and walked casually to the copy machine to make copies I didn't really need. I know I probably should have just handed the original file to Anna to put back, but I couldn't resist taunting Mitchell. Dirty cops piss me off; Mitchell is an Assistant District Attorney for Christ's sake; and he stunk to high heaven. I sauntered back into DA Berghauer's office just as Mitchell was looking through the same file I was itching to get my hands back on and right up beside him before he knew I was there.

"All done with the copies, here's your original file back."

Mitchell actually jumped before snapping the folder closed and glaring at the file I held out to him as though it were a snake about to bite.

"Put that back where you found it."

"Ok."

I put the file back, and then turned to face Mitchell again. He was closing the middle top drawer of the desk. The files that were on the desk were nowhere in sight.

"So I hear DA's got a big conference to go to tonight. Got the entire staff running ragged to get everything done so he can get out of here on time, you gonna be going to that too?"

"What do *you* know about the conference?"

"Me? Nothing much, just the rumor mill gossip."

"Hey, didn't I see you at CPS this morning?"

"Not today, been too busy chasing down paperwork. Why, did you need me to go by there for a case or something?" I asked, intentionally misinterpreting Mitchell's question to throw him off guard. It seemed to work, he relaxed a little.

"No, I'm just over worked today. I had to pick up some files for the DA from there this morning and I could have sworn I saw a county sheriff there that looked just like you."

"Must be the uniform, makes us all look alike, that's kind of the point."

"Ya, like I said, over worked and I better get back to it."

"Me too, good luck with the conference."

I saw him stiffen out of the corner of my eye as I left the office, and held in a laugh. Well, whatever was going on at that conference in Salem, it was most definitely a sensitive subject for ADA Mitchell. I'll have to figure out how to get back into that office and see if I can get my eyes on those files he stashed.

Back in the cruiser, I called the therapist's number to see if she was in and get an exact address. Turns out the woman has two offices, one in Hillsboro and one in downtown Portland. Of course, since I was currently in Hillsboro, the therapist happened to be at her Portland offices today; perfect. I turned left onto 1st and headed for Highway 26. Traffic on 26 alternately melted out of my way or slowed to a crawl as I came upon it, depending upon how paranoid the particular driver. I wasn't interested in issuing any tickets for the time being so I flashed my lights to get people out of my way and went around the creepers. Once I crossed over into Multnomah County people slowed long enough to figure out I wasn't from their county and then pretty much ignored me.

Youth Counseling Center Portland, where Evin's therapist spent half her workweek, was located in one of the many old brick buildings lining Morrison Street in the older section of downtown. I tried not to jump as a Max train squealed to a stop on the tracks behind me while I waited for a light to change in the on-going hunt for a parking space. Some things didn't change no matter what time of day it was. When the light turned, I took a left and managed to snag a parking spot a hand-painted neon striped VW bus was vacating, only in Portland.

According to Krysta's notes, Cate Veda had been Evin Mallory's counselor since she was in foster care. Apparently, she had seen a number of other counselors during her stint in the 'system', but Cate Veda was the first one with whom she connected. When Evin returned home, she continued to see Cate Veda even though the state no longer mandated it. Evin had a regular weekly appointment with the psychologist every Monday afternoon, but for some reason the counselor had cancelled on the afternoon that Evin had gone missing.

When I entered the seventh floor offices of Youth Counseling Center Portland, the receptionist, who was talking on the phone and busily taking a message, pointed one perfectly manicured finger at a sign-in sheet on the counter and went back to her call without missing a beat. I don't think she noticed the badge or uniform. I glanced at the sign in sheet briefly, and then tapped the counter to get her attention. When she looked up, I pointed to my badge. The receptionist shook her head and picked up the sign in sheet, pointing to the lettering at the top of the page where the words, "EVERYONE MUST SIGN IN" were in bold capitalized letters, and then promptly went back to ignoring me. Irritated, I gave in and signed the stupid form. She smiled at me as though she'd been watching the entire time and motioned to a table at the side of the room with hot drink dispensers on it. I went to make a cup of coffee and wait for her to get off the damn phone.

Taking my coffee and a three months old copy of National Geographic

Magazine, I sat in the waiting area across from the reception desk and feigned interest in the torn up periodical until she had time to acknowledge me. Somehow, I imagined a youth counseling office would be dead quiet in the middle of the afternoon, but the phone in this place rang off the hook. After nearly a half an hour of endless phone calls, the receptionist finally picked up the sign in sheet and read off my name.

"Sheriff Al Truman, how can I help you today?"

"I need to speak with Cate Veda about one of her clients, is she available?"

"Do you have an appointment?"

"No, I don't have an appointment. One of her clients went missing yesterday; I need to know if she has any information that may help us find her."

"She's extremely busy, but I'll see if she's available, just a moment."

She disappeared around a corner and down a hallway; I presume to check with Cate Veda out of my range of hearing. Her demeanor was one of prim superiority. The kind of woman that always thinks she's better than everyone else is. I hate women like that. Hell, I hate *people* like that. A few moments later she returned with a slightly older woman following her, she looked pissed, the receptionist did I mean. The older woman looked like the kind of person you might drink hot cocoa with and easily confide everything, the kind of woman that embodies the true meaning of the word 'mom'. At least what we all really want our mom to be like. She had a friendly face punctuated by smile lines around eyes and mouth and set with the warmest brown eyes I've ever seen. She looked to be in her late forties, but the only real give away was the un-dyed streaks of silver in her soft, medium-brown, shoulder length curls. She didn't wear makeup, but with the natural smile that was obviously her usual expression, and gentle features, she didn't need it. I could see why Evin connected with her. I could instantly tell this woman was a good person.

"Sheriff Truman, Liza says one of my kids is missing. What can I do to help?"

"*I* didn't say a girl was missing, *he* did, and they *aren't* your kids!" Liza said.

Cate Glared at the woman briefly. "Don't you have work to do?"

Liza glowered for a moment longer before returning to her endlessly ringing phone. Instead of the usual handshake, Cate warmly clasped my hand in both of hers, a look of gentle concern on her face. I found myself wanting to confess all my own sins to the woman and had to remind myself why I was here. Self-consciously, I cleared my throat.

"Is there someplace private we can talk?" I asked, glancing at the receptionist.

"Yes, of course, in my office; right this way."

I followed Cate down the hallway to a small office, obviously appointed with the comfort of her clients in mind and not her own. Her desk and office chair were old, and only took up one small corner of the room. Utilizing most of one wall was a comfortable looking, if also used, black leather couch. It looked like the kind you could be equally happy on laying down or sitting up. Adjacent to the couch was a matching loveseat, and the sturdy old coffee table showed signs it doubled as a footrest. The walls were soothing shades of blue and cream accented with artwork that felt more homey than office-like. A bookshelf and small table with an assortment of cocoa and teas shared the wall with the door we had come through. She closed it behind us.

"Liza often fails to realize that most of the kids that come here are displaced and often feel unwanted. I try to make them *all* feel wanted *here* regardless of their status or home situation. Therefore, they *are all my kids*."

"I'm sure they appreciate that you care so much about them."

"Honestly, some don't, but I care anyway. I couldn't do this job otherwise. I never understood those that choose this profession and don't *care* about the kids. Now, which of my kids is in trouble and how can I help?"

"Yesterday Evin Mallory went missing. Apparently, you were supposed to have an appointment but had to reschedule?"

"Yes, I had to take my birth daughter to the doctor. My ex-husband had to go out of town at the last minute and was unable to take her as planned."

"Has Evin ever said anything that indicated to you she might just take off on her own?"

"Young man, you haven't *met* Evin, have you? I mean, do you *know* her?"

"No Ma'am."

"Then you wouldn't know how protective she is of her Mama. If nothing else, she would never stray too far from her, she'd worry too much."

"You're certain?"

"I am. Eventually, Evin would like to travel, but she won't do that until she is sure that her Mama is stable and protected, and she doesn't think she is yet."

"Okay, well can you tell me anything she's talked about that might help us locate her? Places she might go? People she might hang out with?"

"Well, I've probably already broken confidentiality, not that I wouldn't risk my license to help *any* of my kids. I'll just pull her file and refresh my memory, I have *a lot* of kids, you know."

I watched, somewhat bemused, as Cate rummaged through the overstuffed file drawers attached to her desk searching for Evin's file, muttering under her breath about things being out of order while she looked. Finally, she stopped searching and closed the drawer, a somewhat puzzled look on her face.

"Well, that's odd."

"What's odd?"

"Evin's file is missing. I filed it myself after finishing my notes after our last session it *should* be here. I'll just check with Liza, maybe she pulled it for some reason."

I noticed the glint in Cate's eye was *not* a happy one as I followed her from the small office back up to the reception desk where Liza, as always, was on the phone. Cate ended the call for her and took the receiver from her then shocked-limp hand.

"What the hell are you doing?" asked Liza.

"Did you take Evin Mallory's file from my office?"

"Yes, I needed it."

"Why?"

"I had to update the caseworker."

"*What* case worker?"

"The CPS case worker, Violet Skazony."

"Liza, Evin Mallory is *19 years old*, she is *not* a *child!*"

"Well, the caseworker still asks for updates, and *Evin Mallory* never revoked, so as far as *I'm* concerned, I'm still required to send them as requested!"

"Give me her file, NOW."

"Fine, but I was just doing my job." She said as she handed over the file.

"Well, your job is now *done*." Cate took the file, possessively. "Pack your stuff, you're fired."

"What? You can't fire me!"

"I'm a partner in this firm, I *can* fire you. Now, are you going to leave civilly or shall I have this nice Sheriff escort you out?"

I gave Liza my best smile. She glowered at me before pulling a purse out of a desk drawer and stomping out of the office. I held in a laugh. It was obvious from the look on Cate's face that she was fuming mad. I didn't feel sorry for Liza, though, she'd been rude to me from the moment I walked in. Cate turned and walked abruptly back to her office, I followed. Once we were both inside, she closed the door softly behind me, and then paced pensively a moment before sitting and looking up at me.

"What I can't figure out is why Liza would be sending case updates on a client she *knows* is out of CPS care and they no longer have authority over."

"Any idea why Violet Skazony is still requesting those updates?"

"None, though I seriously doubt her motives are altruistic, that woman is a bane to society."

"The head of Child Services Division, why do you say that?"

"Obviously you haven't had the *pleasure* of meeting Violet Skazony. That *woman* has an ulterior motive for everything she does."

"Have you known her for long?"

· "Personally, no, I have much higher standards than that. Professionally, unfortunately, I've had to deal with her quite a lot over the years. She's always rubbed me the wrong way, and I haven't met a child yet with her as their caseworker that likes her either."

"That's interesting. I tried to go by and speak with her this morning but she's apparently in Salem for some big Social Services Conference she, and a number of other bigwigs are attending."

"What Social Services Conference? There's no conference in Salem that I've heard of, and as a licensed child psychologist and registered child welfare advocate I'm on just about every mailing list there is. I attend conferences all over this coast, some even further, and I've heard of *nothing* in Salem."

"Really, are you sure an invitation wasn't just misplaced or something? Say, by a surly receptionist?"

She laughed. "Well, I guess that's a possibility. I could make some phone calls and find out for sure."

"That's alright; I already have someone checking into it, actually. So, was there anything in Evin's file that you think might help us find her? Places she likes to go or people she might be with?"

"Oh, right, sorry!" She said opening the file in her hands. "We *did* discuss her going to Forest Park to sit and write with some frequency. I even suggested a spot to her once that I'd taken a liking to on my own hikes and she seemed to have taken to it herself. It's called 'The Stone House' on Lower MacLeay Trail. In fact, she mentioned she would probably go there to write yesterday since we wouldn't be meeting. What time did you say she went missing?"

"It would have been somewhere between noon and six pm."

"Our appointment would have been at 2:00pm, so it's very likely she was at least headed there."

"And this information is in the notes from your last session?"

"Yes – oh my God. I've never liked the woman, but it couldn't be..."

"It has to; somehow Violet Skazony is connected to Evin's disappearance, or your ex-receptionist, Liza, is. But somehow I don't see her having the brains to pull off an abduction."

"Trust me, she doesn't."

"Then it has to be the CPS worker."

12 TUESDAY LATE AFTERNOON
EVIN MALLORY

Consciousness dawned like the worst acid trip ever, combined with a terrible hangover. The room I was in swirled in an oily slick of colors, the sparse furnishings dripping off the walls and pooling on the floor. I closed my eyes and fought off the overwhelming urge to vomit. Whatever I was laying on had the feel of dry hay on a concrete slab. I squinted to shut out the violent spinning of the room, tried to roll into a sitting position and fell onto the floor with a thud. The nausea won out and I vomited onto the burlap-textured carpet. At least I wasn't nauseous anymore. I wiped my mouth on my sleeve and ventured another look around the room. The spinning had slowed some, but everything still seemed to be made of slick oil paints instead of real materials.

What the fuck did I do last night? My head throbbed in protest as I tried to focus my thoughts on the prior night. The rancid taste in my mouth was atrocious. The fact that it felt like I hadn't had a drop of water in a decade was worse. Using the edge of the unforgiving bed for leverage, I fought my way to my feet and managed to get a few steps before the world tilted and I came face to face with burlap floor. Fuck. Water, I *have* to have water. Resigning myself to hands and knees, I crawled toward the only open doorway I could see. It took a millennium to get there, but finally I made it to the blessedly cool stone tile. The bathroom vanity as my backrest, I slouched, waiting for my pulse to slow, and gathered the energy to pull myself back to my feet. I don't know how long it took to get my legs to cooperate, but the light from the other room had definitely changed by the time I pulled myself up to the sink. After fighting the faucet with sweaty, vomit-incrusted hands for an indeterminate amount of time, I managed to get the water on. I leaned on the sink for support, and drank directly from the faucet, stopping to gulp breaths of air between mouths full of water. I managed to get the vomit off my hands and face, and then gratefully sank back to the cool tile floor. *Why was I so Goddamn tired?* Vague images of Forest Park and strange faces flashed but wouldn't coalesce. Maybe if I slept a little longer...

The loud *crack* of a door slamming nearby jarred me awake. It was dark in the room I was in – a bathroom; a *strange* bathroom, I remembered. As my eyes adjusted, I realized it wasn't night, just dusk and the bathroom I was in had no windows, dim light filtered in through the doorway. I got up and cautiously looked out into the attached bedroom. A king size bed dominated the room, with matching dresser, nightstands, and a chair in the corner. Memories crept back from my earlier awakening. The carpet was a plush beige pile, not burlap as it had felt to my over-sensitized nerves. The walls were a matching shade with a fancy antiqued effect added. It was actually somewhat pretty – except I didn't want to be here. The window looked out on nothing, juniper trees and wilderness. There was some sort of coating on it, as you would put on car windows. The kind where it shaded the interior and you could see out through, but made it impossible to see inside.

Raised male voices outside the bedroom door drew my attention away from the window. The voices triggered another flash of memory, and I recognized them as those of the men who'd taken me from Forest Park. I wasn't sure *exactly* what their plans for me were, but from the little bit I remembered, I knew they couldn't be good. I had to get out of here. My lace-up shirt was torn and had dried vomit on the sleeve and front. I didn't know exactly where I was, but my sweatshirt was missing and it was edging toward dark. I knew being out at night in the wilderness of what I guessed to be some part of central Oregon, judging by all the Juniper trees, was probably going to get very cold, very fast. I kept an ear on the voices fading in and out of coherence outside the closed door, and checked the dresser for something warm and clean to change into. The first drawer held various types and sizes of flimsy lingerie. *Not* going to happen. The second and third drawers were completely empty. The fourth drawer was too. I closed my eyes and prayed to whatever God would listen, as I slowly pulled open the bottom drawer; it had some weight to it. I opened my eyes and looked. I almost closed it again in horror before even digging through it; it was filled with sex toys and S&M crap; *fucking wonderful. Who the fuck are these people?* Instead of closing the drawer, I took a deep breath and dug through the contents. I set aside ball gags, leather straps with spikes on them, a *fucking whip*, along with a ton of dildos and vibrators of every kind imaginable; and then I saw them and smiled. Idiots – it probably never occurred to them that *any* girl would know what to do with a set of Nun chucks. I wasn't just any girl though – I had training, *lots* of training. Mixed martial arts classes teach more than just how to kick a good roundhouse. At least if you think to *ask* for the 'more' anyway.

So, no wearable clothing, but a weapon was definitely a good start. I heard the doorknob rattle and the door started to open before someone yanked it closed again. I jumped. The voices got louder for a moment, then quieter like they were moving down the hall. I closed the drawer, tucked the chained together end of the Nun chucks into my back jeans pocket, and went to investigate the closet. The first thing I saw when I opened the closet door was my boots, shiny and clean. Why the hell would they bother to clean my boots? Shrugging, I pulled them from the closet floor and sat down to put them on. Now I had shoes again, and *two* weapons. My boots had steel toes beneath the shiny new leather. I went back to the closet to investigate further; it was full of dresses. Beautiful dresses of all sorts and sizes. Dresses for formal events and dresses for dancing; in private, ballroom style, *and* the sort you would wear clubbing. Most girls would *love* to have a closet full of dresses like this. They even all had the tags still on them. I lifted the tag of one of the dresses I actually liked and mentally whistled $450.00. I knew I was wasting time, but I couldn't resist, I checked the tags on several more; the prices only went up from there.

A large crash coming from another part of the house brought me back to my senses and I closed the closet. There was nothing in it I could actually use. I could layer them for warmth, I guess, but that would be bulky. My pack had to be here somewhere, if I couldn't find it or something better; maybe I'd try to come back for some of the dresses. I crept to the bedroom door and listened earnestly for a moment before trying the knob, surely they'd have locked it right? When the knob turned I concluded in the heat of whatever argument they had been having outside the door they must have forgotten. My good luck. Slowly turning the knob in case anyone was paying attention, I cracked the door and peeked out. The hallway was empty, but the clear sounds of a fight grew louder with the door open. Cautiously, I crept into the empty hallway. There were more doors lining the hall, most of which were open and dark inside. I got the quick impression my two captors and I were the only ones in the large house, which seemed odd, if convenient. Someone had obviously spent a lot of money on this place and on preparing the room I was in. The two brainiacs that had kidnapped me definitely didn't seem the type to qualify for the kind of bankroll required.

I moved quietly to the nearest open door across the hall. Floor to ceiling bookshelves covered most of the walls. A large modern desk sat under a window next to a set of curtained French doors. A separate door off the back I assumed led to an attached bath. I went to the doors and moved the curtains aside; bars covered the exterior and a double-keyed deadbolt secured them. I would need a key to open them even from the inside. The next room contained numerous empty cribs, creepy. The next door down the hall was another bathroom. The one after that held double sets of twin bunk beds; also empty. The room I had come from, at the end of the hall, had obviously been the master suite. I was about to investigate another open doorway when I heard another loud crash. Obviously, the two men that had taken me were having some sort of major disagreement. Abandoning my room search, I went to the end of the hallway and cautiously peered around the corner. A richly appointed living room, the kind you would see in a model house, sat empty beyond. The crashing and shouting came from an archway off the far side. Another archway opened off closer to my left. I moved through the living room as quietly as possible and went through the closer exit from the living room. I found myself in a wide, marble-floored foyer, complete with high ceilings, couches and tables. There was another arched entry to the far right side, which looked like it might lead into a kitchen. Directly across the large room from where I stood was a table where some sort of poker game had been interrupted, probably by their argument. Hanging on the back of one of the chairs was a man's black leather jacket – it looked expensive, and beside that, the doublewide front doors.

Checking the open archway to the kitchen, I dashed across the room, grabbed the leather jacket, and put it on. It was too long, and a bit larger around the waist and chest than I really needed. It must belong to the tall guy, but it was better than nothing. I moved to the front doors and was about to try one of the handles when I heard an angry shout from the kitchen area. Too close for comfort, I ducked back across the foyer into the hallway I'd entered it from just before the tall guy came striding into the room. I stepped back a little further into the hall, but he hadn't even noticed me. Instead, he went to a bureau next to one of the couches and pulled out a drawer. Taking a large silver gun from the drawer, he tucked it inside the back of his pants under his shirt, and then moved to the front doors, unlocking them with a key and opening one. So, they *were* locked, well that could be a problem.

"Hey, Alan," he yelled, startling me, "I think I heard something out side, you'd better come help me check it out."

"It's probably a fucking raccoon or something, Charlie," said Alan as he came into the room. "Let's get back to our earlier *discussion*."

"It was definitely human; besides, I thought about it, you're right – what the boss doesn't know…" Charlie's gaze met Alan's and both men smiled coldly. I felt a shiver run up my spine.

"Come on," Charlie said, "let's find out what that noise was outside, and *then* we can get back to the girl."

"You got it." Alan laughed, clapping Charlie on the shoulder before following him out into the darkening night.

They left the door wide open. I waited long enough to hear their crudely joking voices fade into the distance some, then ran to the door and looked out. I couldn't see them, but there was a large red horse barn off to the left of the house and the door was cracked open just enough for a man to enter. I saw a light go on inside. I kept glancing toward the barn as I moved across the columned porch and down the front steps into the night. The house was huge, fronted by a giant circular drive and columned front entrance. A gravel drive connected to the circular one, stretching off into the trees. I could see light posts way off in the distance to the right, what had to be a road of some kind. I hurried across the circular part of the driveway towards the wilderness in between. Just as I got to the far edge, the loud *BANG* of a gunshot echoed behind me. I glanced over my shoulder as my heart skipped a few beats, and saw Charlie outlined in the light from the barn just before he shut it off. As fast as my booted feet would carry me, I raced through the woods toward that distant road.

My lungs burned by the time I reached the source of the street lamps I had seen. It wasn't a real road; at least not what I would consider a real road anyway. Instead, what I had come upon was a long gravel and dirt affair stretching as far as I could see in either direction. I decided to follow it to the right, away from the house I had fled, but stayed along the tree line in case I needed to hide in a hurry. Who knows what other kinds of psychos are out here. I'm sure that Charlie had lured Alan out to that barn and killed him. If he was able to kill his partner so easily, I definitely didn't need to stick around and see what he had in mind for *me*. I didn't think he'd seen me when he was coming out of the barn, though, so I should have at least a little bit of time before he discovered I was gone. I quickened my pace.

After what felt like an eternity, but was probably only about 15 minutes, the gravel road met up with a real one. The signs declared it as US-20, and there was actual traffic on this one. According to one of the green Highway signs, the town of Sisters, Oregon was about six miles away. So I was right, Central Oregon, they'd taken me all the way to Sisters. I was a long way from home. Once I started walking down the side of the highway, a brisk wind kicked in. I zipped up the leather jacket and stuffed my hands in the pockets. My right hand encountered a roll of hard paper. Pulling it out, I examined it under a streetlamp, a roll of hundred dollar bills: sweet. I just may make it out of here after all.

I decided to hitch a ride the rest of the way into Sisters. I didn't know how long it was going to be before Charlie figured out that I was gone, but I didn't want to stick around and find out. Once I was in town, I might be able to find a bus back to Portland or maybe someone else that was going that way. With money in my pocket, the prospects were definitely better. At least I would be able to get some clothes that weren't torn up and reeking of sweat and vomit.

The first several cars I tried just ignored me. I continued to walk towards my destination as I tried to hitch a ride to escape the cold. People around here must not be very trusting. I mean, I know I looked a little rough, but come on I'm one girl. It was starting to look like I was going to have to walk the whole six miles after all when I saw another set of headlights. It was full dark now, and I wanted to get into town. I stuck out my thumb. I could hear the brakes squeal as they engaged. I smiled my relief as the vehicle slowed. Then it got close enough for me to recognize it – the white delivery van. As the van screeched to a stop on the side of the highway, I screamed and took off running into the woods. I heard the slam of the van door echo behind me in the dark as I ran.

Fucking nightmare! What the hell was I thinking? I should have stayed hidden in the woods alongside of the road until I got into town. Of *course* he would come looking for me in the van. How could I be so fucking stupid? I don't know why I thought I'd have more time. I could hear Charlie running behind me as I raced through the Juniper trees and brush. My pulse pounded in time with my feet as I tried to out-distance him. It was no use; he easily had six inches or more in height on me. I cast about for somewhere to hide. All I could see in the darkness was the shadowed outline of more trees, rocks, and bushes. I ducked behind the next large tree and pulled the Nun chucks from my pocket, thankful I hadn't managed to drop them. I peeked around the tree to see how far away my pursuer was.

Charlie was maybe a hundred fifty or so feet off and closing fast. He'd slowed to a walk and was carefully inspecting the area around him as he progressed. As he neared, I noticed he was carrying something in his right hand. It was the gun I'd seen him take from the bureau at the house. The memory of gunfire rang through my mind and I involuntarily drew in a sharp breath. The gun raised in my direction. I ducked back behind the tree and readied the Nun chucks.

As Charlie neared the tree I was hiding behind, I could hear the dry ground cover crunching beneath his feet. Suddenly the sound of his movements stopped. I held my breath and waited for him to step forward into view, but he didn't. A twig snapped almost directly behind me and I let out my breath, spinning in place. There stood Charlie, gun held loosely at his side, eyeing me speculatively.

"You've caused me a fair amount of trouble, little girl." Charlie said.

"There's your first mistake." I taunted, holding eye contact, hoping to keep his on my face.

"What's that?" He asked cautiously, raising his gun hand.

"Thinking of me as a 'little girl'." I replied as I swung the Nun chucks into motion. He didn't even have time to look down before the whirring Nun chucks knocked the gun from his hand. Unfortunately, the nun chucks ricocheted off the gun and went flying too.

"You little bitch!" He screamed diving after the gun as it skittered across the ground into the dark.

I had no doubt he'd shoot me if he got his hands back on that gun. He was crouched on his knees searching the ground. I couldn't believe he'd turn his back on me so easily, but I couldn't let him get his hands back on the gun. I launched a spinning kick and steel-toed boot connected to ribs with a sickening crack. Charlie went over into the dirt and pine needles with a soft 'oomph'. I ran for the bush I'd seen the gun slide under. I got to the bush and felt under it frantically until my hands closed around the cool metal. Just as my fingers closed around the grip of the gun, I felt Charlie's hands around my ankles. Rocks dug into my stomach as he dragged me backwards. I twisted over onto my back and brought the gun up to point at him, it was heavier than I expected. Before I could aim the giant silver handgun, Charlie was straddling me, his gargantuan hands wrapped around mine trying to take it. I bucked to the side trying to dislodge him but he only laughed a horrid rasping sound. Failing my first attempt, I pulled myself up and sank my teeth into his forearm as hard as I could. He screamed in rage and rolled sideways taking me with him, as I tasted blood. Now *I* was straddling *him*. I spit blood in his face and kneed him as hard as I could in the groin.

"Aaargh – FUCKING BITCH!"

Letting go of the gun with one hand, he slapped me hard across the face. It hurt like a son of a bitch; I felt my lip split and tasted blood, but I was prepared. Using my increased leverage on the gun, I twisted it sideways, trying to wrench it out of his grip. The barrel swiveled around to point directly at his chest. Surprised, he grabbed for it again with his other hand and tried to regain his advantage – and the gun went off with an ear shattering *BOOM!*

Charlie's body went still under me. My heart thundered in my chest and I could feel the sickening heat of his blood covering my face, and hands. It took a few minutes for me to realize my hands – and his, still gripped the handle of the heavy, blood-soaked gun. I let go in horror and struggled to my feet, backing away from his body slowly.

Now, what the fuck do I do? Well, I sure as hell was *not* spending the night in the woods with a fucking *dead body*. There was a perfectly good vehicle sitting on the side of the highway back there waiting for me. Gritting my teeth, I checked Charlie's pockets for keys, and didn't find any.

When I didn't find the keys in Charlie's pockets, I assumed he'd left them in the ignition, but they weren't there either. Which means the keys were probably somewhere on the forest floor around where we had been struggling for the gun. Well, there's *abso-fucking-lutely* no way I was going back to search around his dead body in the dark for the damn keys. I guess I'd be walking to Sisters after all. At least the fucking van was good for something. I found half a case of bottled water in a cooler between the front seats. Using the bottom half of the curtain separating front from back and several bottles of water, I was able to get most of the blood off my hands, face, and the leather jacket. I snagged another and gulped it down before exiting the van and continuing on the remainder of my six-mile hike into town. It was going to be a long fucking night.

13 TUESDAY 10:15PM
CADEN NEELY

The girl behind the glass stared at it as though she could see me, and even though I could tell it was one-way glass, I still found it unnerving. I let out a breath I didn't realize I'd been holding and lowered myself into the chair in front of the bidding station. There was an item number and brief description blinking on the screen of the monitor next to me. They had this terrified girl reduced to an item number; it pissed me off. Was Evin locked in one of these rooms, terrified like this girl, while strangers bid on her like a piece of property? My head started to throb. I rested my face in my hands for a minute; I had to think. I couldn't just buy every kid in the place; I didn't bring that kind of cash. Hell, I didn't even know how many were here. I looked back at the girl behind the glass, and then glanced at the bidding terminal. The girl looked a little ragged, as if she'd been sleeping on the streets. I looked a little closer at the 'item number' - WF18R1329. It started to make sense. W= white, F= female, 18 probably her age, R = runaway maybe, and the last string of numbers – all I could speculate is that she was somehow number 1,329, which was really fucked. The bidding terminal gave a little more information such as eye and hair color and then at the bottom of the screen in bold it said 'STATUS: UNTRACEABLE'. I'm not sure what that meant. I debated whether I should try to save the girl by bidding on her and concluded it was too early for that. I didn't even know if Evin was here yet. I at least had to check some more of the rooms first. If Evin was here, I had to try to get her out first. Feeling like a piece of shit for leaving the girl behind, and promising myself I'd do whatever I could to put a stop to this madness *after* I found Evin, I slid my key card in the door lock and let myself back out of the room.

The next three rooms I went into were variations on the first, except the second one had a teenage boy in it. They were all at least 18 from what I could tell from their item numbers, but I got the impression that they were only barely so, and that none of them came from stable situations. They all looked like kids you might find on the streets. The kind of kid no one was likely to go looking for. Somehow, that just pissed me off more. Life had probably thrown these kids all kinds of hard balls and somehow a human trafficking ring snatched them up. All of their terminals had the 'STATUS: UNTRACEABLE' thing at the bottom and I'd started to think I understood what it meant. That no one was going to miss them when they were gone. No missing person reports. No families to come looking for them.

I turned the corner into another corridor of temporary walls and rooms and slid my keycard, expecting yet another dismal teenager; and stopped cold as the door clicked shut behind me. This room was easily four times the size of the others. The entire first hall was lined with small identical rooms the same size. This room, the first door off the second corridor, was completely different. There was no plate glass separating bidder from 'auction item' for starters, and the room was crawling with people. Literally and figuratively, I'd walked into a nursery. The confusion must have shown on my face, because a woman approached me and pointed toward another of the terminals that said 'Bidding & Adoption Procedures' in bold across the top. I nodded my thanks and went to read the screen. Apparently, this was a multi-purpose human trafficking auction. You could pick up your street kid to torture or enslave and adopt your black market baby all in one trip. The nursery was full of infants and toddlers as well as a number of auction participants 'browsing' through them. According to the terminal if there was a child you wanted, you placed your bid. If your bid was the highest, they drew up adoption papers – it didn't *say* the papers were forged but I'm sure they were. I don't know, considering the crowd that ran this place, maybe the adoption papers printed up all nice and legal. How they chose the adoptive *parents* definitely was *not*. Some of these babies may have ended up in perfectly loving homes that way – but my guess is that most of them ended up with people of the less savory variety. People the law would never let adopt a child. Or else why not go the more traditional and legal adoption route? I suppressed a shudder and left the nursery. I wasn't getting any closer to finding Evin.

I'm not exactly clean, but this place was really starting to give me the creeps. Maybe I should give Al the heads up and see what he had to say. I pulled my cell out and flipped it open to send him a text: no signal. Fuck, they must have a signal blocker. I decided I needed a smoke instead. I hadn't seen a single person light up since I got here, so I wandered back toward the front lobby area and asked one of the guards where I could smoke. He pointed to a blocked open side door that two of his twins bracketed. I headed in that direction. One of the guards stopped me before I could go out.

"Hold out your hand." The guard said.

"What?"

"You need a stamp."

"Oh."

I held out my right hand. He stamped it under the black light shining down over the doorway. A fucking cigarette – cute. As I walked out into the smoking area, the stamp disappeared. Even the smokers stamp was invisible ink; paranoid mother fuckers. A ten-foot construction fence surrounded the outdoor smoking patio.

My phone vibrated in its holster and I jumped. Apparently, the cell signal blocker didn't extend to the smoking area. I was the only one out there, so I turned away from the door as I lit my smoke, and then pulled out my phone to look at it.

It was a text from Truman. "Get out – feds on the way. Got intel girl is in central OR somewhere."

Fuck! I checked the timestamp on when the message: ten minutes ago. I crushed my smoke beneath my boot then strolled casually back into the lobby area blending into the crowd before making my way to the exit.

As I gunned the Harley up the on ramp onto I-5 North, I saw the long line of identical black SUVs' taking the off ramp. I wondered if the feds caught wind of what was happening on their own, or if Al found something at the DA's office and called them himself before I could get back to him. Either way, I was grateful he thought to warn me instead of leaving me there for the feds to haul in with the real scum at the auction. At least I knew those kids would be safe now.

Normally I would have taken the back roads to Cornelius from Salem, but since I had to book it out of there, I took the closest exit and that landed me on I-5 North. Not that there's anything wrong with the freeways, you just have to watch out for cops more along the I-5 corridor. Although, between the dirty cops acting as guards at the black market auction, and all the feds I just passed getting onto the freeway, I wasn't sure there'd *be* many cops out running basic traffic patrol. I decided to play the odds and gunned it up to 80.

I'd made it all the way up I-5 and most of the way up Highway 217 nearly to my exit when I heard the blip of a police siren. *Fuck!* All I could tell from my mirror was that it was one of the new black Camaros issued this year. The cop flashed his lights at me and blipped his siren again. I sighed and pulled over into the emergency lane. He pulled to a stop behind me. I checked my watch – a little after midnight. I couldn't even believe there were any cops awake out here on a Tuesday night. Especially with so many of Washington County's *finest* down in Salem pretending to be security guards. Cutting the motor, I gently leaned my bike onto the kickstand and sat forward to get my wallet out. That's when he came up behind me, silent as could be.

"Going a little fast out there, weren't you? Is there some sort of an emergency or are you just in a hurry?"

Biting off the first smart-ass response that came to mind, I managed to get my wallet loose, and pulled out my ID and insurance card as I replied.

"As a matter of fact, Sir, there is an emergency –" And that's when I actually *looked* at the cop standing next to me.

"I really don't need your ID, Caden."

"Al – you son of a bitch! What the fuck, man?"

"I figured you'd be coming this way, since you would probably take the most convenient escape route, and that was I-5."

"True – wait; how did you know that? I didn't even know the location of the auction until I got to Salem and met with my contact. So it *was* you that sent in the feds?"

"Yes, I'm not sure exactly how far the corruption extends, but what I found gave me the impression that I shouldn't trust anyone in district. So, I called in the FBI. I guess they'd already been checking into the DA's office and some of the local precincts. They knew there was a black market auction but they haven't been able to track it down. I just gave them a time and place. They refused my offer of assistance in the raid."

"Did they mention *what* was being auctioned? Or did what you found mention it?"

"No, I figured guns, drugs, the usual stuff, why?"

"They're selling kids, Truman. Teenagers, babies – you name it. So you're sure Evin isn't down there."

"Well, I was, now I'm not. But if she is the feds will find her and bring her home."

"They better."

"Kids – seriously? I didn't see that one coming. Even with your friends' kid missing."

"Me either."

"Well, maybe the Central Oregon tip I got was a mistake. If they're auctioning kids at that thing in Salem, I'll bet Evin *is* there and you just didn't have time to find her. The FBI will bring her back. She'll be fine. Go home, fill in Krysta on what's going on and get some sleep. I'll give them Evin's photo and let you know when they have her."

"Okay, I will, thanks man."

"No problem. Oh, and Caden?"

"What?"

"Keep it under 70. You were doing 85, that's a *federal* speeding ticket."

I winced. "Fuck."

Al walked back to his cruiser. They must have issued him one of the new Camaros sometime today; fucker, I bet he was just itching to pull me over with it too. I chuckled to myself as I put my wallet in my pocket and revved the Harley back to life. Just because I *knew* he wouldn't actually ticket me, I burned out before taking off, making a ton of noise. About a mile down the highway, I heard a single blip of his siren as he gunned it past me in his new police Camaro, flipping me the bird as he passed. I grinned into the wind and merged into the turning lane to exit onto T.V. Highway.

It was 1:00am when I let myself back into the shop. As I disarmed the alarm just inside the hidden doorway, I was thinking about what I might find when I entered my apartment upstairs. I half expected it to be in shambles, Krysta sitting guiltily among my belongings after having gone through every nook and cranny, waiting to demand answers of me the second I opened the door. For some reason this image made me smile. I was still smiling when I walked through the front door. Krysta was sitting on the couch with the comforter off my bed wrapped around her like a cloak, watching TV. When she saw me, she sprang off the couch and met me half way across the room.

"Is it good news? You're smiling. What did you find out? Do you know where Evin is? Is she with you?" She paused and looked behind me; seeing no one there, her enthusiasm sagged a little.

"Whoa, hold on a minute." I said, holding up both my hands. I don't think the woman took a breath since I walked in. All of her questions just flew out of her the second she saw me.

"But you were smiling, you have good news right?"

I motioned towards the couch. "Let's sit down and I'll tell you everything, okay?"

Krysta nodded and exhaled slowly, confirming my impression. We both took a seat on the couch and I waited as she curled back into my comforter, and then nodded that she was ready.

"I'm going to start from the beginning, Okay? That way I don't have to backtrack, or leave anything out." She nodded again. "I got to the auction location a little after 9:30pm. They didn't let us into the auction area right away, just some sort of lobby, so I spent the first half hour just casing the guests and the guards trying to figure out what it was all about, but no one was talking. I didn't recognize anyone I could actually identify, but some of the guards looked familiar and they *all* had the bearing of cops."

"I *knew* the police couldn't be trusted."

I patted her leg and gave her a look that meant 'stop'. They aren't all dirty; one of my best friends is a cop. When I was sure she was going to let me talk I continued.

"The auction area wasn't set up like a regular auction. Everyone exchanged a key card for their buy in and we had to use these to get in and out of temporary rooms where the auction items were. Most of the rooms only allowed one person to enter at a time. When one person left the room, a light above the door would show it was unoccupied and allow another to enter, view and place a bid."

"So, what were they auctioning?"

I squeezed her leg. She clamped her mouth shut.

"The rooms, as far as I was able to determine in the short time I was there, were separated into categories by age group." Krysta sucked in a breath. "There were several long corridors comprised of temporary walls and each corridor was lined with the item viewing and bidding rooms. They were auctioning kids down there. I –"

"Evin – they have Evin? Did you find her? Where is she?"

I squeezed her leg again. She looked defiant, but she shut up.

"She wasn't in the rooms I entered."

"But—"

Squeeze – glare, I continued.

"*BUT*, I only went into four rooms and there were easily over a hundred. —"

Krysta shot off the couch, instantly furious. Tears streamed down her face. "*YOU LEFT HER THERE!*"

"I'm *NOT* finished, Krysta, *NOW CALM DOWN!*"

She sank back to the couch, somewhat deflated, but still seething.

"The first three rooms held teenagers right around Evin's age, *BUT*, it was pretty obvious they were all street kids, not taken from home or family." Angry nod from Krysta. "The fourth room I entered was much larger than the others and set up as a nursery, full of infants and toddlers.

They had a slightly different set of procedures for that group, but they were still auctioning them off. The winning bids just came with adoption papers. After seeing the nursery I was sick to my stomach and needed some air – so I went out for a smoke."

Even mad, Krysta laughed outright at the logic behind this. I grunted and gave her a grim smile.

"Before I left the bidding area I tried to send Al a text to let him know what I had found but there was no signal. I'm sure there was a signal blocker in place because the building itself wasn't constructed of anything that would cause a total disruption. Luckily for me, the block didn't extend to their smoking area outside the building, or I would be explaining myself to the feds right now instead of talking to you."

"What?"

I smiled. "Al found some info on the auction at the DA's office and called in the feds. He sent me a text warning me that they were on the way and that I should get out of there."

"Couldn't he have just told them he had a guy inside?"

"He may have thought about it, but then, the auction seems to be *run* by cops, so he probably figured it was safer to just get me out of there."

"The FBI would think he was dirty too?"

"Probably."

"But then why would he give them information?"

"Who knows, I'm sure they'd have their theories. He may have just decided he didn't want them knowing I was tied to him. I can't say I blame him. So, anyway, on my way out, I pass this long line of standard Government Issue black SUVs', exiting I-5 as I got on."

"You barely made it out of there."

"*Exactly*; so I didn't really have time to search every room. But, the feds probably busted in on the place pretty soon after I left, so if Evin is there they will find her and bring her home."

Krysta's whole body seemed to relax, and then she dissolved into tears. I'm so fucking confused. I thought I just gave her *good* news. Evin was probably in the custody of the FBI as we spoke or at least about to be rescued. We should have her back sometime tomorrow – well, actually today as it was nearly 2:00am. Exasperated, and at a total loss, I leaned forward and put my arms around her. The sobs wracked her entire body, as she cried *whatever* she was feeling out of her system. Not knowing what else I could do, I just held her tight and rocked her gently back and forth.

"It's going to be alright," I said softly, "they'll bring her home. It makes sense that's where the kidnappers would take her; finding out about the auction was no coincidence."

Finally, after what seemed like an eternity, her sobbing subsided and she smiled up at me, wiping her tear-streaked face as she did so.

"I know, I've just been holding in all this fear and rage since she went missing. Hearing that it's almost over and she's going to be safe is just such a relief."

If the mood swings I've witnessed over the past 24 hours were evidence of Krysta *holding in* her emotions, I was afraid of what it would look like if she just let it all out. The woman cried when she was angry, she cried when she was sad, scared – and now when she was happy and relieved? I will never understand women's emotions. I *still* think tears are a weapon they use to immobilize us. There's not a man alive that knows how to react to a crying woman. She must have seen the confusion and irritation on my face, because she took mine in both of her hands and made me look her directly in the eyes.

"Thank you." She said, and then kissed me.

She started out soft and tender, and it *felt* like a 'thank you' at first. Then something ignited, and the kiss transformed into a scorching heat. Her hands moved from my face to the back of my head and neck as she shifted herself up onto my lap and wrapped her legs around me. I *tried* to respect the fact that this probably wasn't the best time to be taking her to bed – but she was making it *really* hard. I groaned inwardly at the mental pun and verbally at the effect she was having on my body. Her kisses moved to my ear and neck, leaving behind a trail of fire in their wake.

"Off – I want these *off!*" She said, pulling at my jacket and shirt.

I disentangled from her arms long enough to remove my leather jacket and shirt and tossed them aside, and then she was back. She ran her hands over my bare chest and shoulders, then leaned in and followed the caresses with her mouth before bringing it back to mine in another fevered kiss. What started as a simple thank you kiss had erupted into a thunderous passion. I didn't stand a chance against a woman like this. It was more than I could take. Giving in completely, I repositioned my grip and abruptly stood, lifting her as I did, and carried her into the bedroom. I hadn't planned to take her to my bed tonight, but she started it, and I *would* finish it.

After carefully setting her on the edge of the bed, I shed my riding boots and socks, and then entangled my hands in her hair and plundered her mouth savagely. In an unexpectedly sudden and agile move, she wrapped her arms and legs about me and toppled me to the bed on top of her. The impact, combined with the kiss, momentarily winded us both and she grinned up at me wickedly. So, *that's* how she wanted to play, huh? My pulse quickened as I repositioned so I was straddling her and pinned her arms above her head. She uttered a soft '*ohhh*' before I dove back in to devour her mouth and throat. In response, she struggled to free her hands and arched her body into mind, bringing us as close as clothing would allow. I tightened my grip on her hands and smiled knowingly.

"Not yet," I whispered, and leaned in to tease her lips with my tongue and teeth.

"*Now*," she demanded plaintively.

I repositioned my grip so that I could hold her hands in one of mine, and stole her breath with another deep kiss. Her body arched and ground against mine, only heightening the level of torturous pleasure. Using my freed hand I pulled her shirt over her head to her wrists, where it only helped me contain them, and then leaned down to tease her breasts through the soft lace and satin of her bra. Krysta moaned her pleasure, and I added my teeth to the mix, as I reached down and unfastened her jeans. My fingers slid beneath denim, and discovered she wasn't wearing panties. My eyes met hers, and this time it was *she* that wore the knowing smile. I felt myself stiffen, and plunged my fingers deep inside of her, swallowing her gasp with my mouth. She sucked in my breath and ground against my hand as I lifted my face to nibble her bottom lip playfully. I could *feel* she was close, but I wanted her to beg, so I removed my hand and released her wrists long enough to remove her jeans. She tossed her shirt and bra aside as she scooted further onto the bed, motioning me to her.

Instead of complying with the subtle request, I gripped her ankles and pulled her to the edge of the bed, placing her feet on my shoulders, and then sank to my knees in front of her. Her protests died on her lips as my tongue connected with the most sensitive flesh on her body. Her scent and taste was an aphrodisiac that caused my own desire to scream for release, but I pushed that aside as I used tongue, lips and skillfully moving fingers to bring her to the edge. I felt her body gathering, arching, and muscles tightening in anticipation, and she cried out.

"Please –"

That is what I was waiting for. I pulled back, gently massaging with my fingers to keep her on the edge, but not enough to send her over.

"Please *what?*" I asked teasingly.

"Just please –"

"Tell me what you want."

Instead of answering, she sat up, pushing me back and then pulling on my arms to get me to stand. I complied and she tore at my belt and jeans, trying to get them loose. I allowed her to get everything unfastened; reveled in her hands urgently seeking and her lips on the hollow of my hips just above the pant line, and then stayed her hands and stepped back.

"*Tell* me what you want, Krysta." I said, meeting her gaze in challenge.

"Why?"

"I want to hear you say it."

"I want –"

"Yes?"

She pulled her hands free of mine, and reached once again for my jeans. I recaptured her hands, leaned down and kissed her softly, slowly.

"*Tell me.*" I whispered before stepping back again.

The desire on her face, in her eyes, was almost too much to bear, but I

140

held out, keeping her gaze locked in mine.

"I want to feel you inside of me."

The second the words left her mouth, I released her hands and together we removed the rest of my clothing. Then I was entangled in her, above her on the bed, my hands seeking to feel every inch, hers leaving a trail of heat along my body. Our mouths found one another in a fevered pitch, her legs encircling me, hands pulling me to her, as our bodies molded together and I buried myself inside her. We instinctively found the perfect rhythm, slow and deep; fast and hard, and then back again as we drove each other higher until we both cascaded off the edge in simultaneous release.

Exhausted, I fell against her, where I laid panting for a moment before rolling onto my back and snuggling her into my chest. After a while, our breathing slowed and I felt her shiver, so I got the comforter off the couch before reclaiming our earlier positions. *This* was where I wanted to be; lying in bed, Krysta molded against me, both of us worn out and completely content. A small smile on my lips, I closed my eyes and allowed sleep to take me.

The insistent ring of my cell phone pulled me unwillingly from a deep and fitful sleep, and I rolled out of bed in search of the irritant. It wasn't in its customary place, plugged into the charger on my dresser. Groggy, I surveyed the room and spotted the tangle of discarded jeans from early this morning. My eyes traveled up to the bed where Krysta was still sleeping, firmly cocooned in my comforter, which she had managed to steal the entirety of sometime after I passed out. The phone beeped its message that I'd missed a call. Searching my pants and belt, I discovered the phone holster missing. I heard the phone beep again and followed the sound under the bed where the holster apparently rolled in our hurry to remove my pants. I dug it out and flipped it open, looking at the display read out; three missed calls. I must have *really* been out of it; my ringer is extremely loud. Switching to the missed call log, I noted that it was Al; I selected the number and hit send. He answered on the first ring.

"About fucking time," Truman answered.

"What?"

"You aren't gonna fucking believe the results of the FBI raid last night. Can I come over so we can talk? You're gonna want to hear this in person."

"I have company."

"*Really?* Wow; well wake her up, she's gonna want to hear this too."

"Fuck — Okay."

"I'll be there in twenty."

I closed the phone and went to wake Krysta, trying to shake the feeling this *wasn't* going to be good news.

14 WEDNESDAY 10:00AM
AL TRUMAN

Yesterday was long as hell, and as I hung up with Caden, I was thinking today would be longer. I was operating on next to no sleep. This little missing person's case he'd gotten me involved in had turned into a giant clusterfuck with more corrupt officials than I'd ever even *dreamed* of taking down. Coming from me that's saying something. Here I was, thinking I was finally going to have what I needed to take down one – count em – *one*, corrupt cop from my past that I'd been after most of my life, and it turns into some major conspiracy. Its headache making, that's what it is. Caden owes me fucking big for this one; and I know just how he's going to pay up. But we'll get to that later.

Nothing yesterday went as planned. Oh, I spoke to the counselor, and that was revealing. However, not at all in the way I expected it to be. The CPS worker, Violet Skazony, was looking more suspicious by the day. Too bad she's missing in action. All the dots seemed to connect in pointing to her involvement in this somehow, as well as District Attorney Berghauer, and ADA Mitchell. I *swear* all of their names, as well as Richards, were on the header of the document in that folder Mitchell so quickly stashed after he walked in on me. When I managed to convince the night clerk to let me back in after everyone else was gone, the only names listed were Berghauer's, a bunch of random cops, and others I didn't recognize. Maybe I just *thought* I saw the other names on that email print out. I guess it could have been my subconscious trying to fit evidence to the nagging feeling in my gut that they are involved. I *did* only get to look at it for a minute or two before Mitchell walked in. This case is going to drive me crazy. I had this constant feeling that everything I did was being monitored – and not in a good way. Then there was the random tip showing up on my desk at the Sherriff's office written in the strong pen of a male hand. That's why I was confident the girl was in Central Oregon. I figured someone on the inside felt guilty, figured out I was checking into it, and decided to point me in the right direction. *Now*, I think it was more likely someone just fucking with me – an intentional misdirect. Pulling onto the gravel drive of Caden's shop, I ground my teeth with frustration. It felt like the closer we got – the further we were from finding Evin.

Caden was standing in front of the first bay door smoking a cigarette when I got out of the car. He was wearing a pair of beat up black sweatpants and nothing else. I shivered just looking at him. It might technically be spring, but it's still Oregon and its fucking cold outside.

"You're nuts, Caden, its freezing out here."

Caden laughed. "You're a pussy, Truman."

"Fuck you, it's cold, let's go inside. Besides, Krysta should hear this too."

"She's upstairs."

"So let's go upstairs."

Caden looked at me for a minute as if he was sizing me up, and then shrugged.

"Fine, but keep your nose out of my shit. You aren't a cop when you're in my house."

I nodded and laughed, but really, I was pissed. I mean, if Caden knew the number of times I could have hauled his ass in and didn't because he's my friend and I know deep down he has a good heart; he wouldn't say such a thing. He should know better. I followed him into the shop and through the first two bays into the office. It occurred to me that as long as I've known Caden, I've never made it past the office even though I knew he lived upstairs. I've never questioned it. We just always hung out in the shop and out front. It never occurred to me that it was strange until now. I'm not even sure how to *get* upstairs. Caden stopped in front of the closet door and gave me that look again.

"Forget what you're about to see. You won't be able to get in without me anyway, it's always locked and alarmed."

"Wow, Caden, you're getting paranoid in your old age."

"Fuck off."

I just laughed. I guess that if I collected for the drug dealers and other scum I'd probably be a little paranoid too. So, then he walked into the closet. I stayed where I was and waited for him to come back out, until he called to me irritably from inside.

"Truman – are you coming or not?"

I followed him into the closet. He pulled the door closed behind me and locked a deadbolt with a key he produced from somewhere. As soon as the door closed, a light blinked on overhead. It was a rather large supply closet, but still a closet.

"Why are we locked in a closet, Caden?"

Caden graced me with a look of impatience as he pushed past me to the back, then reached in between the shelves; the back wall swung open.

"Fucking sweet – but you *are* paranoid."

"I don't like people in my house. You make number two. This thing with Krysta is making me break all my fucking rules." He said as he closed the hidden door.

I had to laugh at his obvious discomfort. He's totally gone on the woman. I've never seen him bend like this for anyone. I clapped him on the back, and followed him up the adjacent staircase.

"You're head over heels, man, it's about fucking time."

Caden grunted his response. I laughed again.

"Please tell me you have coffee?" I asked. "I've been up since the crack of dawn with no caffeine."

"Of course I have coffee. Now, wait here while I go inside and make sure Krysta is decent. I'll come back and get you in a minute." He said before closing what I assumed to be his apartment door in my face with a slam. I guess he was a little touchy about his feelings for Krysta.

I tried to contain my curiosity at Caden's hidden apartment entrance, but it was somewhat difficult when he left me sitting out there for twenty minutes straight waiting for him. I suspected he was doing more than making sure Krysta was clothed; like hiding anything incriminating. The landing to his apartment was in a little hallway at the top of the stairs. The hallway formed a reversed "L", with some shelving on the back wall, mostly bare. There was only the one door at the end of the small part of the L. Considering the size of the shop below; I figured his apartment had to be huge. Either that or he had more hidden rooms up here. I wouldn't put it past him. I was examining the wall of shelves lining the end of the long arm of the 'L' when Caden tapped me on the shoulder; I jumped.

"Find anything interesting?" He asked.

"No." I answered, my smile chagrined. He *did* catch me snooping.

"You won't. Come on, Krysta is ready and the coffee is brewing."

I followed him into the apartment. The layout was simple. A fair sized living room connected to an open kitchen with an eat-in bar as the divider. There was a closed single door off the far side of the living room. I presumed this means he didn't want me in there. It was probably the bedroom. The apartment was relatively small. As in two thirds, the size of *one* of the shop bays downstairs, kind of small. That meant there was a lot of floor space up here that was unaccounted. I was itching to explore and I'm sure Caden knew it judging by the smirk on his face. The cop in me wondered what he was hiding. The kid in me just wanted to see more of the cool hide out. I resigned myself to being curious and shrugged my indifference to Caden. Satisfied, he went into the small kitchen and got out two cups, started pouring coffee.

"How do you drink your coffee, Truman?"

"Black – with a pound of sugar."

"Seriously?"

Krysta laughed from where she sat over on the leather couch, curled into a giant comforter. She already had a cup of something steaming in her hands. Honestly, I hadn't really even paid attention to her being there before then I was so focused on the size – or rather *lack* of size, of Caden's apartment. I suddenly felt guilty for ignoring her.

"Hi, Krysta, it's nice to see you again."

"Good Morning, Truman." She smiled.

"Truman – coffee?" Caden asked impatiently.

"Oh, right, I'll make it. Just show me where the sugar is." I said went into the kitchen and inhaled the first glorious scent of caffeine in more than 24 hours.

Caden got a five-pound bag out of a cupboard above the coffee pot and set it in front of me. He leaned back against the counter sipping his straight black coffee as I dumped in about ten spoons of sugar – and it wasn't a small spoon. Finally, gauging it close to the correct bitter – sweet ratio, I stirred, tasted, and then added two more. Caden choked on the drink he'd just taken and spit it everywhere.

"How the fuck can you *drink* it like that?" He got out after he stopped choking.

Used to the reaction, I calmly sipped my superbly syrupy coffee while he sputtered before answering.

"I like it this way. How can *you* drink it *like that?*"

"I like my coffee to taste like coffee."

"Are we all gathered for 'coffee shop' talk or was there something more important you wanted to share with us, Truman?" Krysta asked pointedly.

Caden and I exchanged a guilty glance and simultaneously went to join Krysta in the living room. He sat next to Krysta on the leather couch. I really didn't want to be that cozy with Caden, so I dragged over one of the kitchen bar stools and set it next to the immaculately clean coffee table. Too clean actually, if you asked me, not even a magazine on it. That's when I noticed there was a couple of nicotine outlined squares on the walls around the living room.

"Really, Caden, you took the time to take down *Artwork?*"

He bristled, "Maybe."

"Whatever, man, like I give a fuck what you hang on your walls."

Caden shrugged.

"So what did you want to talk to us about, Truman," Krysta asked, "did the FBI find out anything about Evin last night? What happened?"

"Honestly, they're still not sure if Evin was there or not. They were still processing the kids last I heard. We probably won't know if Evin is one of them for a little while yet. I made sure that the FBI agents involved all have a copy of her photo and her information. They called a bunch of Children's Services Department workers in to come help them try to identify the kids that were either too young or too traumatized to talk. Apparently, *none* of the kids, as far as the FBI could figure out, have been reported missing. That's odd, because there were well over a hundred, ranging from infancy to about 19 years old. I told them I suspected Violet Skazony, the head of the Washington County CPS office might have something to do with that. Maybe the kids were *from* the foster system, but the FBI openly scoffed at me. They asked if I had any proof – actual documentation. I don't of course, just a hunch, and I can't even track the woman down to talk to her. They laughed in my face – told me not to mess with CPS."

"Whoa – backtrack, I'm confused," Krysta said, "I've never liked the woman, hated her even. But you think *she's* involved somehow in all of this? You think my *CPS Worker* had something to do with kidnapping Evin. Why?"

"I think the woman is involved for several reasons. She's been involved with you since the beginning." I started ticking off the evidence, circumstantial though it was, on my fingers. "She hand-picked Evin's case when you attempted suicide. She's the *head* of Washington County CPS so it's strange for her to be taking cases at all. She was supposed to be at a 'conference' in Salem that turned out to be the black market auction of kids and teens. They didn't find her there, either, by the way, I'll get to that in a minute. Evin's counselor *really* dislikes her, and says that every kid she's ever counseled feels the same way, and Violet was still requesting copies of all of Evin's counseling session notes from the receptionist – without the counselor's knowledge or Evin's consent even though CPS no longer had legal jurisdiction to do so. And," I paused and met Caden's eyes and then Krysta's, "the last notes made it clear Evin was going to the Stone House in Forest Park the afternoon she disappeared."

"Oh my God," Krysta gasped, "she gave them Evin."

"That's my theory. I think she's the rings inside person at CPS."

"That would explain why none of the kids have been reported missing – at least the underage ones anyway, if they were all from the Washington County foster system. But what about the older kids – the teenagers?" Krysta asked. "Why wouldn't any of them be reported missing? I understand why *Evin's* report wasn't filed, with the history between Officer Richard and I, but wouldn't there be others? Does this mean that Officer Richard *isn't* actually involved in all of this?"

"I'm not sure if he's actually involved in the human trafficking, or if he's just been stalking you and Evin, but regardless he's corrupt and I intend to take him down."

"He's involved," Caden said, "we just have to figure out how."

"I'm not so sure anymore, Caden," I said, "I think he may just be obsessed with Krysta and maybe knows Evin is his kid. I'm not saying that doesn't make him dangerous, I know for a fact he is, I just don't think we should assume he's involved in her kidnapping until we find something that actually shows he is."

"He only *pretended* to take the missing person's report and threw away the notes he *did* take." Caden said.

"Maybe he intended to look for her himself. Maybe he thought it would help him get to Krysta, I don't know. I really can't tell you his motivation for that, Caden, but whatever it is, we'll find out."

"Wait," Krysta said, holding up her hand for attention. I suppressed a laugh. "Officer Richard aside, did you tell the FBI everything you know about Violet Skazony? Did you point out to them everything you just did to us?"

"Yes, I did, they told me I was grasping at straws."

Krysta gaped at me, Caden just looked angry. I couldn't blame him. I thought the FBI was going to be our salvation on this one. They hadn't heard the half of it yet. Neither of them were going to like what I was *about* to tell them. I got up to refill my coffee while they waited expectantly. They could tell I was about to drop a bomb on them. I could feel it from the tension in the room. I finished adding the sugar to my coffee, stirred, and went back to my barstool. However, I couldn't sit, so I sipped my coffee then set it down on the table so I could pace while I talked.

"With the exception of getting the kids out of the hands of the people trying to buy them and arresting maybe a half a dozen dirty rookie cops from several different precincts, the raid accomplished almost nothing last night. *None* of the actual auction participants would face justice. None of the people actually *running* the trafficking ring was arrested; and nobody is talking. Whoever is in charge of this thing has to have an inside person in the FBI too, because I got the impression *a lot* of people got out of there before the raid – or just weren't 'seen' if they *were* still there."

"What about the District Attorney and the ADA? Didn't you tell Caden they were both supposed to be there? Wasn't the documentation you found *in* the DA's office?" Krysta asked.

"You mean the evidence he got without a search warrant?" Caden added.

I stopped pacing a minute and grimaced at Caden before answering Krysta. "They'll figure a way around that, I think, but yes, they were both *supposed* to be there. District Attorney Berghauer *was* there, but he insisted that the kidnappers have his kids and refused to say who they are because he says that 'they' will kill them if he does."

Krysta blanched at this news and if it was possible, Caden looked even angrier.

"I believe him." I added. "He's just never struck me as dirty, but ADA Mitchell does. I think he might be the one putting the pressure on Berghauer."

"So what does the FBI think about DA Berghauer?" Caden asked.

"They think he's lying to cover his own ass. Both his kids are in their late teens, technically adults. One is supposed to be away at college, the other living somewhere in Washington alone. They don't think they're even missing and they aren't willing to check."

"The first three kids I saw down there were in their late teens." Caden said.

I nodded "That's not the only thing. I finally traced that wheelchair."

"Well?" Krysta demanded when I didn't elaborate right away. I knew they wouldn't like this.

"It was ordered in DA Berghauer's dead wife's name – six months *after* she died."

"He's being framed." Caden said.

"The van was also registered to her name around the same time period. I *didn't* mention any of this to the FBI. I think they would take it at face value, and I don't think he's behind this. I think Mitchell is; he stands to gain the most by Berghauer's downfall."

"What does all of this mean for Evin?" Krysta asked.

"If she's among the teens down in Salem they are still interviewing, not much other than red tape, maybe some paperwork, medical evaluation, etc. then they'll let her go home. But if she's *not* among them —"

"We need to find her fast." Caden said.

"I need to figure out the source of the tip that was left on my desk if she's not in Salem. That will be the best place to start. But, first, there is more I want to tell you about the raid."

"What else is there to tell?" Krysta asked.

"What's being done to the auction participants." Caden answered.

"Exactly," I said, "and the answer is nothing. Every single one of the participants arrested during the raid has diplomatic immunity. They all get to go back home."

"No *fucking* way! I *know* not everyone there was foreign." Caden said.

"Not according to the FBI. Only foreign diplomats, no one they can hold, and not many at that. *Apparently*, the place was abandoned, except for the kids, a couple handfuls of diplomats and some rookie cops posing as guards when they got there – plus Berghauer of course. Whom the FBI insists was running the whole thing, and though the bad cops they *did* get aren't pointing any fingers, they aren't *denying* he's responsible either."

"BULLSHIT! I got out of there *minutes* before the feds arrived, and the parking lots were still full!"

"They said the lots were being used for a charity event being held at another warehouse nearby, and that they were able to *verify* which vehicles belonged to the people attending the charity event. They refused to disclose any information on who the participants were exactly, or what charity the event benefited. They told me it was a private event and I had no need to know."

"It sounds to me like whoever set up the auction was prepared with a cover and escape route just in case something like this happened." Krysta said.

"That's what I thought." I said. "The agent I spoke to on the phone didn't see it that way."

"That's ridiculous – it's so obvious!" Krysta was angry, and looked near tears. "So, they're going to get away with this? What's going to happen to all those kids?"

"Well, the older ones, the ones that are over 18 will just be released to go home – or back to whatever version of a home they have. The minors will be returned to their families if they have them, or, as I suspect is the case for most if not all these kids, returned to CPS custody to be placed in foster care."

"But if Violet Skazony is involved in the trafficking ring and she's still at large, won't that just put them right back in danger?" Krysta looked hopeless. "They can't do that!"

"You're forgetting," Caden said, "the feds don't think CPS is involved."

"You have to stop them, Truman." Krysta pled. "You can't let them put those kids back in Violet's hands."

I picked my coffee up off the table and took a sip; it was cold, I drank it anyway. I wasn't exactly sure where to go next. My plan was to concentrate on locating Evin as they asked. As long as ring members were still at large, Evin could be in danger even if we did get her back home. We needed to find the evidence to expose them all and get it into the right hands. I finished my cold coffee and set it back on the table, preparing to go. I had an idea of where I could start.

"You're right, Krysta," I said, "We have to do more. However, it's not going to be easy. By the way, Caden, the FBI has been watching you. They have a file. You might want to take that into account during your 'extra-curricular' activities."

"*Fuck!*" Caden said.

With that, I walked out the door. I got as far as the closet before I realized Caden had locked me in. I really didn't want to go back into the apartment and ruin my dramatic exit. About ten minutes later Caden came down the steps and found me sitting at the bottom waiting for him. He let me out without a word. I don't think either of us was in the mood for more talking. Unsaid was the likelihood that the FBI found him through me because they were watching the local precincts. I heard the deadbolt to the closet lock behind me and knew he was pissed. I hoped these fuckers didn't cost me a friend.

15 TUESDAY APPROXIMATELY 9:00PM
EVIN MALLORY

One of the things small towns seemed to have in common was all the businesses closed up shop early. My legs felt like lead weights as I made my way into Sisters from the East end of town, passing multitudes of darkened shops along the way. The only exceptions to this rule were bars, and there were a fair spattering of those. Something else small towns had in common. I was really hoping to find somewhere to get better clothes tonight – clothes *not* covered in blood. At least I managed to get most of the blood off the leather jacket, my face, and hands with bottled water from the van. The jacket was black anyway, so it didn't show up too bad. I just had to keep it zipped until I could replace what was underneath.

I was cold and exhausted when I finally found somewhere open that looked like more than just a bar. The Gallery was a red brick building with a covered walk, lots of windows, and most importantly, lights on and people inside. The open door greeted me with a blast of warm air and the strong scent of fried fish and other greasy foods. I the number of people present surprised me, and I was suddenly even more self-conscious of my appearance. Stopping only long enough to get directions from the first employee I saw, I made a beeline for the restrooms.

I looked like hell, but not in the manner I expected. My hair was all windblown and knotted, and there were pieces of leaves and debris in it from my struggle with Charlie. My face was dirty. I had a black eye, an ugly scrape across my left cheek, and a split and swollen bottom lip. I looked like I got in a knockdown, drag out fight with someone; and lost – lovely. The water took a minute to get hot, and while I was waiting, I examined my hands. I've never really done much with my nails, other than occasionally paint them black or dark red. After the night I'd had, they were chipped and broken; jagged lines encrusted with dirt, and my knuckles were scraped and swollen. So much for cleaning up with bottled water. I guess I just got the surface stuff off. Finally, the water running into the sink turned hot. With a ton of soap from the commercial dispenser, I scrubbed at my hands and nails until they were truly clean, before attacking my beat up face. It hurt like hell. Judging visible skin clean as possible with what was available, I tore at my hair; pulling out twigs and leaves, and finger combed until it was *nearly* acceptable. *God*, I wish I had some make up. I guess this was the best I was going to get. With one last look in the mirror, I squared my shoulders and left the restroom to brave humanity.

The hostess was looking down at her little pad or seating chart and not paying attention when she asked how many in my party.

"Just me," I said, "and can you give me walking directions to the closest motel?"

"Sure," she said, then looked up and gasped. "Oh my *God*, what happened to you?"

"I got kidnapped," I quipped, "you should see the other guy."

The hostess stiffened. "That is *so* not funny. Your table is this way."

I followed her to a booth in the back of the restaurant, where she set down a menu and then abruptly walked away. I guess I offended her. I was still looking at the menu when the waitress came over. I was having trouble deciding between their bleu cheese burger and their classic deluxe. It felt like I hadn't eaten in days. Hell, I probably *hadn't*.

"Have you made your selection or would you like a little more t – *are you okay?*"

Wow, I must look bad. I couldn't even order a burger without freaking out half the staff. I decided to take a more tactful route this time, and maybe not scare her off.

"Yes, it's a long story. I'm tired could I please just order? Also, do you think you could tell me how to get to the closest motel in walking distance?" I realized I was near tears. Apparently, it showed because the waitress got this look of utter sympathy on her face and flopped down on the bench across the table from me.

"Oh, sweetie, I'm sorry. Tell me what you'd like and I'll have it right up for you. Would you like to talk about it? I'm a real good listener."

I fought the tears. The last thing I needed was to cry in public. The waitress was about mom's age and she smelled like citrus. Her sandy colored hair was done up in a French twist held in place by a pretty silver clip with pink crystals on it. Her kind blue eyes were warm and inviting. I bet she had her own kids my age. It made me want to break down and tell her my completely horrible ordeal. She seemed to divine my thoughts in that way only a mother could. She reached across the table and patted my hand.

"You just tell me what you want to eat. We'll get you fed then I'll come back and keep you company for a bit. I'll take you to the motel myself; my shift is almost over anyway."

"I think I want the bleu burger, with bacon, and some hot chocolate, please." I said, still trying not to cry.

"That's an excellent choice. I'll bring it right out." She stood and walked toward the kitchen.

I didn't think telling a stranger everything that had happened to me in the last few days was such a good idea. The simple warmth and kindness the waitress showed helped buoy me in a way I couldn't quite grasp. After the terror I'd just experienced, a little kindness went a long way. Only a few minutes had passed when the motherly waitress set a steaming cup of hot chocolate on the table and plopped down across from me again.

"Your food will be ready in ten minutes. I'm Abby, by the way," She said, pointing to a nametag I hadn't even noticed. "Would you like to talk about it?"

"I'm not sure that's a good idea, Abby. I mean, I really appreciate how nice you're being, but I don't want to get you into any trouble or anything."

Abby pensively regarded me for several minutes. She had that 'worried mother' look on her face. She appeared to come to an inner conclusion and sort of nodded to herself, then reached across the table and took one of my hands in hers. Her hands were soft, warm, and comforting.

"How about this," she said, "I'll tell you what I think, and you can tell me if I'm right and fill in the gaps or not if you want to. I just want to help."

"Okay."

"When I look at you I see an independent but terrified girl. I think you are far from home, and running from someone very bad. I think that 'someone' you are running from is responsible for the beat up face and defensive wounds on your hands. I also think you don't want to tell me because you are afraid if you do, it will put me in harm's way, or worse. Am I right so far?"

"How do you know?"

"Because it wasn't that many years ago that I sat where you are. Honey, you did the right thing by leaving him. Now you have to stick to your guns and not go back."

I tried not to laugh at the misconception and nearly choked on my cocoa. She obviously thought I was running away from an abusive relationship. "Not a chance," I managed.

"Good girl, you'll get through this. We women are a lot stronger than those abusive assholes make us out to be. Now, were you able to get out with clothes or anything?"

"I got his jacket, the clothes on my back, and his money stash. I really need new clothes – these aren't in the best condition." I unzipped the jacket and let her see my ripped and bloody shirt.

"Oh, goodness, you had quite the struggle didn't you? It looks like you were lucky to get out alive. How far behind you is he?" Abby looked around as though she expected some big scary dude to bust in looking for me.

"Don't worry; he won't be along any time soon. But ya, I barely made it out."

Abby absorbed the implications of my statement and her demeanor changed to one of mild approval. She squeezed my hand.

"Well, good for you. I wish I'd have had the guts to fight back like that.

Your food should be done," she said rising, "I'll be right back."

As I took a ginormous bite of my bleu cheese and bacon burger, I concluded that it was the best I'd had in my *entire* life. Of course this could be due to the fact that the last time I ate anything was Sunday night at home in Forest Grove; at least as far as I remembered anyway. As I took another bite, I considered a little longer, nope, definitely the best. Abby dropped off my food before being called away to help clean up before closing. She made promises to come back and give me a ride to the hotel as well as anywhere else around town I needed to go as soon as she was done. I doubted anywhere else was open, but thinking about it, even Forest Grove had a couple of super markets and such that were open late. Maybe there was somewhere I could at least get basic toiletries. It would be nice not to have to walk.

I'd finished all I could of my burger and fries and was working on the last of my cocoa when Abby reappeared beside me. She was one of those people that seemed to have endless energy. I wanted to ask her to share. She sat back down across from me and smiled.

"Well, I'm all done for the night. You ready to go or would you like to sit here and talk for a while?"

"I'm ready," I said, pushing my cup aside. "Is there any place open this late I can buy something else to wear?"

"Not in Sisters. The closest anything is likely to be open this late is Bend."

"How far is that?"

"About half hours' drive each way. It's not too bad we can go to Walmart. They're open 24 hours."

"It's alright; I don't want to put you out. I can wait until tomorrow."

"You aren't, I won't be able to sleep for hours yet. I'm always wired and bored after work. There's nothing do but go to the bars and I don't drink. It will be fun. Come on, we'll get you some clothes and stuff at Walmart then I'll bring you back here and find you a place to spend the night."

"Are you sure?"

"Absolutely positive," Abby said. She grinned and pulled me after her by the hand.

The night air was frigid and I zipped the leather up a little further as I followed Abby to her car. She led me around the block to where she parked on one of the side streets. Her car is a little red Mini Cooper with white racing stripes. It suited her perfectly. She unlocked it with the key fob and we both piled inside. It felt bigger than it looked. She blasted the heater and the stereo, grinned at me again, and then did an illegal U-turn to get back out to the main street through town. As we came to a stop at one of the lights, a police cruiser crossed the intersection in front of us.

"They're a long way from home." Abby said.

"Huh?" I responded, confused. The warmth of the heater already had me sagging in my seat.

"That police car," she explained, "it said Portland Police on the side."

An inexplicable chill traveled up my spine. "Oh, weird," I replied.

I was too tired to contemplate why a Portland cop would be all the way out here, and I didn't really care anyway. Where the hell did that chill come from? I leaned forward and adjusted the heater vent so it blew more directly on me, and then snuggled back into my seat. It wasn't long before I felt my eyelids drooping again.

Darkness shrouds the woods, and a thick fog makes the ground treacherous with unseeable hazards. A gunshot rings out in the night somewhere behind me. Adrenaline surges through me, and I force my legs to pump faster, harder, as I try to outdistance my pursuer. My breath leaves me in viscous puffs that mix indistinguishably with the fog. The thick air burns my lungs as I drink it in with each rasping gulp. Another gunshot echoes nearby and I feel the spray of shattered bark rain against the side of my face as it embeds in the tree next to me. I bite my lip to keep from screaming and pump my legs even harder.

"Evin..."

The voice is taunting in its singsong manner. He's playing with me. He could have hit me with that last shot if he'd wanted to. Sharp pain lances through my chest, forcing me to stop. My lungs are objecting to the strain, the liquid air. I slump down behind a tree, hoping he's as blinded by the night and the fog as I am. *Knowing*, somehow, he isn't. I force myself to relax, my breathing to slow, trying to reduce the pain in my laboring lungs.

"Evin... Evin – I only want to talk to you, Evin. Why must you keep running?"

My legs rebel as I force them under me again, make them propel me forward. Black looming shadows of trees whip past me in the fog as I dodge left and right around them, jumping over rocks and sliding on leaves and slick pine needles. The terrain slants into a downhill grade and I start to slide. Up ahead I can see the fog is starting to lift. I regain my footing, racing forward; and windmill my arms as I slide to a stop on the edge of a cliff to keep from falling off into the endless depths below. The dark maw stretches as far as I can see to either side of me. I have to turn back. Heart thudding in my chest so loud I'm certain he can hear it; I turn around.

"There's nowhere to go, Evin."

He's standing in front of me; towering there smugly. His eyes glow eerily blue in the moonlight. The cast of the shadows make him seem even taller than he is.

"It's you." I whisper.

"*So it is,*" he says, stepping towards me.

A scream lodges itself firmly in my throat, and then his hands are on me, shaking me.

"Evin! Evin wake up, you're having a nightmare!"

Abby was shaking me by the shoulders. She had a concerned look on her face. We were in a parking lot in front of a Walmart store.

"What happened?" I asked groggily.

"You screamed. You were having a nightmare. Are you okay?"

"I'm fine."

"Are you sure? Do you want to talk about it?"

"Nah, I'm ok, let's go inside."

Really, I was shaken up by the freaky dream, but I wasn't about to tell Abby that. I just met the woman. Even if she *did* give super strong 'mother' vibes. It was like a weird mix of my chase through the woods with Charlie and some kind of subconscious foreboding. I had to wonder what it meant. I guessed all this shit would probably haunt me for a while, even though I managed to get away from those maniacs. I would probably need more therapy, fucking great. I groaned at the thought.

"Are you *sure* you're alright?" Abby was at my elbow, examining my face worriedly. We'd just entered Walmart. It was bright as fuck after the dark.

"I'm fine, I just have a headache, and it's really bright in here."

"Probably from the shiner that jerk gave you. We'll get you some pain killers while we're here."

"Okay, thanks."

Not all Walmart's are created equal and the one in Bend was completely different from the one by where I live. Apparently, Abby frequents this place though, and she led me though the store like a whirlwind on a mission through clothing, cosmetics, and the pharmacy section. By the time we were done I was sporting two sets of clothes, totally *not* my style, but wearable, some comfies, make-up, basic hygiene stuff, head-ache medicine, Duct-tape, (you can never have enough Duct-tape), and a new backpack to put it all in. I debated changing in the bathroom but decided I really wanted a shower first so we headed on back to Sisters. Half way there I realized I should have bought a throw away phone. Oh well. I was sure I'd be able to find one in town the next day. I fell asleep in the car again. No more nightmares, thankfully.

Abby woke me up when we got to Sisters Motor Lodge. It was one of those cute little mom and pop motels comprised of several buildings that looked like little cottages. There was a little pond that I'm sure was pretty in the day light and plenty of other decorations that were hard to see clearly in the dark. It was all very quaint and country. It looked like the kind of place where you had to reserve a room way in advance.

"Are you sure they have a room?" I asked.

"I called ahead while you were sleeping" Abby smiled. "My brother stayed here when he came out to visit a few months ago. You'll like it. They have one room left."

I shrugged and followed her inside to check in. The 'one room' they had left was the honeymoon suite and it turned out to be due to a cancellation. They gave me the room for a discount. I'm not sure if the discount was because of the cancellation or the lady just felt sorry for me. Abby gave the woman the rundown on her version of what happened to me. The two of them combined efforts to get me settled into the cozy little second story suite as if they were mother and daughter, or *my* mother and grandmother. The lady that checked me in was easily old enough to be Abby's mom. Finally the proprietor, concierge, or whatever she was called went back to her office and left Abby and me in the room by ourselves. Abby sat down on the bed beside me.

"So, what are your plans from here?" She asked.

"Tomorrow I plan to go to the police and report what happened –"

"Sheriff."

"Huh?"

"We have a county Sheriff's station not a police department; and?"

"Anyway, I'm going to go report what happened, then I plan on going back home to my mom's in Forest Grove after that."

"They may want you to hang around for court or something."

"Well, I'll come back out with my mom if they need me to. I'm *not* staying out here by myself."

"That's smart. How do you plan to get home?""

"I figured I'd ride the bus."

"Greyhound? You may have to go into Bend to do that, I'm not sure. They should be able to tell you at the Sheriff's station. Here's my number," Abby scrawled a number across the pad of paper from the bedside table and handed it to me. "Call me if you need a ride to the bus station or anything. Good luck, sweetie, it takes a lot of guts to do what you're doing. I'm proud of you."

She wrapped her arms around me and squeezed me tight. I realized she was crying. It was somewhat strange but sweet at the same time. I barely knew this woman and she rather adopted me right off the bat because she thought we had this horrible thing in common. I hugged her back briefly and then she stood up, wiping her eyes.

"Sorry," she said, "I don't know what came over me. I'll let you get some rest."

"Thanks for helping me, Abby. I'll call you."

She gave me another quick hug before darting out the door. Strange woman, nice, but strange. The honeymoon suite consisted of a medium room with a king sized bed, draped in what appeared to be a handmade quilt, lacy pillow shams, and afghan. A braided oval rug in hunter green graced the floor at the foot of the bed, and various other 'country home' décor accented the feel. It had a bathroom with a bathtub/shower combo, a microwave, mini-fridge, coffee maker, and its own deck overlooking many trees and other landscaping that was too dark to see.

A good long soak in the bathtub sounded glorious. I was cold, tired, achy, and covered in – I didn't even want to *think* about the kinds of grime encrusting the majority of my body. After shucking my boots and jacket, the rest of my clothing, sans bra, went directly into the bathroom trashcan. Since I didn't want to leave my bloodied up clothing for the cleaning staff, I tied off the bag and stuffed it into the new backpack. The cops would probably want it anyway. There was probably evidence of my kidnapping in the folds, in addition to my own and Charlie's blood.

I let the bath water run steaming hot as I examined the damage to my body in the free standing full length mirror. I looked even worse naked than I did clothed. I bruises covered me. They blossomed across my back and side, over my hips in the front, probably from Charlie's weight, and decorated my knees, thighs, and shins in ugly shades of blues, greens, and purples. There was a giant scrape down the length of my back from my left shoulder blade all the way to just below where the waist of my jeans would have been. Raw scrapes and bruises covered my knees. I also had dark, rope-patterned bruises forming on my wrists and ankles I hadn't noticed before. I looked like a bus dragged me. Where was a fucking camera when you needed one? Maybe I should go buy one tomorrow, come back here and take pictures of the damage. I didn't like the idea of the cops shooting photos of my naked body – evidence or not. I wondered how much of that money I had left. I hadn't even counted it. I'd have to do that after I got the grime off my body.

The steaming water burned like hell on my abused skin. I closed my eyes against the sting as I sank into the tub, laying back to submerge all the way up to my neck. It was a deep tub. Gradually, I felt my muscles relax into the warmth and the stinging subside as my body adjusted to the temperature. I opened my eyes to search for soap and stifled a scream. Blood *filled* the tub. An image of my mother floating in a blood-filled bathtub flashed unbidden to the front of my mind and I couldn't get out of the water fast enough. Dripping sickeningly pink water, I closed my eyes and willed my thundering heart to quiet. Intellectually, I knew it was from the dried blood caked to my body from my struggle with Charlie. The bath water was the same gruesome color it was when I found my mother with her wrists slit so many years ago. Forcing myself to breath, I yanked the chain on the drain and let out the offensively colored water. So much for taking a relaxing soak in the tub.

Thankfully, the motel had a decent water heater. The second the tub finished draining I ran the shower, rinsing the last of the crimson drops down the drain, and then stepped under the steaming spray. I scrubbed the rest of the blood and grime off me as quickly as possible, leaving my skin raw in the process. I would never view cleaning rituals the same again. No lingering baths or showers. In and out would be my motto from now on.

The women's long johns I got in lieu of pajamas were soft and cozy against my skin – except where I was cut and scraped, which was just about everywhere. Oh well, at least I was clean. Flopping down on the oversized bed, I dragged the leather jacket onto my lap to dig out the cash and count it. Something hard inside bounced off my bruised and battered knee and I let out a small yelp of pain. It didn't even occur to me to search the jacket for other pockets. The outside only had the two traditional ones and there was only money in them. The inside lining of the jacket was black too, so it was hard to see. I got up and turned on the rest of the lights in room then laid the jacket out on the bed. There were two regular slanted pockets aligned with the ones on the outside, only these had small zippers holding them closed. There was also a large square one inside the right breast of the jacket with a Velcro patch at the top. I opened the square and felt around inside. My hand came out with a few wadded receipts, an old gum wrapper, and a piece of gum *without* the wrapper covered in lint; ewww. I tossed the gum and the wrapper in the bedside trash and looked at the receipts. They were all for useless stuff, cigarettes and a soda, a fast food receipt, and one for a pack of gum – figures. The receipts followed the gum into the trash and I opened the right zip pocket, nothing. When the left zip pocket yielded nothing as well, I picked up the jacket and carefully felt around the back of it until I found the shape of the object that smacked me in the knee. It *felt* like a cell phone. There had to be a hidden pocket somewhere. I checked both of the outside pockets, taking out the cash and dumping it on the bed, feeling around inside each of them, normal pockets. I decide to pull the inside pockets out, one reversed easily, the other didn't, bingo. Pushing my hand all the way inside, I felt around until I found a hard seam – Velcro. I got the Velcro strip open, reached around inside the back of the jacket until I felt the object, and wrapped my fingers around it. It was definitely a phone. Once I got it free of the jacket, I examined it closely. It was a Samsung phone with a slide out QWERTY keyboard and it was off. Why would he hide a phone from his partner? Of course, I was sure he killed his partner so maybe he used it to communicate with their boss behind Alan's back. Once the phone powered up I could see by the minute readout on the screen that it was a prepaid. It had over 3500 minutes on it. I guess he didn't like to reload.

I was still examining the phone, checking out the features, when the thing started vibrating like crazy. I nearly dropped it. When it finally stopped vibrating, I looked at the screen. A bunch of text messages just came in at once. I opened the inbox and started reading the messages.

Text number one: 'Charlie – did you find her yet?'

Text number two: 'That girl's worth a lot of money – you better get her back!'

Text number three: 'Charlie – what's taking so long? I better not have to come out there!'

Text number four: 'Call me as soon as you get this!'

Text number five: 'We're on our way – if you know what's good for you you'll have the girl ready.'

All of the messages were from the same number. The phone didn't have any names in the contact list to identify it. There was no doubt the 'girl' in question was me. Maybe Charlie only texted from this phone or used it to receive discreet messages from his boss. It was obvious he reported that I got away to whoever that boss was before he went looking for me, before I killed him in the struggle over his gun. Those messages were sent while the phone was off in the back of the jacket I stole. Now, whoever was in charge of this whole nightmare was on their way to that house. Well, they wouldn't find Charlie and they definitely wouldn't find *me*. Maybe they would think he found me and decided to keep me for himself. Who knew how these people thought? First thing in the morning, I would go to the Sheriff and turn in my report, then get on a bus back home. By the time they figured out what happened the *cops* would be looking for *them*.

I fell asleep to some stupid horror movie and of course, it followed me into my dreams. I tossed and turned all night. The nightmare was a combination of Charlie chasing me through the woods and killer psychotic clowns from outer space hunting me in a circus tent. I woke up with the quilt tangled around my legs and drenched in sweat. I rinsed the sweat off in the shower as quickly as possible and got dressed in a new pair of jeans, powder blue pull over hoodie, (*so* not me), my boots, and the leather. My gothic knee high boots and the blue hoodie totally clashed. At least I had make up; which didn't come close to covering the shiner, scrape, and fat split lip. Oh well. Now I just looked like someone trying to *hide* that they got into a fight and lost. I gave up.

After repacking my backpack, I headed down to the office to get directions to the Sheriff's station. It turned out the Deschutes County Sheriff's Department was the equivalent of about 14 blocks from the little motel where I spent the night. That was a walk in the park compared to my six-mile hike yesterday. It took me twenty-five minutes to get there, and that was with stopping for a Carmel Mocha Macchiato on the way. I counted the money this morning before I left the room. Even *after* buying clothes and crap, I still had $1,845.02 left, which meant there was $2000.00 before dinner and my little shopping trip last night. I should have given Abby some gas money but I didn't think of it until this morning. If I see her again, I will. I turned the cell phone back off. I was hesitant to use the thing with it being Charlie's, and there was no telling if his boss has some sort of tracking device or something on it. I'm not giving them any advantages. I figured I could call mom from the Sheriff's station when I finished talking to them and let her know I was safe, and how I was getting home. She could meet me at the Greyhound station in Portland. If her car was still broken down, I was sure she could get *Caden* to take her.

When I got to the Sheriff's Department, there was a Portland Police cruiser parked out front. It was weird but I didn't really think much of it. Hell, maybe I could hitch a ride back with the cop. I found them creepy, but it's their job to rescue people, right? When I walked in there was a lady in a Sheriff's uniform behind a desk answering the phones and doing paperwork. It was a small station, but I guess that's what you'd expect in a 'blink and you miss it' kind of town. From what the woman at the little motel told me, the main station is all the way in Bend, and I sure as hell was not walking to that one. The lady Sheriff at the desk finished her call and I hesitantly stepped forward. I wasn't sure how to proceed and was somewhat nervous. I fidgeted for a minute and didn't say anything.

"Can I help you with something?" She asked with a look of mild irritation on her face.

"Um, ya, I don't really know how to do this."

"Do what?"

"I need to report a crime."

"Okay." She pulled out a thick form and a notebook from her desk and motioned me to take a seat in a chair next to it. "What's your name?"

"Evin Mallory."

"And you were a witness to this crime?"

"Um – yes, and the victim, I was kidnapped."

For the next hour and a half, the lady Sheriff peppered me with questions. I answered them all as best as I could. Several times, she stopped me half way through an explanation to ask a new question, all the while taking notes. I told her all about how they took me, drugged me, waking up sick, Charlie and Alan fighting, how Charlie shot Alan and I got away. I told her about Charlie finding me, chasing me through the woods, and struggling over the gun. As well as how it went off and killed him while I was fighting for my life. I ended up giving her my bloodied clothes *and* letting her take photos of all my cuts and bruises – humiliating. She made me wash off my make up so she can get good shots of the damage to my face. She also chastised me for not going directly to the police last night *before* washing off any evidence; and then hugged me when I started sobbing. People out here are so weird. After I'd told her everything I could think of, and she had taken photos of every inch of my body, she allowed me to go into the bathroom and reapply my makeup. She said she'd get the report filed and when her partner got back, she'd send me out with him to locate Charlie's body and the house where he left Alan's. Once he had the GPS co-ordinates down, he could call it in to their headquarters in Bend.

When I came out of the bathroom the lady Sheriff was talking to a man also in a Sheriff's uniform. There was another man standing behind the first, but my view of him was blocked. When I reached the desk, they all turned towards me. I don't know why, but I had to suppress the urge to turn and run. The cop from Portland was standing there next to the two

Deschutes County Sheriffs; it was Officer Richard. I saw him everywhere. He was the cop that took the report when mom tried to kill herself, the cop that drove me to the hospital. My boyfriend, Sean, and I, ran into him all over Portland, I guess he transferred there recently. What the *hell* was he doing in Sisters? It was like he was fucking following me. The dream I had in Abby's car came back with crystal clarity and I inadvertently quoted my subconscious self.

"It's you." I whispered.

"I'm sorry," the lady Sheriff said, "do you know Officer Richard, Ms. Mallory?"

"We've met before," said Officer Richard, "it was a sad circumstance."

"Oh, well, at least you know each other." Lady Sheriff said. "It seems Officer Richard took a missing persons report on you and followed up a lead that you might be in this area. He came to our Department to check in and let us know he was here looking for you, as well as to enlist our help. It appears his timing couldn't be more perfect."

"Great." I said unenthusiastically.

Something about Officer Richard has never sat right with me. I wasn't sure what it was, but he was just so – *creepy*; and not *normal* cop creepy, but *creepy*, creepy.

"Alright, Davis," the other Sheriff said, "why don't you fill in Ms. Mallory while I take care of a phone call, then we'll get on the road."

"You got it, Troy." She said.

Apparently, 'lady Sheriff' is Sheriff Davis and her partner is Sheriff Troy. Sounded like some kind of action film, '*Davis & Troy*'. I subconsciously pictured blazing guns and stupid ninja moves featuring the small town County Sheriffs and tried not to smile.

"So," Sheriff Davis said, pulling me out of my reverie, "Sheriff Troy and Officer Richard are going to accompany you to locate this 'Charlie' fellow's body so that we can call it in to the crime scene guys, then to the house you were held in if you can remember how to get there. After that, you can call your family and then Officer Richard here will take you back home. If we need to get in touch with later on in the investigation we have all your information."

"Umm, okay, but won't you be coming with us?"

"Nope, I'll be staying here to get the paperwork filed and man the office. Sheriff Troy and Officer Richard will take good care of you, I promise."

Somehow, that's what I feared. I had no clue what Sheriff Troy was like but I didn't trust Officer Richard as far as I could throw him – and that would be not at all. Officer Richard volunteered to drive and for some reason Sheriff Troy went along with this as though it was perfectly normal. It made no sense to me at all. I mean, wasn't Sheriff Troy the one that knew the area? Richard climbed straight into the driver's seat of his cruiser and left it to Sheriff Troy to get me situated in the back. The cruiser had those hard plastic seats in back with the weird cutouts made especially for criminals with their hands in cuffs. They're uncomfortable as hell.

It only took Officer Richard about five minutes to drive us out to where the van should be along the side of the highway. It wasn't there. I seriously doubt it would have been towed that fast and Charlie sure as hell didn't drive it anywhere. My best guess is that someone who had access to another set of keys moved it for him. Officer Richard and Sheriff Troy took their time studying the skid marks the van made and Troy questioned me repeatedly about what the van looked like. Richard let him take the lead and kind of hung back and watched me intently while Troy questioned me. It was weird and started to freak me out. After a while, Sheriff Troy radioed Davis to have her check and see if any services towed a van matching my description from our location any time since last night. He told her he suspected some kids probably took it for a joy ride.

We combed the woods in and around where I left Charlie, following the same route I took running from him, but there was no body. It was obvious it was here, there's still a *ton* of blood. It leaves Sheriff Troy scratching his head. Who would steal a van *and* a corpse? Sheriff Troy studied me quizzically while Officer Richard just studies me; creep.

"Well don't look at me, *I* didn't move him! That guy was as tall as you guys and probably weighed over 200 pounds. Besides, I was freaked the fuck out – I just wanted out of here!"

"She does have a valid point," Sheriff Troy said, "it would either take someone big, or with the proper training to move a body that size. I don't see any other tracks besides the two, though, so whoever it was knew how to cover them."

"You're right, Sheriff," Richard said, meeting my eyes, "it would take someone big. Why don't we go check out that house?"

Fucking creepy. We trekked back to the cruiser in silence. Officer Richard walked slowly behind Troy and I the whole way and I could *feel* his eyes on me. I didn't know what his deal was but he was really starting to freak me out. I got this whole stalker vibe from him that I couldn't seem to shake. Sheriff Troy didn't seem to sense anything wrong. I quickened my pace so that I was walking right beside Troy. Officer Richard didn't hurry at all. We had to wait for him at the cruiser to catch up to us; it was like he was taking a fucking country stroll.

By the time we got to the house I escaped from, I was really beginning to think Officer Richard knew more than he was letting on. I mean, I barely even gave directions, he practically drove us straight there. It didn't seem to faze Sheriff Troy, but I thought it was damn suspicious. We pulled into the big circular drive and I shivered involuntarily. I thought I'd never see the place again. At least I was *hoping* anyway. Sheriff Troy let me out of the back and I did my best to stay close to him. I didn't know the guy but he felt a lot safer than the alternative.

"So, where was it that you thought you saw the other guy shot?" Troy asked.

I pointed to the large red horse barn to the right of the huge house. "I saw Charlie coming from there right after I heard the gun go off."

"Okay, wait here; I'll go check it out." He said walking towards the barn.

"I'm coming with you." I said, "I don't like it here."

"Just stay behind us." Richard said, "You're safe now."

Ya right, he *totally* wasn't even going with Sheriff Troy until I said I wasn't going to stay there. The three of us made our way into the barn, first Sheriff Troy, then Officer Richard, and then me. The first thing we found when Troy opened the giant sliding door was the missing van. It was just inside the giant barn, and there was blood dripping down over the back bumper from under the twin doors as well as from the handles. There was really no question what we would find when we opened it up. I figured this was where we should backtrack and call in the troops. Well, apparently Sheriff Troy didn't get the memo. He reached on up and opened the back doors to the van to look inside. No gloves or anything – even *I* knew better than *that*! Maybe he thought there was a chance someone was still alive in there, I don't know. The first thing that hit me was the stench. It hadn't been 24 hours since my struggle with Charlie and his death, and God only knows how long he'd been in the van parked in that barn. I deducted that since it was a heated barn, it probably sped the decomposition of the body – hence the horrible stench. After Sheriff Troy finished emptying his stomach next to a stall over to the left side of the barn about fifty feet away he came back to actually take a peek inside. He still looked a little green.

"Heated barn," he said weakly, "that's why it smells so bad."

"Really," I said, "I would never have guessed that." *Fucking idiot.*

He pointed inside, "This the guy you shot last night in the woods?"

"Yes," I replied, "that's Charlie, one of the guys that *kidnapped* me and was trying to *kill* me last night in the woods."

"And that you consequently shot?" he asked.

"While trying to get the gun away, yes, I *consequently* shot him."

"*Thank you*," he said, as if I'd answered some great riddle. "Now, shall we see if we can find the other one?"

Sheriff Troy led us slowly around the van further into the barn. It didn't take long to find Alan. We turned left down an isle lined with stall enclosures off the back of the main part of the barn. At the end of the wing full of stalls, we found Alan slumped up against the wall with a single bullet wound to the head. He stank pretty badly too. Sheriff Troy dry heaved for a minute before getting control of himself. I don't know how you become a cop with a weak stomach.

"I better go call these in," Troy said, turning to walk back out.

"I'm afraid I can't let you do that." Richard said.

Officer Richard somehow managed to move around behind Sheriff Troy *and* me, and was standing between the way out and us. He had a gun leveled at Sheriff Troy's head. It took me a second to realize it was *not* his service weapon but the gun I fought with Charlie over last night.

"That's Charlie's gun. *You* moved the van and his body."

"Officer Richard," Troy said, "Let the girl go, this isn't about her."

Wow, didn't Lady Sheriff, I mean 'Davis', tell him *anything*? It was *all* about me. They fucking *kidnapped* me! They'll take good care of me my ass. I tried to inch sideways and Richard pinned me with his eyes. The gun stayed focused on Sheriff Troy, but the message in his gaze was clear; I didn't move another inch.

"Oh," Richard said mockingly, "it's *all* about the girl. *My* girls are *always* the most coveted."

I tried to swallow the sudden lump in my throat. "*Your* girls?" I asked. "What do you mean by 'your girls'?"

"Didn't you know?" Richard smiled coldly, and then shot Sheriff Troy in the head. I felt the hot stench of blood soak my face for the second time in less than 24 hours. "I'm your father."

16 WEDNESDAY APPROXIMATELY 11:30 AM
CADEN NEELY

After letting Truman out I headed back upstairs and put my apartment back together. Krysta watched me with a worried look on her face but didn't say anything. Once everything was back in their rightful place, I got in the shower. I was standing there, eyes closed, letting the hot water pour over me, when I felt her arms wrap around me. She had to be brimming with questions. I hadn't filled her in on my past, on my 'extra-curricular activities' as Al called them. All of those things that would be in the file the FBI had on me; fucking wonderful. Now that I had a good reason to walk the straight and narrow I was about to see my whole fucking life go down in flames. I seriously doubted Al could get me out of this. Krysta started massaging my neck and shoulders under the hot water and I moaned and leaned into her. How am I going to make this right? Turning, I pulled her to me.

"Come here."

Her mouth was hot as I took her in, greedy as it mated with mine. The pending doom hanging over what we'd just found translated into a desperate hunger as we devoured each other under the hot spray of the water; clung to one another trembling. There had to be a way.

"We can run." I said, holding her eyes with mine. "I have money. We can get Evin back and then run."

"No," she looked sad, resigned even. "I've spent half my life hiding. I'll be damned if I'm going to spend the other half running. I'll wait for you if I have to. We'll figure it out."

"Krysta –"

"No, Caden, I won't run. We'll find another way."

I didn't even know what kind of time I would be facing. Theft, drug trafficking, assault, an assortment of firearms charges, breaking and entering; the list could go on. Not only that, but multiples of each, I was sure. Unless Al could somehow convince them that everything was in the process of helping him with cases. However, a lot of the shit in my past pre-dated my association with Al. Just how much did the FBI have? I felt a future with Krysta slipping through my fingers and we'd only just started. She wasn't going to wait for me. Why would she? I wasn't worth it. She didn't even know what she was getting herself into. I turned off the shower and got out, handing her a towel and picking one up for myself. I'd find her daughter. Maybe if I saved Evin I would have a chance.

I was tying my boots when my phone rang. I glanced at the caller ID and flipped it open; it was Al.

"Ya?"

"We've got a body."

"Fuck, is it her?"

"They've been unable to identify the girl so far. They found her in a dumpster behind the warehouse where the auction was. She was tortured and beaten pretty badly. All of the vital stats are right and it looks like someone ripped out a couple of facial piercings. Her attacker removed her fingertips as well. They'd like Krysta to come down and see if she can identify her. If not they will try dental records. Her face is beaten too badly to tell from the photo, Caden, I'm sorry."

"Fuck."

"Do you know how to get here?"

"Get where, the FBI office?"

"No, the State Medical Examiner's Office, it's in Clackamas."

"Oh, Fuck no, give me directions."

The last place I expected to find myself, or to be taking Krysta, was the morgue. I'd never been there before, and I never wanted to go again. When I broke Al's news to Krysta, she collapsed at my feet, making the most disturbing sound I'd ever witnessed. Not quite a sob, not quite a scream, but a horrible combination of both. After a few minutes of this, I was scrambling to dig through her bag for an inhaler as she suffered the most horrific asthma attack I think I'd ever seen. For a terrifyingly slow few minutes, I thought I was going to be dropping off a body instead of going to identify one. When I said I was taking her to the hospital she held up her inhaler and waved me away. Finally, she got her breathing under control and lapsed into normal tears. I've never been so happy to see a woman cry in my life. After several moments of quiet crying and mumbling words I couldn't quite hear, she looked up at me; determination on her face.

"It won't be her, I didn't feel her die."

"If you know it's not her, then why are you crying?"

"Because I know it *will* be if we don't find her soon. *Somebody's* baby is lying on that table. Let's go. The sooner we prove it's not Evin, the sooner they can figure out who she is, and we can find *my* baby."

I decided not to state the obvious. That she's a mother in mourning and she's probably in denial. It very well may be Evin waiting for us in the morgue. I hoped Krysta was right. I hoped Evin was still out there. I had a very bad feeling she was wrong. I helped Krysta into her jacket and we headed down to the truck. It was nearly an hour drive to Clackamas from my shop. We made the entire trip in silence. We arrived at the Coroner's office at 1:00 pm. It was the longest fucking drive of my life.

Al met us at the front lobby and escorted us to the actual morgue. The place was swarming with FBI in addition to its normal staff. Apparently, the girl Al told me about wasn't the only body they found. Ordinarily, they would take Krysta to a viewing window where she would see the face of the victim needing identification. This situation, however, was far from ordinary and it wouldn't be so easy. Not for the staff, and definitely not for Krysta. However, someone had cut or burned all obvious identifying marks from the body. Whoever this monster was, removed her fingers at the second digit and there were a number of strategic burns about her body indicating the removal of tattoos, scars, or birthmarks. In addition to this mutilation, the girl had obviously been tortured and beaten as well. Her face was a swollen, unidentifiable mess of ugly bruises, cuts, and burns. Krysta answered the Coroner's questions in a sort of numb daze. I'm not sure if she still though it wasn't Evin or if she saw something that told her it was. I honestly couldn't tell at that point. The girl was the right height and weight. She had the right hair, though sections of it were singed, others torn out. The poor girl went through hell. I heard irritation in the voices around me and returned my attention to the conversation.

"With the exception of the bruising to the face, most of the mutilation was done post-mortem." The Coroner was saying. "What other identifying marks did your daughter have, Mrs. Mallory, besides the tattoo that was cut from her bicep?"

"It's *MISS* Mallory, and I *told* you, that's *not* Evin!"

"*Miss* Mallory," the Coroner said, "I'm sorry, but as I told you, I'm afraid her wallet was found shortly after Officer Truman called you over here. It was in the same dumpster. We still need to prove it conclusively, and that's why we need you here, but all evidence points to this being your daughter, Evin Mallory."

"Krysta," Al reached for her hand, sorrow in his eyes. "Please, let's just get this over with. I know it's hard."

"Was the back of her head mutilated or damaged in any way?" Krysta asked exasperated. "The skin on it, I mean?"

"No, it wasn't," the Coroner said, "why?"

"Evin has a birthmark at the base of her skull, beneath her hair," Krysta said, "a strawberry. It's very pronounced. Turn her head and pull her hair out of the way. Let me see."

I held my breath as the Coroner carefully repositioned the head of the dead girl so that they could examine the back. Krysta shoved him out of the way and I expelled it in an inappropriate laugh at the look of indignation that crossed the little man's face. He'd been rude to her the whole time. Krysta carefully combed through the dark hair at the base of the dead girls head; there was nothing there. She glared at the man triumphantly.

"You see, no birth mark, this is *not* my daughter!"

"You're *certain* about the birth mark being there?" he asked.

"Are you fucking serious?" I said.

"I'm her *Mother*, of course I'm certain! Have you even done a blood test yet? What is this girl's blood type? Evin is O positive."

"We're still waiting on the birth records from the vital statistics office, so no; we haven't done blood typing yet."

"Perhaps," Truman piped up, "you might like to do that *now*? Or do you also doubt a mother to know her daughters blood type?"

"Of course not!" the little man hurried off to get his equipment.

"Fucking imbecile!" Krysta said.

I can't help it, I barked out a laugh at Krysta's righteous rage. The guy *was* a moron. I was just glad wasn't directing her anger at me. She glared him down the entire time he was running the tests. It turned out the girl wasn't even O blood type; she's AB negative. We knew conclusively the dead girl was *not* Evin. Before Krysta was willing to leave, she got one of the FBI agents to oversee the Coroner in doing dental molds and running her general description and blood type through all the databases looking for a match. She insisted that *'that fucking moron'* (her words not mine) not be left alone to fuck up the identification on his own and put another mother through the torture session she'd just gone through. I think I even heard her threaten to sue somebody. It was fucking funny. It was after 3:00 pm by the time we made our way out of there. Krysta fumed a trail of wreckage all the way out of the Coroner's office on the way back to the truck. Al and I followed at a safe distance trying not to chuckle at the discomfort of the FBI agents and Coroner's staff she left in her angry wake.

"You *do* realize," Al whispered, glancing anxiously at Krysta, "someone went to a lot of trouble to make that girl *look* like Evin Mallory. Removing skin where identifying marks would be, the appearance of ripped out piercings – the wallet. Someone's trying to get us to stop looking for her."

"They obviously didn't know Krysta very well. Or bother to match the blood type."

"They may not have known Evin's blood type." Al shared a worried glance. "Or they only needed a little more time and it didn't matter."

"Let's hope it's the first option." I replied. "I'd appreciate it if you didn't share this with Krysta."

"Somehow," Al said, studying her as she terrorized another staff member on our way out. "I think she's smart enough to figure it out on her own."

"Ya," I grimaced, "I get that feeling too."

"Hey, about what I mentioned last night," Al stopped me just shy of the truck. "I have a couple of ideas on how to handle it. Try not to worry, and don't do anything rash."

Don't do anything rash. It was almost as if he was listening in on my conversation with Krysta in the shower. But I knew better than that. I huffed out a laugh and clapped him on the shoulder. He stumbled forward.

"Right – like I would do anything *rash*." I said.

Al laughed outright at my statement before cutting it off midway in a choking manner. I followed his gaze to find Krysta glaring openly at us from next to the truck a few feet away where she stood smoking one of my cigarettes. We both sobered up and closed the distance as if summoned.

"So what do we do now?" She asked between drags.

"I still think Violet Skazony is our best bet, but she's in the wind." Al said.

"What about that Mitchell character you mentioned?" Krysta asked.

"Also missing and unaccounted for," Al answered.

"Why don't we go somewhere we can sit down and go over our battle plan?" I offered, "We can figure out what we need to do next."

"Let's head back to your place." Al said, "It's a good central location and it's off everyone's radar."

I just stared at him. I already let the fucker in once. He was just dying to go through my shit, I could tell.

"Tell me," I ventured, deadpanning him, "how is my place off the radar with you landing me in an FBI file?"

I heard Krysta suck in a breath. I think she was expecting me to deck him. I *was* considering it. However, I'm relatively sure decking my friend, the *cop*, wouldn't help me fix the problem, so I didn't. I just continued to stare him down until he dropped his gaze and let out a defeated sigh.

"I told you I have some ideas. I'll fix it, Caden, I promise."

"You better hope so."

"I will."

"Good. Now let's go back to the shop."

We converged on my shop at a little before 4:00 pm. Against my better judgment, I let Al and Krysta talk me into having the little conference take place in my apartment instead of downstairs. The first thing Al did was dart around the living room looking at the pictures and magazines that had been placed back in their customary locations since his earlier visit before giving me a triumphant grin. I glowered at him. I managed to get the bedroom door locked before he could get that far and he actually pouted like a child when he figured it out. I may let him back there someday but definitely not yet. I was arguing against the logic of coffee instead of beer when Al's phone rang and he insisted upon answering it.

"Officer Truman here," He said.

I watched his face as he listened to the voice on the other end of the line. I couldn't hear what they were saying, but whatever it was, it had him excited. His eyes lit up as he nodded into the phone and smiled toward Krysta. Finally, he hung up and grinned at us both.

"Forget the beer, Caden."

"What the hell was that all about?" I asked.

Krysta watched our exchange, breathless; I could tell she was afraid to ask. Hope written across her face like a mask.

"That was the Secretary from my office. A very lengthy report just came across the wire from a Deschutes County Sheriff's Department. I know where Evin is."

17 WEDNESDAY APPROXIMATELY 4:30 PM
AL TRUMAN

After some not so calm debate we decided, *against* my better judgment, we should all go over the report that came in together. Therefore, I was on my way back to the Department to pick up a hard copy while Caden and Krysta packed for a trip to Central Oregon. Which *begged* the question – who the hell left that tip on my desk and why? Obviously, it *wasn't* a miss-direct as we had previously interpreted. Why didn't they leave more information? Was it someone on the inside feeling guilty? Someone that saw or heard something they shouldn't have? These questions and more were eating away at me. Something told me I was going to want to find this mystery person. Then, of course, was the question of how in the hell Evin came to be in Central Oregon in the first place. Why would they take her there? If the same people took her that were running the human trafficking ring, it would make the most sense for them to sell her at the auction. There are too damn many connections for her abduction and the trafficking ring not to be related in some manner.

Like Violet Skazony. That woman was going to turn out to be the bane of my existence on this case. *Everything* pointed to her being involved in both Evin's kidnapping *and* the human trafficking ring. She *should* have been at that warehouse when the FBI raided it. I'd be willing to bet Caden's big money that hers is on that list of names the feds are withholding of patrons attending the 'oh so convenient' *fund raiser* that was held right next door. Either someone high up was protecting her big time or she had some serious dirt on someone. Regardless, it spelled bad news for her when I finally caught up. The evidence may have been circumstantial so far, but I *swear* I will bust that woman. I thought dirty cops were bad. A dirty Child

Services worker takes the cake. Their *sole purpose* is to protect kids from harm. It was completely unthinkable for a CPS worker to be involved in something of this horrific caliper. My stomach turned just thinking about it. Then you added in the obvious involvement of various corrupt law enforcement officials, ranging from cops, to at least one member of the DA's office, possibly an FBI leak - it gave a whole new meaning to the phrase 'Social Services'.

I'd worked myself into a fury by the time I'd pulled up next to the Washington County Jail building. My teeth ground together as I stalked through the glass front doors and past the security desk, giving the guard only a curt nod as I made my way across the lobby to the stairs. I had too much pent up energy to take the elevator, besides its only one floor up. It occurred to me as I slammed through the door of the Sheriff's department and past Andy at reception, that he probably took the tip message and left it on my desk. Andy, our male secretary, probably took the phone call and didn't bother to take down any additional information about the caller. I turned on my heel and marched back to his desk. He blanched at the look on my face and rolled his desk chair back a couple of inches.

"Who the hell left the tip about the girl, Andy?" I demanded, hands planted on his desk, face mere inches from his.

"Whoa, back up, Truman — what tip are you talking about?"

"The anonymous tip about the girl in Central Oregon left on my desk yesterday — Did you take a call, or did you leave me the tip yourself? Are you involved in this twisted scheme?"

"Ohhh, *that* tip — wait what twisted scheme?" Andy stood, abruptly just as angry as I was. *"ARE YOU ACCUSING ME OF SOMETHING TRUMAN?"*

My stance relaxed, voice quieting to a deadly whisper as I answered his question with a reiteration of my own. "The girl was kidnapped by a human trafficking ring run by a plethora of dirty cops and other officials; *are — you — involved?*"

The room went silent as the handful of other people in the office turned all eyes on us. They all knew the low menacing whisper meant I was at my most dangerous. They also knew I could smell a lie a mile away. I was waiting for Andy's reply, but really, my attention was assessing the reactions of those others in the room; gauging *their* guilt. I *doubted* Andy was actually guilty – I would blind-side if he was, and that rarely happens to me. However, that didn't mean I wouldn't investigate the possibility. Besides, I knew he was afraid of me; he'd be an easy break if he *were* involved.

"*FUCK* no, are you kidding me? I have two daughters of my own! That's *sick*, Truman, how could you even *think* that?" The honest hurt and disgust in his eyes did more to assure me of his innocence than his words did. I kept my body language focused toward him as I noted one of the newer deputies, swallowing nervously, slowly ease his way out the back of the office; bingo. I *knew* I felt eyes on me here since I started this case.

"I believe you. I'll be back in a minute to ask about that tip."

I left a flabbergasted Andy and darted back out the front, trotting around the upside down 'L' of the walkway fronting the office entrances overlooking the lobby. I stopped short of the door into the Sheriff's department at the other end of the walk and waited for Sheriff's Deputy Baern to come through. The Sheriff's Department offices actually wrap around the entire length of the 'L' with an entrance on both ends, one by the elevator and one by the stairs.

The last thing people expect to see is one Sheriff cuffing another one. So when Baern came through the door and I twirled him around before he had time to react, slapping a pair of cuffs tight about his wrists, and then quickly disarming him, all activity in the lobby below ceased as everyone tried to figure out what was going on. In seconds, offices were emptying and I marched Baern back around the walkway and through the front door of the Department to the startled gazes of over a dozen county workers and pedestrian visitors. Considering I was doing this all on gut instinct, I had to break him fast or *I* would be the one in deep shit. Jaws hit the floor as I escorted Baern past Andy, a handful of other Deputies and staff and into an interview room, where I locked the door and turned on a recorder.

Baern is the new guy on the block. If he'd spent any *decent* length of time in the Sheriff's department, he'd know that *I* was the one that liked to bust dirty cops. It was an extreme rarity for one to crop up in our department since I'd been there. My nickname with the girls may be 'Pretty Boy', but my nickname in the Department was 'Cuff Buster'. If you were in law enforcement and dirty I was the last one you wanted to be working with. I decided to use my reputation around the office to my advantage.

"Do you know what the other Deputies like to call me, *Deputy* Baern?" I asked slurring his title like it left a foul taste in my mouth.

He sneered. "*Cuff Buster* – like you can't keep em in one piece." He snorted a laugh.

"That's right," I said, smiling, "but not because I break my cuffs." I leaned over the table so we were nose to nose. He swallowed, but the sneer came right back. "They call me 'Cuff Buster' because I'm *really good* at busting *bad* cops. In fact – I pride myself on it." The sneer disappeared as Baern blanched white. I stood up and started pacing. "I know about the human trafficking ring. I know there are dirty cops spread throughout the precincts as well as a leak in the FBI, and involvement in the DA's office and CPS. *You* are going to fill in *all* the blanks, *Deputy* Baern, or I will make sure you are housed with all those criminals that *love* to take their aggression out on people that hurt kids – and that they know *exactly* what you were involved in." I stopped pacing and graced him with a cold smile. He sweated visibly.

It took all of five minutes to break Baern. Frankly, I was surprised they even used such a wuss. His primary role, according to the rather lengthy monologue I had beautifully recorded as evidence, was that of 'breeder'. Just the thought made me cringe. Baern was a good-looking guy with a quick temper and a holier than thou attitude. It turned out he grew up in foster care, big surprise there. Violet Skazony was his primary caseworker at the end, God she must be old. Before her, he told me, CPS transferred his case among many, but she was the one that 'saw something in him and singled him out for a greater purpose'. She groomed him for his future role as a breeder and made sure he did all the right things to ensure he would land a position in law enforcement, making it all that much easier for him to stalk and prey on their unsuspecting victims. Once I got Baern talking, it was difficult to shut him up. He couldn't tell me much about who the other bad cops were or exactly who was involved in any of the extended branches of law enforcement, such as the District Attorney's office, or if anyone besides Violet Skazony at CPS was a part of it. But he gave me a boatload of info on his role as a 'breeder', how it came to be, and Violet Skazony's role in making it happen. With his testimony alone I could take her down. If only I could find her.

The 'breeders', as he called himself, were chosen at a young age for their beauty, silver tongues, and cruel hearts. They were always boys. Then taught from a young age to appear guileless, while *being* cunning, quick witted, masters of deception. Their primary purpose was to *create* subjects for the trafficking ring by targeting women that would either easily fail under CPS scrutiny, or break with a little guided torment. The result was the progeny of these breeders and their targeted women – usually rape victims that didn't report because their abusers held positions of power – ended up in the custody of Child Protective Services, and Violet Skazony's hands. Her *exact* role in the ring hierarchy was yet to be determined, but it was obvious at this point that she was the primary supplier of its 'wares' if not at the top of the food chain. I couldn't wait to take her down.

Baern would be begging for a deal. He hadn't been in place long enough to rack up many of these targets, but he'll still be facing some hefty charges. He didn't know enough to acquit DA Berghauer of the charges the FBI were still holding him under, but his statement definitely reinforced my suspicions that *he* was telling the truth. Someone, probably Skazony, was holding his kids hostage to keep him from talking while she very neatly framed him. I formally arrested Baern and personally escorted him downstairs to the county jail intake. He tried to back pedal when it really sank in he was about to be *in* one of those tiny little cinder block cells. I hoped I could clear Berghauer in time to hear his case personally – although, I'd bet he'd recuse himself due to involvement in the case – he struck me as the sort of man that would. Still, that probably wouldn't keep him from offering his two cents on suggestions for sentencing.

Finally, I had some solid fucking evidence. The puzzle pieces were starting to fit disturbingly together. I still had to figure out exactly how Mitchell played into all of it, Violet Skazony's exact role in the ring hierarchy, and who the hell the leak in the FBI was. Hopefully, I'd be able to track down where that original tip came from. Something told me it was vital. Whoever that person was had access to one of the major players, I was sure. I turned my phone back on as I took the stairs two at a time back up to the department to pick up the report and have another chat with Andy. Several missed calls and one text from Caden asking where the fuck I was; the missed calls were all him too. I hit send and called him back as I made my way to my desk and grabbed the report. I was flipping through it when he answered.

"What the fuck is taking you so long, Truman?"

"Holy shit!" I inadvertently let slip as I came across the photos of Evin's injuries in the report. She'd suffered some serious damage. Caden was going to be out for blood; hell, I felt mine boil.

"Sorry, that wasn't directed at you. I'm not so sure Krysta should see this report."

"Why? And you didn't answer my question."

"I ended up making an arrest when I got here. I'll explain when I get back to your place; it's connected. The kidnappers beat Evin up pretty bad, Caden; there are photos. At least she got away in one piece."

"Fuck."

"I have one more thing to take care of and then I'll be on my way."

"Make it quick. Krysta's chomping at the bit to get out of here. She wants her daughter back."

"I know I'm just trying to make sure we take down *all* of the people responsible."

I disconnected and headed up to Andy's desk.

"So, about that tip, do you know who left it?"

"What the hell was all that about earlier, Truman? Why did you just arrest Baern? What did he do?"

"You know that human trafficking ring I mentioned?"

"You mean the one you *accused* me of being a part of?"

"Exactly – well, he is; a part of it I mean. Sorry about all that earlier. I was pretty sure you *weren't* involved but I knew *someone* in the department was and I needed to draw them out."

"Gee, thanks, clue me in next time."

I shook my head. "It had to be genuine. Now, about that tip, what do you remember?"

"You're an asshole, you know that Truman?"

"The tip, Andy?"

He glared at me for a minute. "It was a woman, she called, didn't leave a name."

"Did you *ask* for her name?"

"Did I ask for her name – of course I fucking *asked*! I know how to do my job."

"Well, what did she say when you asked? Did she just refuse or did she give you an excuse? The least little thing could help me find her. It's important Andy."

"She gave me a smart ass reply and hung up."

I swear it was like fucking pulling teeth. "*What* was the reply?"

"She said, 'tell him it's his Guardian *Angel*', just like that – with angel said real mockingly. She was just mouthing off. Then she hung up on me. And before you ask, the number was a payphone in downtown Portland, it could have been anyone."

"Thank you, Andy. Oh, call the Sisters Deschutes County Sheriff's Department and let them know that I will be bringing Evin's mother out to pick her up tonight."

"Will do; and whatever, Truman, I *told* you IT WAS USELESS!" He raised his voice to follow me out the door.

It *wasn't* useless. I knew *exactly* who called in that tip, and I guess I made an impression after all. I guess the pertinent question was; did I track her down now, *before* going to Central Oregon, or when we got back? I had to wonder just how she came across the information Evin was in Central Oregon when she did. I *knew* she didn't suspect Violet of anything untoward before my little visit to CPS that first afternoon. I must have I planted a seed of doubt in Angel's pretty little head; got her wondering. I just hoped I hadn't put *her* in any danger.

When I pulled into the shop Caden's Harley was out front, bags strapped to the back behind the seat for travel. I guess he decided his bike would be the quickest means of transportation. That probably made me the ride back for Evin when we picked her up, either that or a rental. Caden sure as hell wasn't going to fit Krysta *and* Evin on that thing. Frankly, I was surprised Krysta agreed to it. However, Caden usually got his way when his mind was set on something. He'd come back out of the shop and was putting extra gloves in the handle bar bag when I approached him.

"You gonna be able to keep up in that thing, or do you want to go get your bike?" he asked.

"I'm not sure a motorcycle is going to be the best transportation for Evin in the shape she's in right now. Let's go upstairs and talk." I held up the inch thick file in my hand. It wasn't a small report.

Caden glowered at me while he lit a cigarette and then led the way up to his apartment. I couldn't believe I'd managed to get inside the place three times in a row. I managed to contain my curiosity at the open door into the bedroom and sat down on the couch, setting the thick report on the coffee table in front of me. Krysta and Caden crowded in close.

"I haven't read through the whole report yet," I said, looking at Krysta, "but I think you should know before I even open this that I thumbed through it and there are some rather disturbing photos of Evin in here. Are you sure you want to see it?"

"She's ok isn't she?" Krysta asked; worry etched on her face.

"Well, apparently, she walked into the Sister's branch of the Deschutes County Sheriff's Department all on her own and filed this report, so I would say yes, but she sustained some ugly wounds."

"I want to see it," she said, "it's better to know what to expect in advance than to be surprised by it when I see Evin in person."

"Okay, don't say I didn't warn you."

The three of us poured over the entire report together, reading it in silence. By the time we were done Krysta was in tears and Caden and I were both seeing red. Evin is one *tough* little girl. She'd gone through hell. They kidnapped her, drugged her, and took her nearly 300 miles from home. Yet she fought them repeatedly, ultimately killing one of them in a life and death struggle to escape after he had apparently already shot his partner for trying to mess with her when they had orders not to from some unknown higher up. Evin managed to glean a fair amount of information about her situation regardless of them drugging her half the time. The girl has a level head.

"She killed a man." Krysta whispered, tears streaming down her face. "What's going to happen to her?"

"It's obvious her life was in imminent danger, Krysta, it's a clear cut case of self-defense. There won't be any charges."

"Are you sure?"

"Well, assuming the investigation supports her report, yes. I don't see how any DA in their right mind would want to prosecute. Let's get out there and talk to the Sheriff that took the report. I want to get a look at the scene too. We'll know more then."

"So what took you so long, Truman?" Caden asked. "You said something about making an arrest."

"You arrested someone while you were gone? Was it connected to Evin?" Krysta asked.

"Yes, I did, and it was. I was thinking about that tip I got a couple of days ago about her being in Central Oregon and how we ended up discounting it because of the whole human trafficking angle and expecting her to be found at the auction by the FBI."

"Where they *did* plant a body meant to look like her," Krysta said.

I met Caden's eyes. "I told you she would figure it out."

"Uh-huh, and?" Caden prompted.

"Anyway, it got me wondering where the hell that tip came from, and then it occurred to me that our secretary, Andy, probably took it over the phone and didn't get a name. I figured there was a remote possibility that he may have left me the tip himself. Regardless, I'd had a feeling someone in my department had been watching me since I started working on this case so I decided to confront Andy about the tip."

"So, you arrested your secretary?" Krysta asked.

"No – long story short, I used the confrontation with Andy to flush out the person that's been watching me. Turns out it was the newest Deputy, Sheriff Baern. Violet Skazony was his last caseworker when he was in foster care and she molded him into the treasure he is today. I got one hell of a confession – on tape. He gave me enough to take Skazony down if we can find her."

"So this cop was just a mole?" Caden asked.

"No — that was the smallest part of his role. His *real* role was what he called a 'breeder'." I paused and looked at Caden before meeting Krysta's eyes. "I think it's the same role Richard plays in all of this. Baern told me all about these 'breeders'. Skazony picked them at a very young age, and then groomed them into adulthood. They gain positions of power. Their role is to seek out and impregnate women who will easily fail under the scrutiny of CPS or break and attempt or commit suicide under target pressure — stalking, various forms of tormenting, all difficult if not impossible to trace, since no one has documented it. These women don't report the crimes because their abusers are cops and other men in positions of power. The breeders only choose women that don't have outside resources, no other family to take the kids. So, when they break, CPS takes custody, and Skazony has an endless resource for her black market kids."

"Oh my God," Krysta's eyes teared at the horror of the realization. "I was a target from the beginning. They meant to take Evin all along."

"Son of a Bitch," Caden said, fury written on his face.

"I don't have any proof that Richard is a breeder, but it makes the most sense. Everything fits."

"If Baern is one of these breeders, why would he leave you the tip? Did he have a change of heart?" Krysta asked confused.

"Oh no, Baern didn't leave the tip. The caller was anonymous; or so Andy thought. It turns out it was called in from a payphone in Portland. The caller was a woman. When Andy asked her name she told him to tell me it was from my 'Guardian Angel'."

Caden laughed, "Guardian Angel?"

I smiled, "Andy thought the information was useless so he didn't put it on the message. But the woman leaving the tip knew it would tell me exactly who she was — Angel Fairbairn."

"Who's Angel Fairbairn?" asked Krysta.

"She's a CPS case worker. Her desk is in the cubicle directly across from Violet Skazony's office. When I went by there to try to talk to Violet and she wasn't in, I ended up speaking with Angel instead. I gave her my card. I got the impression that she really disliked me and that she thought Violet was the salt of the earth. I guess I was wrong. Anyway, if she found out where they took Evin, she may know more, or even be in danger. I'd like to swing by there on our way out if it's ok with you. You can go on ahead if you want, I'd understand."

"We'll follow you over." Caden said, "If it look like it's going to take too long then we'll head on out."

"I appreciate it, she's a nice girl – I want to give her a heads up so she can get out of dodge."

Krysta and Caden shared a smile.

I grimaced. "I'm just doing my job."

"She's pretty isn't she?" Krysta grinned.

"You spend too much time around Caden."

Caden busted up laughing.

"Shut up, Caden." I said, heading for the door. Couple of fucking smart asses.

It was technically after hours before we even left to go by the CPS office. I called ahead and convinced Alice to wait for me, letting her know it was important. She didn't look happy when we got there, but then, she never does.

"I said I'd wait to let *you* in, Al, not a bunch of hoodlums." Alice said eyeing Caden and Krysta disapprovingly.

I rolled my eyes at Alice's exaggeration and motioned the two of them inside. "Alice, this is Krysta, the mother of the missing girl I told you about, and Caden, a friend helping out with the case."

"Humph. Well, what do you need? I have things to do you know." Alice said.

"Do you know if Angel Fairbairn is still in?" I asked, "It's very important that I speak with her."

"She never came in today." Alice said, "She was still here working when I went home yesterday. But she didn't come in at all today. Didn't bother calling in sick either. *Some* people have no work ethic at all!"

"I don't think she's sick, Alice."

"Probably just playing hooky!" she said.

"I don't think so." I said, "I think she may be in danger. Do you mind if I go look around her desk? See if there's anything that might tell me where she is?"

"I don't care." Alice said, "But if you ask me she's probably at home being lazy. I suppose you'll be wanting her address and phone number. I'll jot it down for you while you're snooping around her desk."

"Thanks Alice."

I punched in the security code and went through the heavy metal door. Thankfully, I managed not to get lost on my way to Angel's desk. To the casual observer it probably looked like someone with less than great organizational skills just sat there. I still had the image fresh in my mind from yesterday, and I knew what her workstation was *supposed* to look like. Everything was out of order. It was obvious to me someone other than Angel was digging through her files. The inbox and file sorters, yesterday perfectly neat and organized, were in total disarray. There were a number of miscellaneous papers strewn haphazardly across the work surface of the desk and several of the drawers were ajar. Her chair was up against the side of the cubicle, facing out, not towards the desk, the way I'm sure Angle would have left it. I had the very bad feeling Angel didn't leave here under her own accord. Or if she did, she was running from someone.

"This doesn't look good." Caden said.

"Do you think something happened to her?" Krysta asked.

"I think she found out something she wasn't supposed to know – and maybe got caught with the information." I answered.

"Oh God," Krysta said.

"Let's check Skazony's office." I said walking the short distance.

Violet Skazony's office was dark, the door locked. "Oh well, it was worth a try."

We managed to make our way back out of the maze without too much time loss. Alice was sitting at her desk tapping a pen when we come through the security door. She handed me a piece of paper.

"Here's Angel Fairbairn's address and phone number. Do you mind if I lock up now?"

"Thank you for letting us in, Alice." I said taking the proffered slip. "Have a nice evening."

Alice is quick to usher us through the door, following us out and locking it behind her.

"Well, she's a lovely woman." Krysta said.

"Alice was a friend of my mom's. I've known her since I was a kid. She only likes men and children, unless it suits her. She's a fickle beast."

"She shouldn't be working with people if she doesn't like them." Krysta said.

"I've always thought so too," I replied, "but it's what she does."

Caden and Krysta got on the Harley and I got back in my cruiser to head out. It was after seven so it would be close to 9:30 by the time we rolled into Sisters. I decided I had better check in with Andy to see what the Sisters Sheriff's department said when he let them know we were coming out tonight. I dialed his direct line from my cell and hit send.

"Washington County Sheriff's Department, how may I help you?"

"Andy, it's me, Truman."

"What do you want, Truman?"

I got the distinct impression he was still pissed at me. "Did you call the Sisters branch of Deschutes County Sheriff's Department and tell them I'm coming out?"

"You told me to didn't you?"

"Yes – what did they say?"

"Sheriff Davis said they'd wait for you."

"Thanks, Andy."

"You're still an ass, Truman."

When I hung up the phone, Caden was standing outside my car window. I nearly jumped out of my skin. Fucker snuck up on me when I wasn't paying attention. I rolled down the window to see what he wanted, and glared until he stopped laughing.

"A little jumpy, aren't you, Truman?"

"Fuck you, Caden, what do you want?"

"A Tony's gonna meet up with us for the ride – just in case."

"In case of what? Evin's already in custody, it's just a pick up and some paperwork, Caden."

"I have a bad feeling about this."

"Whatever, Caden, let's go. They're staying late for us so we need to haul ass."

"Just try and keep up."

"Keep up – fuck you, I'm leading the way. Someone's got to clear the road for you degenerates."

Caden just laughed as he walked back to his bike and got on. He revved the motor while he waited for Krysta to climb on behind him, and then gunned it out of the parking lot. I followed close on his tail. Other traffic melted out of our way as if they were expecting me to pull him over. It *did* make the commute easier. I followed Caden to a little dive bar in a strip mall along TV highway where there were a bunch of Harleys in the lot surrounded by bikers. He pulled up in front and I stopped right behind him. I flashed my lights for the hell of it and watched the momentary panic on half their faces before they looked closer and figured out it's me.

"Truman, you asshole!" Tony said.

"Like my new car?" I asked innocently, "427 horses – officially of course."

"What kind of torque does that thing have?" Tony eyed the Camaro cruiser appreciatively.

"I have no idea, but it's fast as fuck."

"You're clueless, Pretty Boy." Tony quipped.

"Fuck you, Tony, I know bikes not cars. Speaking of which, we need to hit the road."

I climbed back in the cruiser to the sound of Harley's revving their motors. It's a long ass drive to Sisters Oregon, Down I-5 south to 20 and out East. I led the way in the cruiser with Caden and Tony on the Harleys following closely behind me. Any time we encountered a traffic snarl I flashed my lights and led the procession through at high speed. For once, the guys appreciated having a cop along for the ride – especially when it cut a two and a half hour ride down by forty-five minutes. It was a quarter to nine when we pulled into the Sisters branch of the Deschutes County Sheriff's Department. There was only one county vehicle in the lot. The lights in all of the surrounding buildings were off with the exception of the tiny office holding the Sheriff's department. I instructed Tony to stay put and walked up to the front door of the little office with Caden and Krysta close behind me. The door was locked but I could see a woman sitting behind a desk. I knocked hard on the door and waited for her to come let us in. She didn't look happy.

"Are you Sheriff Truman?" She asked, motioning us inside.

I nodded and extended my hand. She shook it firmly and let go. "This is Krysta Mallory, Evin's mother, and Caden Neely; he's been helping out with the case."

"Sheriff Davis," She nodded by way of greeting. "Why don't we go have a seat and I'll fill you in. I'm afraid there have been some new developments since I sent the report to your Department this afternoon."

"What kind of developments?" I asked, taking one of the indicated seats. Caden and Krysta followed suit as Sheriff Davis sat back down behind her desk.

"Well, I sent Evin out with Sheriff Troy and your Officer Richard to go show them the exact location of the body so Troy could call it in to the crime scene guys —"

"*WHAT?*" Caden, Krysta, and I all demanded in unison. The three of us stood up so fast that chairs went skittering across the tile floor.

"You gave her to *Officer Dick?*" Caden asked.

"*HE'S ONE OF THEM!*" Krysta Shouted.

Sheriff Davis rubber necked between Caden and Krysta, mouth agape at their outbursts, while I tried to get a hold of the sudden temper that had bubbled up in me so that I didn't rip the woman's head off like they were about to do. *One* of us had to keep a level head. Fists clinched at my side, I leveled a glare at Caden and a quelling glance at Krysta before focusing my attention back on Sheriff Davis.

"Sheriff Davis," I said through gritted teeth, "you have quite successfully; I'm afraid, put Evin right back into the hands of her kidnappers."

"But he said she was missing and he was here following up a lead; that he wanted to take her home." She said white faced.

"Did your other Sheriff; Sheriff Troy, ever check back in?" I asked mildly.

"No," she said slowly, head down like an errant child. "That was the new development I was going to tell you about. After reporting that the suspect's vehicle was missing I never heard from them again. I sent the crime scene investigators to the coordinates he gave me but by the time they got there, they were gone. And the crime scene guys reported the body was missing too, though they found lots of blood."

"How long ago was this?" I asked.

"It was early afternoon when they left. They should have been back here by five at the latest. She was only supposed to show them the two locations and then they were supposed to come right back here."

"Your partner is likely dead. We've pretty much determined Officer Richard is directly involved in the human trafficking ring responsible for kidnapping Evin in the first place. I just don't have enough evidence to take him down yet."

"And I handed her right over to him."

Krysta was listening to our exchange in a rage with tears streaming down her face. At Sheriff Davis's quiet proclamation, she stepped forward and laid a right hook square across the woman's jaw. Caden was quick to pull her back. I *wanted* to applaud, but striking an officer of the law is a criminal offense.

"*Krysta!*" I admonished sternly, then turning to Sheriff Davis, "I'm sorry, this has been exceptionally difficult for her. Just this morning she had to identify a body we thought might be Evin."

Sheriff Davis rubbed her jaw. "It's ok – she's right, I should have checked him out better. I just took his word for it. Now her daughter is missing again and my partner is as well."

"I *told* you I had a bad feeling about this." Caden said.

"I know, Caden," I said, "and God forbid, you're always right."

18 WEDNESDAY 4:15 PM
EVIN MALLORY

All I can do is gape at Officer Richard in disbelief. I mean, he *has* to be insane. *He's* my father? I don't *think* so. The dude just shot a Sheriff in the fucking head. Of course, he's insane. Before I can collect my thoughts, put words to his delusion, he has me by the arm dragging me out of the barn and toward the house. The second I see the useless Portland Police car sitting there, the realization hits me; no one is coming to help. My Goddamn *rescuer* is the bad guy! I plant my heels and try to break free. The last couple of days have taken its toll on my body. He tightens his grip on my arm as he pulls me and all but ignores the kick to his shin.

"Come on," he growls, giving my arm a painful yank as he pulls me up the front steps. "You've been enough trouble."

I don't know how the hell I'm going to get out of here this time, but I figure my best bet is to play nice for now and wait for the right opportunity. I relax into his grip and let him lead me through the front door, which he locks behind us, across the foyer, and into the giant 'Homes and Gardens' worthy living room. There's a woman sitting in one of the chairs across the room with a magazine held at arm's length in front of her face. Richard stops us in the middle of the room and goes to her. She sets down the magazine and stands. Violet Skazony – what is *she* doing here?

"I brought her back to you, Mother Vi," he says, taking her plump wrinkled hand and kissing it, "Just like you asked."

'*Mother Vi*' – what the fuck? As if reading my thoughts Violet turns her beady rodent eyes on me and creases her plump overly rouged cheeks in a gruesome smile.

"Little Billy here *always* does what he's told," she says, gracing Richard with a not so motherly loving look. "He's my *best* Breeder. Give Mama a kiss, now Billy."

I watch in disgusted horror as Richard leans down and kisses Violet in a drawn out passionate display that speaks of something much more sinister and dirty than a mother-son relationship. I choke on the bile in the back of my throat. Oh my fucking God – gross. They return their attention to me after their not so maternal display of affection. I'm trying not to vomit.

"You've been quite the bad little girl, young lady." Violet says in her saccharine fake voice. "*Daddy* here, is going to get you all cleaned up and ready for the customer," suddenly her voice takes on that hard edge I remember from a few years ago, "and *you* aren't going to cause *any more trouble.*"

A whirlwind of images pass before my eyes, Officer Richard standing over me in our apartment after my mother's suicide attempt. Then the creepy way he questioned me at the hospital and the argument with Violet outside the conference room, running into him all over Portland with Sean after starting college, even in the dorm halls at strange hours of the night. Of its own volition, my memory rewinds through childhood and a barrage of images collide before my eyes. I'm a little girl of four or five in the grocery store with my mother. I'm sitting in the cart and an Officer confronts her on the way out of the store. He towers over us. He steps in close, grabbing her wrist and whispers something to her while watching me with those ice blue eyes. She pales and pulls away, rushing me past him and to the car while he smiles at me and waves. Another memory of us playing in a park not far from our apartment not a year later, a police car circles the block and parks alongside where I play. Mom notices and scoops me up, running for home with me on her hip. He laughs as we run away. Then another of us taking a walk when I'm maybe ten years old, the police car pacing us, the officer with the cold blue eyes offers us a ride. Mom tells him no and urges me on faster, I'm crying to slow down, my sides hurt, I don't understand. There are more; many more, so many that they blur together before my eyes, my subconscious *screaming* at me that this man has *always* been there, terrorizing us. I think of the flowers that were on the table the day I found mama in the tub, and remember seeing similar ones in the trash previous years. I realized Officer Richard sent them. Violet's words echo through my mind, '*Little Billy always does what he's told – he's my best breeder.*' Oh my God, it's all true, and *she* put him up to it.'

"You *fucking bitch*!" I scream, and stepping forward, give in to the long-standing urge to plant my fist squarely in Violet Skazony's ugly rodent like little face. She falls back into her chair with a soft 'oomph' and before I can do or say anything else Richard is dragging me back towards the Master suite where I first awoke in this fucking house of horrors. Violet stares at me with contempt as he drags me down the hall, wiping blood from her broken nose and bloodied lip, and I'm satisfied that at least I got to show her how I *really* feel.

Richard locks us in the master suite with a key, which he pockets, then drags me to the bathroom. With my arm still firmly gripped in his mammoth hand he turns on the shower, adjusting the temperature to his satisfaction before letting go of me, closing the bathroom door and standing in front of it.

"Get undressed," he orders coldly.

"Fuck you, pervert," I spit, "I'm not fucking stripping for you."

My knees buckle as a hard slap lands across my already bruised and broken face. I feel fresh blood trickle down my chin where my lip has split back open as I slump against the toilet on the cold tile floor. Richards's mammoth hand extends toward me and I automatically wince away, expecting another striking blow to my throbbing face. He grimaces at me and grabs my hand, pulling me to my feet.

"I'm not going to punish you again unless you deserve it." He says, almost kindly, "I'm your Father, and as such I expect you to do as you are told and speak to me with respect."

He's totally loony tunes is what he is. I can't help it; I just stare at him dumbfounded. I don't know what he thinks a 'father – daughter' relationship is supposed to be like, but I'm sure as hell certain nothing on *his* agenda comes close to the kind of nurturing relationship that occurs in a *normal* household. His eyes turn cold again as they range my body. I shiver at the calculating appraisal he gives me.

"Now," his voice is a menacing whisper, "are you going to remove your clothing so I can bath you or do you need me to do it for you?"

"I'll do it," I say, eyes on the floor, "and I can bath myself."

I feel his breath on my neck and look up to find him standing over me, eyes half closed, as he leans in to inhale my scent. I *have* to smell like blood, it's covering me from standing so close to Sheriff Troy when he shot him. The look on Richards face is a combination of pure malice and utter bliss. I involuntarily try to step backward and land hard on the closed toilet seat directly behind me. He opens his eyes and straightens abruptly.

"Well get to it – and be quick, we don't have all night." He moves back over in front of the door and crosses his arms, watching me.

It's apparent he has no intention of leaving. I freeze. "Aren't you going to go check on Violet? I'll be quick, I promise. Just give me 15 minutes and I'll be done."

"Mother Vi told me to get you cleaned up, and that's what I intend to do." He says with a leer, "you have ten seconds to get out of those clothes and under the shower before I do it for you."

Hands trembling, I fight to get my boots unfastened, yanking them off my feet the second they are loosened enough to do so, and then remove the rest of my clothing before he can step in and *assist* me. When I start to pull the frosted glass shower door closed he's there, hand on the door, stopping me.

"Leave it open," he orders, "and don't skimp with the soap; make sure you clean *everywhere.*"

Tears of shame burn tracks down my cheeks as I follow his directions under the steaming water. There are brand new containers of scented shower gel, shampoo, and conditioner lined up along one of the tiled shelves of the shower; and he instructs me to use these as if I've never done it before. I try to rush through washing the grime and blood off my body, but he won't allow it. Throughout the twisted torturous show, he spouts directions like, 'use slower, circular motions there', and '*bend* down to wash your legs, don't squat like an ape'. He makes me wash my hair *three* times; screaming that I'm not doing it right, making me face him while I'm doing it. Finally, he deems me appropriately 'cleansed' and reaches past me to shut off the water; I jump sideways as his hand brushes against my hip.

"Don't do that," he says, angrily grabbing my arm and yanking me back, "don't *ever* do that."

I stand statue still, eyes clinched shut, as he dries me off like a baby. I try to take the towel so that I can do it, hoping to save myself this one humiliation, but he yanks it back, wrenching my shoulder painfully in the process. I let go and give in; something in his eyes tells me I'll suffer a much worse fate if I continue to defy him. This bastard that claims to be my father lost any semblance of sanity a long time ago. I feel him gently take my hand and I open my eyes, a flood of tears I've held back escapes to flow down my cheeks unhindered. He smirks and leads me into the adjoining bedroom. I snatch the discarded towel off the toilet on the way out and hold it in front of me like a shield, trying to cover my naked body. He either doesn't notice or doesn't care. In front of the dresser he lets go of me, I quickly wrap the towel around me while he digs in the top drawer; lingerie, I remember. He throws a lacy white teddy with garters and sheer ivory thigh-highs on the end of the bed before going to the closet and rifling through the dresses. The one he pulls out of the closet is breathtakingly beautiful. Layers upon layers of white gossamer silk and gauze make up the skirt, cascading down at different lengths, tapering from just above where the knee would be in the front to below floor length in the back, in a feathered effect. The waist of the dress is white silk, and looks like it would hug the body. The bodice is silk also, and covers only the front, with a deep V, tying around the neck. The dress is backless. I take a closer look at the teddy on the end of the bed and realize it's a backless, strapless bustier. After carefully laying out the dress on the bed next to the lingerie, he goes to the other side and pulls a drawer out from below it I didn't even know was there. He removes a pair of open toed three-inch heeled sandals that match the dress perfectly. Great, I'm going to break my neck in those.

"There are cosmetics and stuff to do your hair with under the bathroom sink." Richard says, studying me disdainfully. "Cover up those bruises as best you can and get dressed."

I watch as he walks back into the bathroom, gathers my discarded clothing, and lets himself out of the room, locking it behind him. He left my boots. It's funny how they keep doing that. I'm totally tempted to put on the dress with my gothic boots instead of the high-heeled sandals. For the time being, I go to survey the offerings under the bathroom sink while I contemplate the subtle ways I can defy my supposed *father*. Everything is neat little plastic tubs with clip on lids. There must be twenty of them in varying sizes housing just about every kind of cosmetic and hair accessory a girl my age could imagine and then some. One tub is entirely full of hairbrushes. There is an assortment of styling brushes as well as brushes for every hair type. I pick one that comes as close to what I have at home as possible, and attack my hair. It's when I'm digging through the bin containing various types of hair clips, barrettes, and other accessories that it occurs to me that I just purchased all my own stuff and still have it in my brand new backpack. I know I had it with me when we got here, I just can't remember if I still had it when he dragged me back into the bedroom. My boots, still splattered with blood and encrusted with dried mud are slouched against the bathroom wall behind me under the towel rack. The leather jacket I had been wearing is on the floor between the toilet and the sink, almost completely out of sight. I seriously *doubt* he left *that* intentionally. I don't see my backpack. Walking out of the bathroom, I survey the attached bedroom to no avail. I must have dropped it in the living room or outside somewhere. That means I'm stuck with the fucking dresses, even if I *can* get out of this damn room again. Disheartened, I go back to the bathroom and start in on the makeup. At least the stuff they have here is high quality. It does a *much* better job of covering the damage to my beat up face than my cheap Wal-Mart cosmetics. I debate trying to cover all the marks on the rest of my body and change my mind. Fuck them, I don't know why I would want to make myself look perfect for those perverts anyway, they can't have anything *good* in store for me.

The lingerie and dress fit me perfectly, which is suspicious to say the least, because I am *not* easy to fit. My proportions just don't fit into the standard sizes. It's as if they were tailor made just for me, which is just fucking creepy. By the time I've finished hair, makeup, and dressing, and am contemplating whether to put on the sandals or my boots, an hour or more has passed since Richard left me alone in the room. I'm thinking if I get another chance to run away, I sure as hell don't want to be wearing heels, so I go into the bathroom to get my boots. I'm cleaning the mud and blood off them in the sink when my hand slips and the soap goes flying. It ricochets off the shower door and lands behind the toilet, gross. I crouch down to retrieve it and see the leather jacket again; and that's when it hits me – *the cell phone!* There's a perfectly good cell phone in the hidden pocket of the leather jacket that Richard so obligingly left in my possession. After I drop the soap back in the sink and rinse my hands, I pick up the jacket. I'm about to delve into the hidden pocket and dig out the cell when I hear the distinct sound of the deadbolt unlocking in the bedroom; *fuck*. I stash the leather in the cabinet under the sink and pretend to mess with my hair in the mirror when Richard comes in. I see his gaze travel the length of me from head to toe before meeting mine in the mirror. I feel my skin crawl.

"I guess this will have to do." He says coolly, "Come out into the bedroom, the client is here. He's a very important man, so behave."

"The client," I ask fearfully.

"Of course," he smiles, "you didn't think all this was for *me* did you? *I* get the mothers; the progeny are for the clients. Now *MOVE.*" He demands.

I do as he says and walk slowly into the bedroom. There's a man standing just inside the door. On the creep factor scale of one to ten, he easily scores twelve and a half. The way his non-descript brown eyes slide over me instantly makes me feel dirty; gives me the urge to go shower again. I size him up while he molests me with his eyes, to keep my mind busy. He's only about three inches taller than I am, which would make him about five foot eight. In the sandals, I'd be the same height as him, my boots an inch taller. He has mouse brown hair and a matching mustache that badly needs to be trimmed. His face is dull and pock marked. His fingers, which he fidgets constantly, show signs that he chews his nails incessantly. He has a nervous tick in his right cheek just below his eye that jumps erratically. The eyes remind me of Violet Skazony's. They have that same, beady rodent – like quality to them. He *looks* scrawny in his brown pantsuit, white button down shirt, and blue tie, but I get the feeling he's a wiry fucker that would surprise anyone that started a fight with him. I decide I don't want to be alone with this man.

"Evin, this is Mr. Mitchell," Richard says, "you belong to him now. Do what he says."

"I don't belong to *anyone.*" I reply.

"Feisty little thing isn't she?" Mitchell says, eyeing me again. "I assume that has something to do with the damage she has sustained? The price will have to be renegotiated."

Richards reply was calm, but his jaw clinched and rage burned behind his eyes. "She made an attempt at escape earlier, caused some trouble with some of the staff. I assure you, she is under control now. You may renegotiate her price with Violet if you feel it is necessary, you know I do not set the prices."

Mitchell blanched. "Of course, I'm sure it will be fine."

The weight of their gaze is heavy on me for a few minutes and I get the distinct impression they are both making their own separate appraisals. After what seems an eternity, Richards's eyes rest briefly on my eyebrow and lip rings before glancing down at my feet. He grimaces in disapproval.

"Remove those piercings." He says coldly, "and put on the sandals I laid out for you."

"I –" I begin but Mitchell cuts me off.

"I rather like them," he says, "She may leave them in."

"Fine," Richard says angrily, "but put on the shoes."

"I was going to wear my boots," I say, motioning to them in the doorway of the bathroom. "I can't walk in heels like that."

"I *said* put on the sandals." Richard says; the threat in his eyes is clear.

"She may wear the boots," Mitchell says, "they go well with the piercings."

"Fine," Richard answers. The look he levels at me is smoldering with rage. "You're in charge."

"Yes," Mitchell says, "you'd best remember that."

I don't know what's going on between these two, but it's clear they don't like each other. There's some sort of major power play going on here, and I'm the unlucky pawn. It's obvious that Richard has to acquiesce to whatever Mitchell wants but that he detests him. I also get the distinct impression that Mitchell is afraid of Violet and Richard knows this. How anyone could *fear* that ugly little bitch totally eludes me, but it was definitely fear I saw. I hurry to grab my boots and lace them on while the two of them glare at each other. I honestly think that Mitchell said I could wear them just to spite Richard. I still think he's a creepy weasel, but that definitely scored him a couple of points in my book. I'm betting he didn't realize he was giving me a weapon when he said I could wear them though. When I've fastened my boots Mitchell extends his hand as if he's asking me to dance or something.

"Shall we?" He asks.

I look at him suspiciously from my perch on the edge of the bed. "Shall we what?" I ask.

"Dinner awaits us on the back patio." He says by way of explanation, his hand still outstretched.

Involuntarily my gaze moves to the bathroom. He notices my reluctance and frowns slightly.

"Forgetting something?" He asks suspiciously.

"N – No, it's just that I; can I use the restroom first?" I ask, keeping my gaze down, as if ashamed.

Mitchell drops his arm back to his side. "Go ahead," he says, and to Richard, "Please let Violet know we'll be along in a few minutes."

Richard fixes me with a look that says I'd better behave before leaving the room. I go into the bathroom and shut the door behind me. I haven't *seen* the back patio, but I've never heard of a patio that isn't outside. I can't ask for the jacket without giving away that I still have it, and the cell is still inside. I flip up the lid to the toilet noisily and sit down, just in case Mitchell is listening for it. I don't really need to go, but I press my fist into my bladder and make myself anyway. I have the sneaking suspicion Mitchell is right outside the door now. As quietly as I can, I open the cabinet under the sink while I'm still on the toilet and feel inside the jacket until I find the hidden pocket, pulling out the cell phone, then I close the cabinet door. I tuck the cell down inside my right boot next to my calf, then flush the toilet and wash my hands. I can hear Mitchell step away from the door just before I open it. Without a word, he extends his hand to me and I take it, playing along. I figure my best chance to escape again is to get out on that patio. Mitchell smiles at me, tucking my arm into his, and I suppress a shudder. In my boots, I'm a good inch taller than he is, but he doesn't even seem to notice as he escorts me down the hall, through the living and dining rooms, and out onto the giant back patio. My heart sinks the second we step through the wide double glass doors from the dining room. The patio is beautiful, paved in granite stones of varying colors, with large planters blooming with flowers placed all about. There are three levels to the outdoor entertaining area. The top tier contains several tables with chairs, two of which are set with white tablecloths and crystal dinnerware. Violet and Richard already occupy the first. I assume this means the other set table is for Mitchell and I. Candles light the small intimate tables. The second tier has a Koi pond; complete with waterfall, benches and beautiful landscaping, and the path about it is dotted periodically with romantic paper lanterns lending just the right amount of light. The bottom tier is the largest of the three, and contains an Olympic size swimming pool as well as a Jacuzzi large enough to seat at least ten people. A ten-foot high black steel, barred fence with spikes at the top encompasses the entire thing. I don't even see a gate. It appears the only way in or out of this patio is through the house. Unless you happen to have a cutting torch handy, which just wasn't on my list when I was at Wal-Mart last night.

Mitchell escorts me to the other table and pulls out a chair for me. I take the offered seat and he takes the one opposite. The next two hours are some of the strangest of my life. Wait staff serves us a seven-course dinner. I don't know when the staff that served it to us arrived, but it's clear they're here specifically to provide this service and know exactly what they are doing. The waiters are both men, one for each table, and dressed in tuxedos. Richard somehow found the time to change into a casual tan suit in the brief time between when he left Mitchell and me, and when we joined him and Violet on the patio. Violet wore a plum chiffon dress that matched her bad hair dye almost exactly. I think it made her look even rounder than she was, but I could hear Richard ply her with compliments and her sallow olive skin glowed with pleasure at his attentions. My inclination was to defy them by refusing to eat, but the scents wafting from the masterly prepared gourmet food reminded my insubordinate stomach that I hadn't eaten since yesterday, and hunger won out. I might as well take *something* good out of this experience. Our waiters presented each course individually. We'd be given time to eat, then it was whisked away to be replaced by the next dish. Following every other course is a 'palate cleanser' of lemon sorbet and a small glass of wine, which I was heavily encouraged to drink. By the time dinner was completed a couple of hours had passed, and my company was more than a little tipsy. I decided it was a good idea to *act* as if I were too. Wine has never really affected me that way, it takes something a lot stronger, but I didn't think it was wise to let them know that. I pretended to laugh at Mitchell's stupid jokes, and tried not to cringe too obviously when he scooted his chair next to mine and rubbed his hand along my thigh.

After the desert course was completed, Violet dismissed the servers and kitchen staff. I could hear the muffled noises of them packing up from the kitchen through the open doors before the distant sound of a vehicle starting and driving away met my ears. I felt myself deflate a little; that would have been a good way to get out, had the opportunity presented itself.

"How about some music," Mitchel says, "I feel like dancing."

His beady eyes travel over me and he squeezes my thigh. It's easy to imagine what he has in mind for later in the evening, and the longer I can forestall that, and possibly call for help or get away, the better.

"Dancing sounds good." I reply.

"Billy," Violet smiles wanly up at Richard, my skin crawls. "Why don't you set some music for us?"

Richard gets up and goes inside the dining room for a moment. I can see him open a cupboard door on the back wall. There's a stereo system hidden inside. He pushes a couple of buttons and classical music comes to life around us. I realize there are speakers placed strategically all around the patio. If it weren't for the fact this was a Goddamn house of horrors this would be a *nice* place. Mitchell scoots back in his chair, scraping it loudly along the granite, and stands up. He wobbles a little on his feet before steadying himself and extending a hand to me.

"Would you care to dance M'lady?" He asks.

I'm not sure if the 'M'lady' is because he's slightly drunk or he truly believes this is some sort of twisted date and it's his attempt at gallantry, but regardless, I don't get the opportunity to answer. Right after he asks there's a commotion coming from the front of the house. We all hear the front door slam shut and a man cussing loudly. The sound of something shattering echoes out to us, followed by a woman's scream, which cuts off half way. Mitchel freezes where he is, a panicked look on his face. Violet looks angry.

"Billy," she says tightly, "go investigate."

We all watch in unison through the windows as Richard disappears through the living room into the foyer. After a few minutes of silence he comes back followed by an older man carrying an unconscious brunette woman in his arms. There's a cut on his forehead and a developing bruise spreading across her temple. I'm guessing the shattering sound was her breaking something across his head before he knocked her out. I instantly feel an affinity for the unconscious woman, who looks to be in her mid to late twenties. When Violet sees who it is her expression changes to one of relief.

"Saul," she says in her saccharine voice, "I see you've retrieved our little problem. Just dump her in the bunkroom. Then come back out and join us for a drink. Billy, give Saul the key."

"As you wish, Vi," Saul says, taking the key Richard hands him and carrying the woman back into the house.

I stare at the entire proceedings slack jawed; it's as if they've forgotten I'm here. Either that or they just don't care. The entire exchange takes place as if it's just an everyday occurrence, a normal household conversation. Violet notices my expression; her eyes harden.

"Is something the matter sweetheart?" She asks me, still in that saccharine voice, but her eyes are hard as steel.

"I've told you," I say coldly, "I'm not your fucking sweetheart."

"Mitchel," she says, "control your property."

I don't even have time to react before he slaps me hard enough to send chair and me sprawling. I feel fresh blood on my chin. My fucking lip is *never* going to heal. I realize he's not nearly as drunk as I thought.

"Why don't we have our drink in the Jacuzzi," Violet suggests, cold eyes resting on me. "Wouldn't that be nice, *Sweetheart?*"

"I don't have a suit." I say, cowering in case she orders one of her cronies to hit me again.

Violet just laughs. "That's alright dear," she says, "You won't need one. Billy, grab the wine."

Mitchell leans down and helps me up just as Saul comes back out. He catches up with Violet as she makes her way toward the Jacuzzi and wraps one arm around her, squeezing her in a hug as they amble forward. I find myself once again wondering who the hell these people really are as Mitchell leads me towards the lower level of the patio after the others. It's become clear that Violet, my old caseworker, is in charge of whatever is going on here. By the various comments I've overheard and interactions I've witnessed I gather that Mitchell, as well as being a client is also a part of the overall scheme and higher in the power structure than Richard is, but clearly below Violet. Thanks to Violet and Richard's own instruction, I know Richard's role is something called a 'Breeder' and the implications there are pretty obvious and disturbing. He also has some sort of twisted incestuous mother – son relationship with Violet. I get the impression that is how she *makes* a 'Breeder'. I feel the bile rise in the back of my throat thinking about it. The newest puzzle is this Saul character. As I watch his interactions with Richard and Violet, it occurs to me that Richard isn't as threatened by Saul, as he is Mitchell. He seems to treat Violet more like a big sister than anything else.

As we approach the Jacuzzi Violet goes through a door into the house right next to it, and I realize as she pushes the door open it's a restroom. She comes out a few minutes later in an atrocious one-piece swimsuit.

"Is there a suit in there for me?" I ask Mitchell hopefully.

"You're wearing it." Richard says coldly.

"What?" I ask, honestly confused.

"Under the dress," he says, "take off the dress and the boots; you can wear the lingerie in."

"You've *got* to be kidding." I say.

Violet gives Mitchell a look and he roughly twirls me around to face him, raising his hand; I cower.

"Okay," I say, "I'll do it; you don't have to hit me again."

By this time, Richard and Saul have both stripped and gotten in the Jacuzzi with Violet. Richard has swim trunks on, but Saul just wears his boxers. They all but ignore me as I sit on the end of a nearby lounge chair to remove my boots. Mitchell starts to undress himself. I casually swivel sideways as I unfasten my boots one at a time and carefully tuck the laces inside. As I'm doing so, I power on the phone, silently urging it to hurry. While it's powering up I unlace the other boot and pull it off. I set it next to the right one and tuck the laces into the boot with the phone, quickly dialing 911 and hitting send before pushing the phone into the toe of the boot and covering it with the tongue.

"What's taking you so long?" Mitchell says irritably, making me jump.

"Sorry," I say, standing and reaching for the dress ties behind my neck. "My boots just take a long time to get off. Could you help me with this knot?"

He crosses the short distance between us quickly and unties the back of my dress, my delay quickly forgotten as he slides me out of the dress and escorts me toward the Jacuzzi. I can only hope what they say about response time being faster when a 911 caller doesn't say anything is true as I fight the urge to pull away from Mitchell and run for the phone.

19 WEDNESDAY APPROXIMATELY 9:15 PM
CADEN NEELY

I'm trying to get Krysta under control while Al is explaining how fragile she is right now, probably in hopes Sheriff Davis won't slap handcuffs on her for assaulting an officer, when the radio blares on her desk making us all jump.

"Dispatch to Sheriff Davis, copy?"

Krysta stops struggling and we all stare at the radio as if it were some foreign body.

"I told them I would be here late." Sheriff Davis says, still just looking at the radio.

"Dispatch to Sheriff Davis, copy?"

The second request blaring from the device seems to snap her out of it and the Sheriff picks up the radio handset.

"This is Sheriff Davis, go ahead."

"We've got a 911 call, no voice on the line, muffled background noise, mobile GPS places the caller at 67544 Cloverdale, and with everyone at the LaPine fires you're the only unit nearby. Can you take it? Over."

"That's the Skazony Estate, there's not supposed to be anyone there right now, probably just some kids messing around. I'll go check on it, over

211

and out."

"Did you just say 'Skazony Estate'?" Al asks the second Sheriff Davis hangs up the radio.

"Ya, why?" Sheriff Davis asks.

"We're coming with you," I say.

"As in Violet Skazony?" Krysta asks at the same time.

Sheriff Davis repeats her rubbernecking performance between us of a few minutes ago and then lets out a slow breath.

"What did I miss *this* time?"

"We're pretty sure Violet Skazony is in charge of this whole thing." Al says.

"Of *course* she is," Sheriff Davis says, strapping on her gun. "Let's go."

When we get outside Tony pulls up beside Al's cruiser and Davis instantly digs in her heals.

"Whoa – just because I acquiesced to you three coming along doesn't mean I'm bringing a bunch of bikers with me. This is a police matter, I'm not about to put my ass on the line."

"Do you have any other back up nearby?" Al asks.

"No, but –"

"Caden, how many dirty cops would you estimate were at that human trafficking auction of hers in Salem before the *leak* at the *FBI* warned them?" Al asks pointedly.

"I didn't actually take count, but at least fifteen that I saw."

"And," Al says, looking Sheriff Davis square in the eyes, "we know at least *one* of them is here, *and* your partner is already missing. *I* know and trust *these* men with my life. We don't know what's waiting for us at the Skazony place, but I'm betting it won't be pretty. How about we take what backup we can get? Wouldn't you agree, Sheriff Davis?"

"Fine," she gives, "but if the shit hits the fan, it's on your ass, not mine."

"I want Krysta to stay here. There's no telling what we're going to encounter and I don't want her in danger."

"Agreed," Says Sheriff Davis.

"I'm going with you." Argues Krysta. "Evin is probably there. There is no way in hell I'm staying behind."

"We don't have time to argue about this." Al points out.

"Fine, but you're riding with Al and you're staying in the car."

Krysta looks defiant, as if she wants to fight about it some more, but instead she stalks to the passenger side of Al's cruiser and gets in. I get the distinct impression I should be locking her in the Sheriff's office. Something tells me I'm going to regret allowing her to come along.

"Here," Al diverts my attention from Krysta by handing me his backup weapon, a slick .45. "You may need this. I'd rather you not use one of your illegal ones."

"Thanks," I tuck the piece into the back of my waistband under my jacket.

"Are any of the others armed?"

"Not that I know of."

"Okay, tell them to stay at the perimeter, just keep an eye on the exits and keep out of harm's way."

"You got it."

"Let's go get this bitch and find Evin."

We share a grim smile and part company, me to instruct Tony and get on my Harley and him for his cruiser. We all follow Sheriff Davis in her Deschutes County Sheriff's Department Blazer out of the parking lot. If there were any traffic to see us we would have been a strange sight, one Deschutes County Sheriff, one Washington County Sheriff, with lights and sirens, and two Harleys all screaming towards their destination together. Not the usual 911-call response team, that's for sure.

The ride to the Skazony place is a quick one, east out of Sisters on Highway 20, then left on Cloverdale and down another mile or so. What I would call a quick trip around the block on the Harley would have been a hell of a walk in the dark for a scared beat up teenage girl that didn't know where she was. The police report she filed indicated she had walked all the way to Sisters from this place before being unknowingly handed right back into the hands of her captors. My opinion of Evin raised a couple of more notches. She's one tough kid.

When we got a ways down the gravel part of Cloverdale Davis shut off her lights and sirens and Al followed suit. A short distance later, we all pulled over just shy of a long gravel drive and cut our engines. Sheriff Davis motioned us over and we congregated by her Blazer to await instruction.

"If you guys are right and Skazony and that Portland cop are in on this – "

"We are," Al says. She nods and continues.

"Well, then there are likely going to be guns in there. You said there were a lot of corrupt cops involved back in your area?"

"Correct," Al answers, "and we know there is at least one FBI leak because someone warned them before the raid on the human trafficking auction they had going."

"Does the FBI know you came here tonight?"

"No."

"Well, thank God for small blessings. So we really don't know how many armed suspects she has in there then. How many of you are armed?"

"Obviously I am," Al says, "and Caden has my back up weapon. Tony is unarmed but he can keep watch out here and make sure no one sneaks off, alert us if he needs to."

"Do you know *how* to use a weapon?" Sheriff Davis asks.

"Do I fu… - yes." Tony answers.

Sheriff Davis glares shortly at Tony before opening the back hatch of her Blazer and pulling out a shotgun and several hand radios. She hands the shotgun and a radio to Tony.

"Watch the exit from the driveway. Only use this if absolutely necessary. Consider yourself deputized for tonight. Radio us if you see anything, channel 4." She gives Caden and I each a radio. "You two are with me. We try the traditional knock on the front door first. If we don't get an answer, we'll figure a way in. You two stick together. Let's go."

I cast one look back over my shoulder at Krysta still sitting in Al's cruiser before following Davis and Al down the long gravel drive. She has a look of determination on her face I don't trust.

"Tony, keep her here and safe."

"You got it bro."

The gravel drive is dark and Juniper trees and bramble blanket the whole area. After a bit, the gravel gives way to a large paving stone circular drive. There are three cars parked along it. The most obtrusive of the three is the white Portland Police car, as we trot quietly up beside it, I can see a partially open backpack in the back seat.

"The girl had that with her when she came in to the station this morning." Davis points at the backpack, "And this is Officer Richard's Police Cruiser."

As a unit, we inspect the other two vehicles. One of them is a slick black Blazer not unlike Davis's, but without any of the standard police accoutrements and the plates are a different type.

Al indicates the blazer, "That's Federal; I think our FBI leak is here too."

"The black sedan has government plates too, do you think its Skazony's?" asks Davis.

"I doubt it. That's not what CPS vehicles look like."

"So we probably have at least two unidentified, and possibly armed, people inside." Davis looks worried at her summary.

"That's my assessment," Al agrees, "As well as Richard, Evin, and probably Violet Skazony."

"Right – let's do this."

I have to give the woman credit, I think as I follow the signal Al gives me and take my place to the left of the giant double door where I'll be just out of sight, considering all we've thrown at her in such a short amount of time, she's taking it rather stoically. Al takes up the position on the right side of the door and we wait for Davis to knock. They deem it best it *not* appear she suspects anything more than an accidental call. They don't want to scare them into firing first and asking questions later. We're hoping we can get through the locked front door first.

It amuses me that all cops knock the same way. The sound of Davis's abrupt pounding across the hardwood of the monumental door echoes out through the night eerily. There is just no mistaking the knock of a police officer. Her first attempt, however, yields no discernible result. We listen intently for a moment before she repeats the effort, this time adding her voice.

"Deschutes County Sheriff's Department, we received a 911 call, is everyone alright in there?" Her projected voice carries clearly out into the night. If we weren't in the middle of nowhere, neighbors would likely be coming to investigate curiously by now. However, there are no nearby neighbors, this 'Estate' as Davis had called it, apparently holds some 26 acres of property. It's comprised of juniper wood and wild, the mammoth house, a giant horse barn, pool, tennis courts, riding trails, and pastures. Davis's second round of knocking, while not getting an answer at the door, definitely yields results. The distinct sound of mixed voices raised in surprised cursing carries across the night air. Sounding just as we hear the voices from somewhere outside is the distinct scream of a woman from within the house.

"Help me – I'm in here!"

"That wasn't Evin's voice," I comment, meeting Al's eyes.

"They have someone else in there too." He replies.

"Well that's all the invitation *I* need." Davis says, "Let's break it down, boys – those other voices were coming from the pool deck, I'd wager, and it's fenced. We have to go in; on three?"

I'm not waiting for Davis to count to three. I don't know who else is in there, but they know we are coming and they have at least two hostages. It sounds like they're out back, the quicker we get in the better. I put my long experience of collecting for dealers into service and kick in the door. It takes two attempts instead of my usual one, it's a big fucking door, but the deadbolt finally gives and we're through. I hear Davis questioning Al behind me as we enter a rather large marble foyer, richly appointed and totally devoid of human activity.

"Where the hell did you find this guy?" She asks. "It would have taken three of my guys to break in that door."

"Pulled him over for a traffic violation ten years ago," Al says, "the rest you don't want to know."

Another scream cuts short the idle chatter, this time it's male and coming from the back. We hear the distinct sound of a door slamming somewhere off to our left and there are sounds of a struggle coming from both the back of the house and to our right. Davis motions that she'll go right and for us to continue towards the back. Guns drawn, we split off and continue forward into what appears to be a formal living room. The windows of the living room show a patio with several tables and chairs. The patio appears to continue down to a lower level but the angle of the house cuts off the view. Davis slowly proceeds down the hall to the right as Al and I move into a dining room to the left.

The sound of something crashing to the floor draws our attention to a doorway off the dining room. Al signals me to stay put as he goes to investigate. Slowly, Al shoulders open the swinging door and steps inside. I get a brief glimpse of an industrial sized kitchen before the door swings closed again. In a split second, the sounds of battle accost my ears from three distinct quarters of the enormous house. Al is struggling with someone in the kitchen, pans crash to the floor with resounding clangs as the fight apparently collides with some sort of pot rack. Davis's voice raises from the other end of the house in consternation intermingled with a man's as a door opens then closes with a slam, followed closely by a single gunshot and the distinct sound of someone hitting a wall. The same voice we heard from outside the front door adds hers to the struggle at Davis's end of the house. The voices and sounds of fighting that draw most of my attention, however, waft in through the open French doors of the dining room from the back patio. There are three distinct voices, one male and two female; and one of them is Evin's. Al and Davis are cops, they can handle themselves; I race through the dining room doors out onto the patio in search of Evin.

The place is designed like a fucking resort or something. Three huge terraced levels, much larger than you could begin to see through the windows from the living room, spread down and back from the house, fenced and landscaped in a manner that had to cost more money than I would ever see. It's the tableau on the bottom terrace, near a very large Jacuzzi, that draws my attention and stops me cold. I almost laugh. Evin is in nothing but some sort of white semi – opaque wedding style lingerie, complete with garters and stockings and she's soaked to the bone. This bit alone makes me want to kill whoever is responsible, but Evin seems to have things in this quarter under control. She's standing behind a short portly woman, also dripping wet and covered somewhat more modestly in an atrocious swimsuit. Evin has one arm wrapped tightly about the woman's throat, the other hand firmly clasping her own wrist, forming a perfect chokehold. The man, a wiry little weasel in nothing but boxers, stands facing them, hands outstretched in supplication, apparently trying to talk her down as the fat little woman in Evin's grasp curses orders at him. Evin is clearly the one in control of the situation.

"Shut up, you fucking bitch!" Evin says fiercely, tightening her arm on the woman's throat.

"Now, Evin My Dear, I'm sure we can come to some arrangement." The weasel says. "Why don't you let Violet go?"

"I'm *not* your fucking dear; *Mitchell*; you *and* Violet can both go to hell." Evin replies.

Their heated banter continues back and forth, as I quietly move forward toward them. So far, they haven't noticed me, so focused are they on each other. The Mitchell character, whom I can only assume to be the Assistant District Attorney Al has spoken of, seems too worried about the potential wrath of Violet to make any sudden moves. I've made it about half way across the middle terrace when a gunshot rings out in the night just behind me, followed abruptly by Al's distinctive '*Son of a Bitch!.*' I turn around just in time to see the tall figure of Officer Dick skirting the outside of the ten foot high fence at full speed, flashing in and out of sight as he runs through the wide spaced flood lights, followed closely by Al. I return my attention to Evin, but the disturbance has already changed the balance for her. Somehow, in the moment I turned my back Violet managed to get free of

Evin's grasp, probably due to Evin being startled by the gunfire. The radio hanging at my hip flares to life with Tony's questioning voice. I grab it and direct him to stay put as I move toward Evin. Even as I race forward, the portly little woman disappears through a door directly behind the Jacuzzi. Evin is fighting with Mitchell now; I mean *actually* fighting. I've never *seen* a girl spar like this before – woman or child. The two of them are facing off like boxers in a ring exchanging blows like professionals. As I come to a sliding stop just short of them, Evin lands a spinning kick square in the middle of Mitchell's chest, and he flies backward into the Jacuzzi with a giant splash, fucking beautiful. I aim my weapon at Mitchell as he sputters his way to the surface, finding his feet, and stands in the middle of the steaming tub. I smile at Evin.

"Nice work kid."

"Thanks, Caden, and I'm not a kid."

"Okay," I quickly scan the immediate area, "see anything we can restrain this punk with?"

"No, - wait, I have an idea." Then, with that wicked smile I'm coming to know as classic Evin, she unfastens the stockings from their garters and begins taking them off. They don't look like much, but when she hands them to me, I realize they're a lot tougher than they appear.

I test their strength. "These will do. Tie him to the fence?"

"The lounge chairs are bolted down." She walks towards one next to which sit the boots I bought her, dirtied and a little rougher for wear. She follows my gaze and smiles again. "They definitely came in handy. I was right, they did some damage." She laughs.

"Glad I could help."

"Are you going to make me stand here all night?" Mitchell whines from the Jacuzzi. Apparently having a gun pointed at his head isn't incentive enough to keep his mouth shut.

"Shut up," I motion with the gun. "Get out of the water, slowly."

"You know I'm an Assistant District Attorney, don't you?" He asks as he slowly makes his way out of the Jacuzzi to stand on the side, eyeing the gun like a snake. "I'm a very important man – Caden, is it? I'm sure we can come to some kind of agreement."

"*Shut up, punk.*" I point to the chair from which Evin has now removed her boots and discarded dress. She moves behind me and starts putting her clothes back on.

"She's a lovely girl, isn't she? Would you like to have her? It can be arranged – completely untraceable too." Mitchell says as he inches toward the chair.

That's all I can take. The idea of him offering up the girl I've begun to think of as a daughter as if she were a piece of meat is sickening at best. "I *said* shut up!" Stepping forward, I hit him across the left temple with the butt of the gun, knocking him out cold. He falls sideways across the end of the lounge. I quickly drag him the rest of the way onto it, using the stockings to bind his hands to the chair behind his back and his feet at the bottom. I turn to Evin, she's clothed, if somewhat scantily, in a white flowing dress more appropriate for some sort of formal affair than what we're facing, and of course, her knee high steel toed gothic boots. Somehow, it suits her.

"Ready?" She nods her reply. "Where's that lead?" I indicate the door through which I'd seen Violet escape.

"It's just a bathroom as far as I know, but I've only gotten a glance in the door, I haven't actually been inside."

"Alright, stay behind me. She's probably just cowering in a corner but we're pretty sure this whole fucking conspiracy is Skazony's brain child, so there's no telling what she's capable of."

"Conspiracy?"

"We'll explain later. First let's all get out of here alive."

"Who's we? Is mom here too?"

"That too," I roll my eyes, enough questions already. "C'mon, kid."

"I'm not a –"

"*Got it* – now c'mon."

I go through the door, gun at the ready, with Evin hot on my heels. It's definitely a bathroom. It's also huge, with stalls, multiple sinks, showers, etc. I slowly check the stalls and the showers – no Violet. Past the toilets and the showers is a short hallway. At the end of the hallway is two doors; the first opens into a sauna, the second lets us into what appears to be a combination office/library. It has double French doors leading outside – to the *un*-gated part of the property; fucking wonderful. Violet is nowhere in sight; neither are Al or Officer Dick. The enormous red horse barn to the right of the house is directly in front of us and there's a light on inside. The huge sliding door is wide open. I'm betting one or all of them are in there. It looks as though there are plenty of places to hide.

"Have you been inside that barn?"

"Unfortunately."

"What do you mean by that?"

"The van they kidnapped me with is in there with Charlie's rotting body inside, plus Alan's body, *and* that's where Officer Richard shot that other Sheriff – when he was standing right next to me, I might add. Splattered brains and blood all over me; it was fucking gross. Do we have to go in there?"

"You could wait for me here."

"*No* fucking way."

"You're just like your mother."

"I *so* am not."

I just laugh. "C'mon kid, and stay back."

She rolls her eyes at me and we head for the barn. We get halfway to the door and Tony comes barreling around the corner from the front of the house. I almost fucking shoot him.

"What the fuck, Tony? You're supposed to be guarding the exit and watching Krista."

"Krista got out of the car and snuck by us somehow during the confusion with the gunfire, I think I saw her run this way. Did you see her?" He pants, out of breath. "Is that her kid?"

"Holy shit, Tony, I give you one fucking job, and you screw it up. There are maniacs with guns running around out here. They've *killed* people. And yes, this is Evin."

"My mom doesn't know how to fight like I do," Evin says. "She shouldn't be here."

"Try telling *her* that." I reply.

"She can be stubborn." Evin admits, as if she's not exactly like her.

"Tony, take Evin back to the cruiser, and fucking *keep* her there. I'll find Krysta."

"I'm going with you to find my mom." Evin argues.

"No you're not. This whole fucking mess is about rescuing you, now GO!"

"*Fine.*"

I watch her stomp off with Tony, obviously pissed, but at least I'm sure she's safe. Hell, the kid's probably just as tough as Tony is. The radio at my hip blares to life again, and I jump nearly half out of my skin. I keep forgetting it's there. I'm not used to working with these things.

"Caden, where the fuck are you?"

"Al? I can barely understand you."

"Who the hell else would it be? Get your ass out to the barn. Richards out here somewhere hiding, I can't find him, and I'm sure I just saw Krysta run by one of the stalls. So far I've found two dead bodies."

"There are three bodies, and I'm on my way."

"What?"

"Three – never mind. The barn is huge, what's your location?"

"Turn left at the 'T' and go up the stairs at the end of the corridor, I followed Richard that way, and it's a fucking maze up here."

"Be right there."

As I jog into the barn, the first thing I see is the white van. The back doors are open and there's a body inside; has to be Charlie. There's another body slumped against a stall to the left of the van, judging by the attire I'm guessing it's the Alan guy Evin spoke of and not the Sheriff Officer Dick shot in front of her. I don't see the third body, but as I noted before, the barn is fucking huge it could be anywhere. I jog down the main isle of stalls from the entrance to the 'T' Al mentioned and turn left, continuing a few hundred feet more to where the stalls end and there's a flight of stairs to the second level. I take them two at a time. The banistered front half of the second level overlooks the front part of the lower level isle and stalls. There's a large open area at the top of the stairs crowded with crates, what appears to be bags of feed, and a number of stacks of hay. There are two large doors, currently bolted shut, on the wall to the right, apparently for loading purposes. With the exception of the large hayloft and a walkway along the front banister that runs from the stairs to just above the main entrance before it ends at a wall, the entire rest of the upper level appears to be comprised of smaller rooms and hallways. Al is waiting for me by the hay, peering apprehensively down the walkway. Some light filters up from the floods on the first level, but otherwise it's dark. I don't see a light switch.

"He got up here before me," Al says. "He seems to know this place pretty well. It's like a fucking maze and I can hardly see shit. I also saw Krysta run by downstairs as I was coming up. We have to take this fucker down before he realizes she's here."

"That's the last thing we need. I knew I should have made her stay behind."

"Well it's too late for that now, let's find this bastard."

Al and I begin a slow and methodical search of what seems to be nearly a dozen little rooms all interconnected by doors and small hallways. Some of them are empty, but miscellaneous crap fills most of them. Boxes entirely fill one room, there's barely space for us to squeeze through. The next appears to be a long disused art studio, with several artists' easels and a bunch of other art supplies. Another of the rooms is full of folding tables and chairs. There seems to be some organization to how the shit is stored in them, but they all have two things in common; they're thick with dust from long disuse, and so far no Officer Dick. The air up here is stale and putrid, making it difficult to breath, and there is very little light. Bits of moonlight filter into a few of them from skylights, which I find a little strange. Who the fuck puts skylights in a barn?

We've worked through what I figure to be about three quarters of the way towards the other end, when we hear a woman's scream. I know immediately its Krysta. It sounds like it's coming from a little ways ahead of where we are. Al is in front of me, and the room we're currently in is full to the brim with antique furniture stacked in no particular order, we have to go through single file, sometimes shoving things out of the way to get around them. He makes it out before I do, and I can hear his feet pounding on the wooden floor away from me. This one must exit into a hall instead of another room like so many of the others. Finally, I make my way out. It lands me in hallway that runs almost to the other end of the barn before cutting to the left. There are only a couple of doors on either side; these are open with the exception of the last on the right. I see Al take the corner at some speed and take off after him, glancing into the open doorways as I run past; these rooms are mostly empty, except for some cots and maybe a chamber pot. I don't have time for a proper inspection, but the first impression makes my skin crawl. As I near the end of the hall, I hear low crying coming from closed room, but Al's voice just around the corner urges me on.

"It's over Richard," Al is saying as I inch around the corner. "Just let her go and put down the gun."

"You always were a cocky little shit." Officer Dick replies. "I'm always telling Saul he should have taken care of you that night we did your mom, but he insisted it was better if you just looked crazy."

I don't have time to contemplate what Officer Dick is talking about, but it's obvious it pisses Al off; at his last statement, Al's grip on his service weapon tightens and he levels it at Officer Dick's head. Dick has Krysta pulled snug against him by her throat, a revolver pressed against her temple. They're precariously perched at the landing of another set of stairs to the first level, and he could either shove her toward Al, and safety, or just as easily send her plummeting down those very steep stairs. On the other hand, shoot her and run. There is absolutely no way I can circle back and come up this set of stairs from behind him before this plays out, and with at least two more of these assholes unaccounted for I don't dare call in Tony. Officer Dick hasn't noticed me yet, so I quietly inch back around the corner and backtrack far enough to use the radio.

"Sheriff Davis are you there?"

I wait for about thirty grueling seconds with no response before I try again.

"Caden to Sheriff Davis; what's your status?"

I wait for a reply as long as I can, which is maybe another thirty or forty five seconds before I decide she has to be out of commission or unable to respond, and then head back to Al.

"He's fucking dead," Al is saying. "He's been missing for over 15 years."

"Missing," Dick taunts. "I don't think so. I'm afraid you've been misinformed. Poor little lost boy; do you miss your father?"

"He was my *Step* father," Al is clearly shaken, "and he *was* an abusive murdering son of a bitch. In fact, you always reminded me a lot of him. "

The scenario hasn't changed much. Krysta sees me come around the corner and meets my eyes. There are tears running down her face as she mouths to me her daughter's name. I nod to her, letting her know Evin is ok, and she relaxes some. Whatever the hell is going on between Al and Officer Dick takes some of Dick's focus off her and he's let his revolver start to sag away. With each new taunt, he throws Al's way, the more he lets his gun arm fall and his grip loosen on her throat. I'd *love* to ask Al what the fuck they're talking about, but now is most definitely not the time. Al is a great strategist, and I'm sure he's egging Dick on to *get* him to take his focus off Krysta. Whatever they're talking about is clearly deeply disturbing to Al as well. I can see his cool exterior starting to crack.

"Still so young and disrespectful," Dick says, waving his gun in emphasis. "Didn't you learn anythi –?"

As soon as Officer Dick waves his gun away from Krysta, she acts, bringing her elbow back hard into his gut and her heel down on his shin. He releases her more out of surprise, I think, than hurt, although his sentence cuts off with a grunt as Krysta ducks out of the way. Al fires his weapon, but the strange conversation has clearly affected him more than I'd realized; his shot misses. Before Officer Dick has a chance to recover, I fire. The bullet hit's Officer Dick in the center of the forehead and he goes down hard, instantly dead. Krysta is in my arms before I can blink. I'm torn between yelling at her for not minding me and telling her how much she *really* means to me. I settle for a fierce kiss before clasping her hand firmly and locking eyes.

"Don't *ever* do that again."

She swallows her tears and nods. I doubt getting her to listen to me will *ever* be that easy, but she just had a major scare, so maybe; but again, I doubt it.

"What were you thinking coming in here anyway?"

"I was looking for Evin," she's defiant, despite the scare. "What do you think?"

"You were supposed to stay in Al's police car and let *us* find Evin. Anyway, why would you think she was in the barn?"

"I thought I saw people in here, and then I heard a girl scream. From up here somewhere and I thought it was Evin, so I came looking for her. Then Richard grabbed me, Al came around the corner, and well – you know the rest. So, is she in one of those rooms back there? She's safe? Take me to her."

"Yes, she's safe, but she's not up here, she's back at the cruiser with Tony where you *should* be."

"Then who did I hear scream?"

"That's a good question." Al says, "And one I'm pretty sure I know the answer to. Someone was yelling in that last room as I ran past it, but I heard Richard's voice around the corner so I kept going because I knew he had Krysta."

"I heard crying coming from there when I went past. You think they have more kids locked up in there?"

"Oh God," Krysta says, "not more kids."

"What I think," Al pauses as he digs around Officer Dick's body for a minute and then comes back with a ring of keys, "Is that it's DA Berghauer's kids, although they're technically adults, locked in that room and that one of these keys will open the door. I think Richard was hoping to kill them before we got to him."

The three of us backtrack to the room together. It takes a few minutes to find the right key; there are a lot on the ring. We probably could have broken in the door, but Al insists we try the keys first. Finally, one of the keys turn in the lock and the door opens. The smell hits me in the face like a ton of shit and nearly knocks me on my ass. The room is windowless, save for a skylight above that doesn't appear to open so there is no airflow. I have no idea how long they have been in here with nothing but a bucket for toilet facilities, but the fumes are thick enough to choke a rhinoceros. There are two metal army style cots bolted to the floor on either side of the room and each of them has a kid in their late teens to early twenties chained to it by an iron cuff attached at the ankle. It's fucking medieval. The makeshift toilet sits against the wall between them. There is no privacy. There's a pile of garbage comprised of empty water bottles and various wrappers to one side of the room. The kids attempted to keep their prison tidy. At the end of each bed are obviously dwindling supplies of bottled water and more cereal bars. Their captors didn't give them a lot of variety. They weren't exactly left to die, but they weren't cared for either, just left in limbo to rot slowly alongside the rest of the treasures stored away up here, lost and forgotten like yesterday's memories. While Al checks them out and makes sure they aren't seriously injured or in need of emergency medical attention, I watch, and see reflected in the faces of the young and abused the countless victims of the people that I went to work for in my 'off' hours. What Al calls my 'extra-curricular activities', and decide that I don't like what I see. These two college kids, all the kids at that auction, and Evin, *especially* Evin – they suddenly all feel like *my* responsibility; and I know it's time to make a change. I can no longer be the hand that collects from, and breaks the downtrodden on the behalf of the dealers, the bookies, and worse. I have to *do* something. More than occasionally helping the random kid get back home instead of taking that next fix. I have to take the fight to the people that have been calling for my services.

I watch as Krysta helps Al comfort the girl while he gets the cuff off her brother's ankle and realize I also want more for myself. I want a family. I want *this* family, Krysta and Evin; I want to make them mine. If only they will have me. She feels me watching her as she helps the girl toward the door, Al and the slightly older boy following her, and she smiles; even amidst all this horror, she smiles. We slowly escort the two back out to where we left our vehicles. Once Al's cruiser is in view, I tell Krysta to go on ahead to Tony and Evin with the kids, and I pull Al aside for a minute.

"What the fuck was that about back there with you and Officer Dick?

I've *never* seen you miss a target, *especially* at close range."

"It's a long story, Caden," he says, obviously more shaken then he's letting on. "But I've been after Richard for a very long time. Even longer than I've known you."

"Did you know he was involved in something like this?" I'm suddenly angry as well as worried about my friend.

"No –," he stops and scrubs at his face. He looks like he's aged years in the last hour. When he looks at me again, his eyes are haunted, torn. "Look, it's not something I like to talk about, ok? Can we just drop it?"

Normally I would agree to such a request, but whatever the fuck is eating him could've gotten one or more of us killed back there, and we're not done yet. I can't back down.

"Not this time, Al, I need to know you're gonna have my back when we go in there, and right now I'm not so sure. So what the fuck is going on? What aren't you telling me?"

"They killed my mother, ok?" Rage is vivid in Al's eyes, his hands fisting. "That bastard Richard and my step father; I came home from school to them raping her. My step dad beat me unconscious, when I woke up blood covered her bed, and she was gone. They never found her body – didn't even look. They shipped me off to a boy's home. My step dad dropped off the map about 15 years ago. I've spent my career trying to prove it – to take Richard down. It's *why* I became a cop. He was trying to say that my bastard stepfather is alive. He was fucking with me. He was a lying bastard – it's impossible, I've looked everywhere for him."

"Jesus fucking Christ, Al. I'm sorry I had no idea. No wonder you were so hot on this case. You could have told me sooner though. Maybe you should stay here while I go back to find Davis and hunt down the rest of these fuckers. I can take Tony with me."

"NO."

"Al," I temporize. "It's ok –"

"I said *NO!*" He nearly shouts it. "I've waited too fucking long. It's clear they were involved in this thing from the beginning. I'm going to see it through. I'm the fucking cop here, not you, and I'm going back in there. I owe it to my mother."

I study him in silence for a minute. Tony, Krysta, and the others gathered by the cruiser a short distance away, and they watch us curiously but keep their distance. I debate locking Al in his own cop car using his cuffs to keep him there, but decide he would never forgive me. Besides, he's more than earned a little revenge. I may live to regret my decision, but knowing the truth, I can't keep him from going back in there after the rest of these assholes, shaken or not.

"Alright then," I clasp him on the shoulder. "Let's brief Tony and get back in there."

"Thanks man. For a minute there I thought you might cuff me in my own car or something just to keep me safe."

I just laugh. The motherfucker knows me too Goddamn well. When we get to the cruiser, everyone is around Evin and Krysta, offering congratulations and commenting on what a badass the kid is. *I've* seen her fight, but the conversation makes it sound more as if they saw something than just listen to a story, so I'm more than a little curious as to what they're referring.

"What the fuck is going on over here?" I demand as Al and I join the group.

"Nothing much," Tony pipes up with a grin. "Your girl Evin, here, just took down the ring leader all on her own when she tried to sneak into that blazer in the driveway and make her escape. Kicked her ass real good too; it was sweet as fuck."

"Skazony?" I ask.

"Ya," Evin says, "that fucking bitch had me kidnapped then *sold*. I saw her trying to sneak to the SUV in the front drive on our way back out here. I wasn't about to let that bitch get away twice."

"We heard the commotion and went running," Dean says, "and there's a real cat fight going on when we get there. Only Evin here fights like a *man!*"

"Fat little cunt didn't stand a chance," Jimmy says. "Not against Evin, here."

"Alright, I get the picture. Where is she?"

"Hogtied with duct tape and locked in the back of the other Sheriff's blazer." Tony says.

"Duct tape?" I laugh, that had to be Evin too.

"I found my backpack." Evin confirms smugly. "It's what I had."

"Okay, well that's one more bad guy down. Al and I are going back in to find Davis, any other kids or hostages, and track down anyone else that's hiding inside. Stay here. Tony, keep that radio handy, we'll holler if we need you."

"That kid of Krysta's is really something." Al says as we trot back up the gravel drive. "You're going to have your hands full with those two."

"I know; if they'll have me."

"They'll have you. I've seen the way Krysta looks at you. And it's clear that kid worships you."

"She barely knows me."

"Like knows like," he smiles. "You both have big hearts and tough shells."

I just grunt. What else can I say? By this point, we're back to the house and conversation drops as we automatically ready our weapons and synchronize our movements. The house is silent as we make our way through the main living areas just to make sure no one has backtracked into them in our absence. Mitchell is still out cold on the back deck when we check on him. We return to the house, make our way through the dining and living rooms, and down the hallway Davis took when we first arrived earlier this evening. The first door on the right has obviously sustained damage in a struggle, its sagging on its hinges and the latch is broken. Al signals me to stop as he carefully prods the door open, gun at the ready. It's only a couple seconds before he motions me silently forward and I follow him slowly into the room. There's a small hall-like entrance from the door, with a wall on one side and closet on the other before it opens up into the main part of the bedroom.

"Shit," Al swears from ahead of me.

"What is it?"

I hurry the last two strides into the main room. On the wall immediately to the left, around the corner from the doorway are a set of heavy wood bunk beds. Heavy bolts hold them fast to the wall. Davis is slumped against the bottom bunk out cold. Handcuffs restrain her to one of the posts that run between the top and bottom bunks and blood runs down the side of her head and neck. It doesn't look like a bullet wound. Al leans down and checks her pulse.

"Strong pulse, she's alive."

"That's good." I survey the damage to the room.

"Why didn't she radio for help?"

"Either she didn't get the chance," I point to her shattered radio on the other side of the room. The wall looks like something large impacted it – like a body. "Or that happened first, or both."

"It looks like she got a shot off." Al says, examining a bullet hole in the adjacent wall to where her radio lay in pieces.

"Or her assailant did."

"Same caliper as standard police issue," Al points out.

"How does that prove it's hers?" I smirk.

"Good point." He unlocks the handcuffs on Davis and then heads out of the room; I follow.

The next two bedrooms we check are empty, though clearly set up to contain multiple kids, and not in a friendly sort of way. There are double-sided deadbolts on all the doors; clearly, they locked the kids *in* the rooms. One of them even has several cribs in it. I don't usually hit women, but it makes me want to go out and smack that fucking cunt Skazony a couple of times – or maybe let Evin at her again. By the time we get to the end of the hall I'm steaming mad. There are only two more doors. The one on the left is the library; it's open and clearly empty. The one on the right is locked. There are voices inside, one male, one female, and the woman is crying. It's obvious from the man's muffled words and her tearful cries that there's a struggle going on and she's trying to fight him off. I mouth to Al that I'm going to break it down. He nods and stands to the side with his gun ready. I kick the door in and Al is through in a heartbeat. I'm only a second behind him. I've never seen the man in the room before, but clearly, he and Al know one another. Al's gun shakes in his hands, which he dropped in surprise. He looks like he's seen a ghost. The man before us wears only boxers; he has a roughed up, dark haired woman held in front of him by the throat and a gun pointed back at Al. He and the girl are kneeling on the severely messed bed, which has splotches of blood on it from the woman's battered face. She's in only a bra and panties, and the bra is torn.

"Well, if it isn't my long lost delinquent step brat." Intones the man mockingly.

Al shakily raises his gun back up to point at him. "You're dead."

"Now, now, that isn't any way to greet your father is it?"

"You're not my fucking father."

"Semantics, now why don't you and your little friend just turn around and walk away? You're in way over your head."

"You aren't a cop anymore you son of a bitch, you've been MIA for 15 years."

"Oh, I wasn't missing," he sneers, "just under cover; for the FBI as a matter of fact. It's come in rather useful too. So much more power than a lowly cop does. Heading up big investigations, coordinating raids; such fun, and rife with opportunity too."

I see understanding dawn on Al's face about the same time I make the connection. This man, Al's *missing* stepfather, is the FBI leak, a man that's been scum from day one. The girl in the man's grasp whimpers. He tightens his grip about her throat, choking her and cutting off her cry.

"Angel —" Al steps forward, concern on his face.

"Oh, so you know this young lady?" He loosens the grip on her throat so she can breathe, and caresses the side of her face with the Glock 22 he holds in his right hand. "Care about her even." He leans in and nibbles, not so lightly, on her neck. She suppresses a sob.

"Leave her alone!"

I'm at a loss. Anything I do is going to endanger Angel, and Al obviously cares about her. Having him in here is a mistake I shouldn't have given in. There's a long history between these two, creating a dynamic that has successfully landed us in a stalemate. All I can do is stand there; gun ready, and wait for an opening. I hate waiting.

"Uh, uh," the man points the barrel of the gun at Angel's temple; Al stops cold. "Don't do anything rash, now *son*, you wouldn't want to cause *another* untimely demise would you?"

"*You* killed my mother; you fucking son of a bitch, after you and that bastard Richard raped her."

"Is that how it happened? So many women, who can keep track?" He sneers at Al, who bristles at his words. "Where is Richard anyway? He should be around here somewhere."

This time Al grins. "He's in the barn, with a bullet in his brain."

The man's face blanches then hardens. He tightens his grip on Angel's throat again. "Haven't I told you not to lie to an Officer, son?"

"Oh I'm not lying, you bastard, he's dead as a doornail."

A look of pure rage consumes the man's face. He tosses angel sideways off the end of the bed, her head collides with the dresser and she hits the floor in a heap. Then he's off the bed, gun leveled at Al, but Al is gaping in horror at Angel's still form. I see my friend about to die at the hands of the same man that killed his mother.

"Hey!" I holler, drawing his attention away from Al and toward me. Al is still between us. "I'm the one that shot Officer *Dick*, not Al."

"Is that so?" He asks menacingly, and points his gun in my direction, Al momentarily forgotten. Al quickly crouches at Angel's side to check if she's ok.

"That's right; I planted a bullet in his forehead, right where it belonged."

"Unfortunate, he was like a son to me." He says, and then pulls the trigger.

My shot was only a fraction of a second behind his, but a fraction of a second is all it takes. I felt the bullet rip through me even as I saw mine hit him. Two for two, I got him in the head, fucking punk. My last thought before everything went black was that I should have cuffed Al to his car.

20 THURSDAY APPROXIMATELY NOON
AL TRUMAN

The FBI agent before me grimaced in disgust as I poured four more packets of sugar into my coffee; these made 20. The coffee at this hospital was worse than the tar that Caden made. I picked up the swizzle stick and stirred absently, long immune to stranger's reactions to how I drink the stuff. Agent Malone was used to crappy coffee; he was drinking it black. We sat at a small table in the corner of the Cascades Café at St. Charles Hospital in Bend, Oregon. The other patrons of the Hospital Café gave us a wide birth. Apparently, an FBI agent and an out of town Sheriff sitting together around here made people nervous. Hell, it would probably make people nervous anywhere not a cop hang out. He wasn't wearing an FBI jacket or anything, but he might as well have been. He wore his position on his sleeve like a badge.

Malone's partner, Breckridge, was currently down in Caden's recovery room waiting for him to come out of Anesthesia for questioning. They'd already grilled the rest of us. It'd been a long fucking night. He kicked me out of the room and Malone volunteered to keep me company, although he didn't seem happy about it. I don't think he trusted me yet. After everything else, I think they were waiting for Caden to confirm my story before they agreed to what I was asking. They honestly seemed interested and impressed with Caden, (*if* what I told them was true), but I don't think they understood how a Sheriff of more than ten years could be shaken so badly that a civilian had to save his ass. Maybe I was transposing my own demons on them. Who the fuck knows. You have to pry information out of these people with a fucking crowbar. Still, pending a positive outcome of the remainder of their questioning, they assured me that what I was asking was feasible; but there would be conditions. The conditions worried me. Of course, they wouldn't tell me what they were. Only that *after* they confirmed my story and got Caden's statement, would they pose the terms of the agreement to both of us. I continued to brood silently while Malone watched me like a hawk watches its prey. He was veteran FBI. He was around Caden's age, about six foot three, and built like a fucking wall. He made me feel like a damn toothpick. The slick black suit didn't help; it only made him that much more intimidating. I'm a Sheriff; I shouldn't *be* intimidated, but I am. It's shameful.

Krysta spent the remainder of the night and the morning in Evin's room. Doctors deemed that even though her bruises and abrasions *looked* bad, she only suffered minor injuries due to her ordeal. Still, the doctors insisted she spend one night for observation, just to make sure. I think this may have had something to do with Krysta threatening lawsuit if they didn't care for her properly. Evin was clearly irritated by her mother's antics but also obviously very happy to be back with her. The sniping comments between them were only halfhearted and seemed to be masking desperate relief. I made the mistake of chuckling at them – once. The resulting united front that raged quickly dissuaded me from ever doing it again. Immediately after, Malone attempted to tell the two of them they must separate for questioning. Needless to say, that didn't happen, and he looked positively relieved to get out of that room when he was done. I think they terrified him.

Davis suffered a minor concussion and had to have thirteen stitches in the side of her head. She was not pleased when they shaved a four-inch swath above her left ear to do so. She made them shave off the rest just so it was even. Then she checked herself out against doctors' orders. They *wanted* to keep her for observation. She told them to go to hell, and then convinced Breckridge to ask his questions while he drove her back to her office in Sisters. It was apparent he was impressed with her when he got back. Even though she was out of action for most of the events of the evening. "That's one tough little cop," he told Malone upon his return. She had awoken soon after Caden and I had broken into the master suite where Saul was holding Angel. Despite the damage to her head, she'd gotten back to her vehicle and called for backup. Three ambulances arrived within fifteen minutes after Caden's shooting. Followed closely by the FBI, whom Deschutes County called in after she apprised them of the situation. It seems they were already watching Skazony's little 'Estate' so they responded quickly.

After interviewing DA Berghauer's kids, it was determined that he was telling the truth and they dropped the charges. He was supposed to be on his way out. Both of his kids were going to spend a couple of days in the hospital. They were severely undernourished, but they would be ok. ADA Mitchel and Violet Skazony would be going away for a very long time. They were both facing lists of charges long enough to make any lawyers eyes bulge. Since the FBI seized all assets for both of them, they would be taking advantage of those court appointed attorneys. Karmas a bitch.

Angel was shaken and somewhat battered but will be fine. All of her wounds were superficial. Although I'm sure she'll never talk to me again. She's decided I'm too dangerous. When I inquired if she was going to be all right, she told me in no uncertain terms to stay the fuck away from her. She answered Malone's questions quietly, but firmly, gave him her contact information, and then left the hospital via taxi. I have no idea if she planned to take a bus home or what but after her earlier comment I deemed it best not to offer a ride back to Portland. Besides, my car was still in Sisters.

Caden was another matter. Of all of us actively involved in the events that took place at the Skazony Estate last night, barring Saul and Richard, Caden was the most severely injured. I don't think he realized that he spoke aloud as he passed out, but he did. His comment of, "I should have cuffed Al to his car," before he hit the ground left me riddled with guilt during the longest fifteen minutes of my life while we awaited the ambulance. The ride to the hospital was somewhat of a daze but I vaguely remember yelling at the driver to hurry the fuck up. I should have made Caden wear a fucking vest. The bullet entered his upper left chest and tore right through him. He lost a lot of blood but we made it to the hospital on time, in large part thanks to Sheriff Davis. Caden was in surgery for six hours. They had to repair his lung and extensive tissue damage. The four broken ribs will have to heal on their own. They said he could go home in a week. He should be nearly back to normal in four months or so. The FBI says it will take at *least* that long to clean up this mess, so that's fine. Not that I expect Caden will sit on his ass and rest as he's should.

The last we heard there were the five bodies we reported, found where we left them, *and* cadaver dogs had located the shallow graves of at least seven more buried in the stalls of the barn. They wouldn't give me any info on age or sex of the victims but judging by what I already knew, it wasn't difficult to speculate. The FBI was bringing in more people, dogs, and equipment to search the rest of the vast property. The enormity of what we had cracked open was mind numbing.

I started to take another drink of my terrible coffee and realized it was empty. I tossed the cup toward a trashcan about ten feet from where we sat. It bounced off the lip and rolled along the floor. Malone glared at me. Sheepishly, I got up and retrieved the cup, placing it in the trash bin. His phone trilled at him. He flipped it open and listened without saying anything and then snapped it shut again. I looked at him curiously. He scooted back in his plastic chair and stood.

"We're up," he said.

"So Caden's awake, then?"

"Obviously."

"Is the deal on?"

"We'll talk about it downstairs."

"Well, is Breckridge satisfied?"

"Possibly."

"What the fuck is that supposed to mean?"

We were at the elevators. Malone stared at me in silent appraisal. I decided I was done kowtowing to these assholes. We fucking broke this case and they were treating us like suspects. I'm a fucking *Sheriff.* I've spent my career busting dirty cops; I was tired of the FBI treating me like one. He put a calming hand on my shoulder; I shook it off. He shrugged and stepped onto the elevator. Left no choice, I followed him. Malone pushed the button for the first floor and then turned to me.

"Relax, Truman, everything is fine."

It was the first time he'd actually addressed me by name. It was a simple statement, but his eyes showed a new respect that wasn't previously present. It was enough. I nodded. We continued the rest of the way to Caden's room in comfortable silence.

I'm not sure what I was expecting to find when we got to Caden's room, but I wasn't prepared. I should have been I'm a cop for Christ's sake; I've seen the results of gunshot wounds before. It's just that I've always rather seen Caden as indestructible. To see him so – reduced, is disconcerting. I braced myself against the frame of the door for a second while my mind tried to come to grips with what my eyes were telling it.

"I'm not fucking *dead*, Truman, don't stare at me like that." Caden growled hoarsely.

I laughed uneasily. "Sorry, man, you look like shit."

"I feel worse. Get in here. This asshole won't tell me anything else without you."

"Close the door behind you, please." Breckridge said.

I closed the door and took the remaining plastic chair next to Caden's recovery bed. Breckridge was sitting on the other empty patient bed in the room. Malone had pulled the other chair up next to the bed Breckridge sat on. The room smelled of alcohol and other disinfectants. It was cold. I never understood how someone could recover from surgery decently in such a cold, sterile environment. I've always hated hospitals. Probably because I spent so much time in them growing up. Malone met Breckridge's eyes and the two of them exchanged some sort of silent communication. Breckridge nodded.

"Once we were aware of the true scope of the situation surrounding the events last evening we had all of the related files from the Portland field office faxed over." Malone started.

Caden grunted, but otherwise kept silent. I knew what he was thinking. The FBI file on his criminal history the Portland office had put together during their investigations into the supposed black market ring involving the area precincts.

"These files, though not as informative as the statements taken from the multitude of witnesses, victims, and involved parties, were still detrimental in deciding the deal we have agreed to place before you."

"I'm not taking any fucking deal. You fucking punks had your heads up your ass. If it weren't for me and Al, here, you wouldn't know shit about any of this."

"Caden –"

"No, Al, this is bullshit and you know it."

"If you would just hear us out, Mr. Neely. I think –" Malone said.

"That's just it, you guys don't fucking think."

"*CADEN!*"

"WHAT?"

"The *fucking deal* is *my* idea. Now, would you shut the fuck up and listen?"

Caden sputtered for a few minutes. He was still fuming. If I had questioned he would make a full recovery before I didn't now. Six-hour surgery or no, he could still argue with the best of them. He was panting a little with the strain of yelling, and his voice was scratchy and hoarse, but he was still most definitely the Caden I knew. I couldn't help smiling. He noticed.

"What the fuck are you smiling about?"

"Five hours out of surgery and already back to your old ways."

"Fuck off, Al."

"May we continue?" Breckridge asked.

Caden grunted. Malone took that as the go ahead and got up to get something out of a file box placed at the end of the empty bed. He handed me a copy. He stood next to Caden but did not give him a copy yet, I think he was afraid he'd tear it up before reading it. I didn't blame him.

"What I've given to Sheriff Truman is his copy of a two part arrangement with the FBI. In order for it to be valid both Sheriff Truman and you, Mr. Neely, must sign and agree to it."

"I wasn't supposed to be part of it." I said.

"We determined, based on your history with Mr. Neely, it would be best." Breckridge said.

"According to this arrangement, you, Mr. Neely, would become a special advisor to the FBI, working undercover, as needed. You would retain your *legal* day job. You will maintain your underground contacts as necessary to complete your FBI duties but *will not* participate in any *unauthorized* illegal activities. Sheriff Truman, you would be leaving the Washington County Sheriff's department. You will become a full time field agent and will be Mr. Neely's handler. These two offers are not mutually exclusive. Neither offer is valid without the other being accepted."

"What if I decline?" Caden asks.

"We have, in the course of our investigations into your past, uncovered a number of unprosecuted crimes that you are guilty of. Some of them are federal." Breckridge states candidly.

"That's fucking blackmail."

"I've been saying you'd make a good cop, Caden. This gives you the best of both worlds."

"You fucking owe me, Al."

"May I take that to mean you will agree to this arrangement, Mr. Neely?" Breckridge asks.

"He agrees." I say.

Malone hesitantly hands Caden the pages he's holding. Caden yanks them free of his hand, cussing as the movement causes pain. Breckridge hands him a pen. I watch, half-dazed, half-amused as Caden signs his life over to the FBI; I can't believe I fucking pulled it off. I hadn't planned to be part of the deal, but hey, it's the FBI. Can't be worse than the Sheriff's office, right? Caden hands me the pen after he's done signing and I sign my papers then hand them to Breckridge. It's official.

"Now what?" I ask.

"You'll start your training while Mr. Neely is recovering, once he has returned home. You won't officially be able to begin until the Skazony investigation is complete, however." Breckridge says.

"I doubt I need to tell you this, Mr. Neely, but don't tell anyone." Malone says.

"What about family?" Caden asks.

"You don't have any."

"Ya, but I might. I'm seeing someone."

"Use your best judgment. Or better yet, use Mr. Truman's."

I laugh.

"Fuck you, Al."

"Gentlemen, we look forward to working with you in the future. Mr. Neely, speedy recovery."

Breckridge signals to Malone who picks up the file box and follows him out of Caden's room, leaving us alone. We sit in silent contemplation for a few minutes. Neither of us really knows what to say at this point.

"I should have —" Caden starts.

"I should have —" I say at the same time.

We both laugh. Caden's turns into a painful sounding wheeze. I pour him some water out of the salmon colored pitcher sitting on his bed table and hand it to him. While he sips it, I take the opportunity to voice both our thoughts.

"I know you should've cuffed me to my car. You said it right before you passed out last night. I should have made you wear a vest. I'm sorry I got you shot, Caden. I thought I fucking lost you for a while there. You were right, I wasn't in my right mind; and I never expected to see Saul alive."

"I understand, man, I wouldn't have let you leave me behind either. A vest might have been nice though. Not that I would've agreed to it at the time."

"That's why I didn't offer."

A knock at the open door interrupted our discussion. Krysta, looking haggard and worn rested her hands lightly on the handles of a wheelchair in which Evin sat. Evin looked defiant. Noticing my gaze, she spoke up.

"Mom wouldn't let me come visit unless I used the chair. Never mind the fact I took *three* of the bad guys down myself!"

"You need to rest. Mind if we come in?"

"Sure, how are you feeling, kid?" Caden asks.

Krysta pushes Evin up next to the bed so she's facing Caden and then takes the chair I abandon. I move to the other bed.

"I look a lot worse than I feel. How are you feeling? Are you gonna have to stay here long?"

"I'll be fine; a little sore. They say I can go home in a week. Back to work in a few months."

"So, after all this you probably don't want to see my mom anymore, huh?"

"Evin!" Krista says.

"What? It's a fair question."

"No, it's alright, I'll answer."

"See, mom?"

"I was actually hoping you; both of you, would be interested in becoming a more permanent part of my life."

"You mean like a family?"

"Yes, I mean like a family. What do you think?"

"I could live with that. What do *you* think mom?"

Krista had tears in her eyes. I noticed she had taken Caden's hand and held it tightly while she searched his face.

"On one condition." Krysta says.

"What's that?"

"All that ugly stuff from your past you were so worried about me knowing stops. Above the law from now on."

"That shouldn't be a problem." I say, laughing.

"And," Krysta continues, "no more gunshot wounds."

"That's two conditions." Caden says.

"Well, if we're going to be a family I want to keep you around."

"I'll do my best."

"Wait, I'm confused, so does this mean you are, or aren't gonna get married?" Evin asks.

"Are." Krysta and Caden both say.

"Yay!" Evin squeals, jumping out of her wheelchair and bouncing a violent hug off her mother and bounding toward Caden. He managed to maneuver the table between them before she could get to him.

"Surgery, remember? Be gentle."

Evin only pouted momentarily before nodding. Caden rolled the table out and held out his right arm. She hugged him softly, and then stood back.

"Are you going to tell them?" I ask.

"You think I should?" He countered.

"Obviously."

"Tell us what?" Krysta asks.

"As of this morning I am in the FBI, thanks to Al. Under cover special advisor."

"Upon full recovery of course. I'll be his handler."

"So no more maintenance?" Krysta says.

"He'll still keep his day job – as cover." I say.

"Cool." Evin says. "So, where will we live?"

21 ONE YEAR LATER – SATURDAY LATE AFTERNOON
KRYSTA MALLORY

Exhausted with the stress and excitement after a day packed to the minute with wedding related errands and meetings I pulled my new Dodge Charger onto the gravel drive to Caden's shop. I didn't get very far. About half way down the drive was an enormous flatbed tow truck. Its giant cab sat dormant as the driver assisted Caden in slowly rolling a motorless, if freshly painted, Plymouth Volare back off the truck. After some debate, Caden talked me into letting him completely overhaul my old car from the ground up – for Evin. He bought me the Charger. I tried to convince him I only wanted an economy car, but he insisted on power. I can't really complain. I love my new car. I knew that with some work the Volare would make a good starter car for Evin. I didn't begin to imagine what Caden had in store for it though. I expected him to go through the engine, make sure it ran soundly, and maybe fix the worst of the rust, if even that. But, no, he wanted to turn it into a hotrod. If I didn't know better, I'd think it was a completely different car they were backing slowly off the flatbed truck. It was no longer a rusted out, pea green monstrosity, but a beautiful flat black, perfectly straight beast with red pin striping. He'd had the engine and transmission completely rebuilt as well. The only thing left was to put it all back together. None of the four people gathered around the car as it was unloaded had noticed me pull in. I sat where I was for a few minutes and just watched the interactions taking place before me with a bemused smile. Evin jumped up and down excitedly and gave Caden a big hug. I couldn't hear what she was saying from within my car but I could see she was talking a mile a minute. Her animated movements and the smile on her face said it all. I've never seen her so happy. Caden was relaxed as he stood looking at the now unloaded car, his arm casually draped across her shoulders as he explained something to her. He signaled to the other spectator, Evin's boyfriend Sean, and he walked over to listen as Caden lifted the hood and pointed to its empty interior. I got the impression he'd be learning a thing or two about cars in the near future. The tow truck driver waved to Caden and climbed back in his cab and I maneuvered back out of the way so he could pass then pulled up next to their project. Evin saw me coming and had my door open before I could even shut off the motor.

"Mommy, mommy, did you see my car? Come look, you can't even tell it's the same one!"

She was tugging on my arm trying to get me out of my vehicle faster. I laughed.

"Alright, I'll come look, don't pull my arm off!"

I quickened my pace as she led me the rest of the way to the Volare. As she pulled me around from side to side, pointing out the pin striping and expertly repaired body damage, my eyes met Caden'. We shared a quiet smile at her enthusiasm.

"Evin, why don't you go show Sean the motor and transmission he gets to help me install tomorrow? They arrived earlier today, they're in the shop." Caden said.

"Really?" Evin asks, and Caden nods. "Yay!"

The two of us watch as she happily drags Sean into the shop. Once they're out of site Caden pulls me against him and wraps his arms around my waist, smiling down at me.

"Hello, Beautiful how was your day?" he asks.

"Busy, but everything is finally taken care of. We're all set for next Saturday."

"Are you nervous?"

"Not in the slightest. Are you?"

"Nope; just happy." He answers and then pulls me into a deep, smoldering kiss.

"Ewww, you guys are gross." Evin says, poking her head out of the shop door. "Mama, come see my new motor!"

"Alright, be there in a second." I say, and then, clasping Caden's hand, "Shall we?"

As we walk together into the shop so that Evin can show off her newly rebuilt motor, her words of a year ago float back into my mind; "Like a real family."

Made in the USA
Charleston, SC
27 June 2014